continued

Close Up

"Holy moly, action-adventure-romance fans! You are going to LOVE this book! I highly, highly recommend it."
—*New York Times* bestselling author Suzanne Brockmann

"A story fraught with intense emotions and danger . . . Kantra clearly demonstrates that she's a talent to be reckoned with."
—*Romantic Times*

"Kantra's first foray into single-title fiction is fast-paced, engrossing, and full of nail-biting suspense."
—*New York Times* bestselling author Sabrina Jeffries

"Honest, intelligent romance."
—*Romance B(u)y the Book*

MORE PRAISE FOR VIRGINIA KANTRA
AND HER BESTSELLING NOVELS

"Smart, sexy, and sophisticated—another winner."
—*New York Times* bestselling author Lori Foster

"An involving, three-dimensional story that is scary, intriguing, and sexy."
—*All About Romance*

"Kantra creates powerfully memorable characters."
—*Midwest Book Review*

"Virginia Kantra is an autobuy . . . Her books are keepers and her heroes are to die for!"
—*New York Times* bestselling author Suzanne Brockmann

"Spectacularly suspenseful and sexy. Don't miss it!"
—*Romantic Times*

"Packs a wallop!"
—*USA Today* bestselling author Elizabeth Bevarly

Sea Witch

VIRGINIA KANTRA

BERKLEY SENSATION, NEW YORK

THE BERKLEY PUBLISHING GROUP
Published by the Penguin Group
Penguin Group (USA) Inc.
375 Hudson Street, New York, New York 10014, USA
Penguin Group (Canada), 90 Eglinton Avenue East, Suite 700, Toronto, Ontario M4P 2Y3, Canada
(a division of Pearson Penguin Canada Inc.)
Penguin Books Ltd., 80 Strand, London WC2R 0RL, England
Penguin Group Ireland, 25 St. Stephen's Green, Dublin 2, Ireland (a division of Penguin Books Ltd.)
Penguin Group (Australia), 250 Camberwell Road, Camberwell, Victoria 3124, Australia
(a division of Pearson Australia Group Pty. Ltd.)
Penguin Books India Pvt. Ltd., 11 Community Centre, Panchsheel Park, New Delhi—110 017, India
Penguin Group (NZ), 67 Apollo Drive, Rosedale, North Shore 0632, New Zealand
(a division of Pearson New Zealand Ltd.)
Penguin Books (South Africa) (Pty.) Ltd., 24 Sturdee Avenue, Rosebank, Johannesburg 2196,
South Africa

Penguin Books Ltd., Registered Offices: 80 Strand, London WC2R 0RL, England

This is a work of fiction. Names, characters, places, and incidents either are the product of the author's imagination or are used fictitiously, and any resemblance to actual persons, living or dead, business establishments, events, or locales is entirely coincidental. The publisher does not have any control over and does not assume any responsibility for author or third-party websites or their content.

SEA WITCH

A Berkley Sensation Book / published by arrangement with the author

PRINTING HISTORY
Berkley Sensation mass-market edition / July 2008

Copyright © 2008 by Virginia Kantra.
Excerpt from *Sea Fever* copyright © 2008 by Virginia Kantra.
Cover art by Tony Mauro.
Cover design by Rita Frangie.
Cover logo by axb group.
Interior text design by Laura K. Corless.

ISBN: 978-0-425-22199-0

BERKLEY® SENSATION
Berkley Sensation Books are published by The Berkley Publishing Group,
a division of Penguin Group (USA) Inc.,
375 Hudson Street, New York, New York 10014.
BERKLEY SENSATION and the "B" design are trademarks of Penguin Group (USA) Inc.

PRINTED IN THE UNITED STATES OF AMERICA

10 9 8 7 6 5 4 3 2 1

ACKNOWLEDGMENTS

I made this story up, so any mistakes are all mine. But I still relied on the expertise, input, and/or support of the following people to get some stuff right:

Sergeant Walter Grzyb, Maine State Police, criminal investigation division, who patiently answered all my questions; Sergeant Charles Libby, Portland, Maine, Police Department, for coming to my rescue under a tight deadline; Lieutenant A. J. Carter (ret.), who treats even the craziest questions seriously; and Wally Lind, senior crime scene analyst (ret.), of the crime scene writers loop.

Thanks to the incredible Suz Brockmann for sharing her wonderful community of readers with me; to Alyssa Day, Ed Gaffney, Cathy and Rob Mann, and Eric Ruben; and to First Lieutenant Sarah Frantz of the North Carolina Army National Guard.

I am also grateful to Eileen Dreyer, who knows her fairies and asked all the right questions; Melissa McClone, who made this a better book; and Kristen Dill, for her amazing friendship and for not objecting when I rechristened her dogs Buster and Brownie.

Huge and heartfelt thanks to my brilliant, hardworking editor, Cindy Hwang, for never once saying, "You want to write a book about *what*?" and for thinking up kick-ass titles.

To Damaris Rowland, who believes in me and the magic of the sea.

To my children, who (mostly) schedule their crises and celebrations around my deadlines.

And always and forever to Michael, who took me to Maine.

My father was the keeper of the Eddystone light
And he slept with a mermaid one fine night
Of this union there came three . . .

—TRADITIONAL SHANTY

I am a man upon the land;
I am a selchie on the sea.

—ORKNEY BALLAD

"So I shall die," said the little mermaid, "and as the foam of the sea I shall be driven about never again to hear the music of the waves, or to see the pretty flowers nor the red sun. Is there anything I can do to win an immortal soul?"

—HANS CHRISTIAN ANDERSEN

Sea Witch

1

IF SHE DIDN'T HAVE SEX WITH SOMETHING SOON, she would burst out of her skin.

She plunged through the blue-shot water, driven by a whisper on the wind, a pulse in her blood that carried her along like a warm current. The lavender sky was brindled pink and daubed with indigo clouds. On the beach, fire leaped from the rocks, glowing with the heat of the dying sun.

Her mate was dead. Dead so long ago that the tearing pain, the fresh, bright welling of fury and grief, had ebbed and healed, leaving only a scar on her heart. She barely missed him anymore. She did not allow herself to miss him.

But she missed sex.

Her craving flayed her, hollowed her from the inside out. Lately she'd felt as if she were being slowly scraped to a pelt, a shell, lifeless and empty. She wanted to be touched. She yearned to be filled again, to feel someone move inside her, deep inside her, hard and urgent inside her.

The memory quickened her blood.

She rode the waves to shore, drawn by the warmth of the

flames and the heat of the young bodies clustered there. Healthy human bodies, male and female.

Mostly male.

*   *   *

Some damn fool had built a fire on the point. Police Chief Caleb Hunter spotted the glow from the road.

Mainers welcomed most visitors to their shore. But Bruce Whittaker had made it clear when he called that the islanders' tolerance didn't extend to bonfires on the beach.

Caleb had no particular objection to beach fires, as long as whoever set the fire used the designated picnic areas or obtained a permit. At the point, the wind was likely to carry sparks to the trees. The volunteers at the fire department, fishermen mostly, didn't like to be pulled out of bed to deal with somebody else's carelessness.

Caleb pulled his marked Jeep behind the litter of vehicles parked on the shoulder of the road: a tricked-out Wrangler, a ticket-me-red Firebird, and a late-model Lexus with New York plates. Two weeks shy of Memorial Day, and already the island population was swelling with folks from Away. Caleb didn't mind. The annual influx of summer people paid his salary. Besides, compared to Mosul or Sadr City or even Portland down the coast, World's End was a walk on the beach. Even at the height of the season.

Caleb could have gone back to the Portland PD. Hell, after his medical discharge from the National Guard, he could have gone anywhere. Since 9/11, with the call-up of the reserves and the demands of homeland security, most big-city police departments were understaffed and overwhelmed. A decorated combat veteran—even one with his left leg cobbled together with enough screws, plates, and assorted hardware to set off the metal detector every time he walked through the police station doors—was a sure hire.

The minute Caleb heard old Roy Miller was retiring, he had put in for the chief's job on World's End, struggling upright in his hospital bed to update his résumé. He didn't want to make busts or headlines anymore. He just wanted to keep the peace, to find some peace, to walk patrol without getting shot at. To feel the wind on his face again and smell the salt in the air.

To drive along a road without the world blowing up around him.

He eased from the vehicle, maneuvering his stiff knee around the steering wheel. He left his lights on. Going without backup into an isolated area after dark, he felt a familiar prickle between his shoulder blades. Sweat slid down his spine.

Get over it. You're on World's End. Nothing ever happens here.

Which was about all he could handle now.

Nothing.

He crossed the strip of trees, thankful this particular stretch of beach wasn't all slippery rock, and stepped silently onto sand.

* * *

She came ashore downwind behind an outcrop of rock that reared from the surrounding beach like the standing stones of Orkney.

Water lapped on sand and shale. An evening breeze caressed her damp skin, teasing every nerve to quivering life. Her senses strained for the whiff of smoke, the rumble of male laughter drifting on the wind. Her nipples hardened.

She shivered.

Not with cold. With anticipation.

She combed her wet hair with her fingers and arranged it over her bare shoulders. First things first. She needed clothes.

Even in this body, her blood kept her warm. But she knew from past encounters that her nakedness would be . . . unexpected. She did not want to raise questions or waste time and energy in explanations.

She had not come ashore to talk.

Desire swelled inside her like a child, weighting her breasts and her loins.

She picked her way around the base of the rock on tender, unprotected feet. There, clumped like seaweed above the tide line, was that a . . . *blanket*? She shook it from the sand—*a towel*—and tucked it around her waist, delighting in the bright orange color. A few feet farther on, in the shadows outside the bonfire, she discovered a gray fleece garment with long sleeves and some kind of hood. Drab. Very drab. But it would serve to disguise her. She pulled the garment over her head, fumbling her arms through the sleeves, and smiled ruefully when the cuffs flopped over her hands.

The unfamiliar friction of the clothing chafed and excited her. She slid through twilight, her pulse quick and hot. Still in the shadows, she paused, her widened gaze sweeping the group of six—*seven, eight*—figures sprawled or standing in the circle of the firelight. Two females. Six males. She eyed them avidly.

They were very young.

Sexually mature, perhaps, but their faces were soft and unformed and their eyes shallow. The girls were shrill. The boys were loud. Raw and unconfident, they jostled and nudged, laying claim to the air around them with large, uncoordinated gestures.

Disappointment seeped through her.

"Hey! Watch it!"

Something spilled on the sand. Her sensitive nostrils caught the reek of alcohol.

Not only young, but drunk. Perhaps that explained the clumsiness.

She sighed. She did not prey on drunks. Or children.

Light stabbed at her pupils, twin white beams and flashing blue lights from the ridge above the beach. She blinked, momentarily disoriented.

A girl yelped.

A boy groaned.

"Run," someone shouted.

Sand spurted as the humans darted and shifted like fish in the path of a shark. They were caught between the rock and the strand, with the light in their eyes and the sea at their backs. She followed their panicked glances, squinting toward the tree line.

Silhouetted against the high white beams and dark, narrow tree trunks stood a tall, broad figure.

Her blood rushed like the ocean in her ears. Her heart pounded. Even allowing for the distortion of the light, he looked big. Strong. Male. His silly, constraining clothes only emphasized the breadth and power of his chest and shoulders, the thick muscles of his legs and arms.

He moved stiffly down the beach, his face in shadow. As he neared the fire, red light slid greedily over his wide, clear forehead and narrow nose. His mouth was firm and unsmiling.

Her gaze expanded to take him in. Her pulse kicked up again. She felt the vibration to the soles of her feet and the tips of her fingers.

This was a man.

*   *   *

Kids.

Caleb shook his head and pulled out his ticket book.

Back when he was in high school, you got busted drinking on the beach, you poured your cans on the sand and maybe endured a lecture from your parents. Not that his old man had cared what Caleb did. After Caleb's mom decamped with his older brother, Bart Hunter hadn't cared about much of anything except his boat, his bottle, and the tides.

But times—and statutes—had changed.

Caleb confiscated the cooler full of beer.

"You can't take that," one punk objected. "I'm twenty-one. It's mine."

Caleb arched an eyebrow. "You found it?"

"I bought it."

Which meant he could be charged with furnishing liquor to minors.

Caleb nodded. "And you are . . . ?"

The kid's jaw stuck out. "Robert Stowe."

"Can I see your license, Mr. Stowe?"

He made them put out the fire while he wrote them up: seven citations for possession and—in the case of twenty-one-year-old Robert Stowe—a summons to district court.

He handed back their drivers' licenses along with the citations. "You boys walk the girls home now. Your cars will still be here in the morning."

"It's too far to walk," a pretty, sulky brunette complained. "And it's dark."

Caleb glanced from the last tinge of pink in the sky to the girl. Jessica Dalton, her driver's license read. Eighteen years old. Her daddy was a colorectal surgeon from Boston with a house right on the water, about a mile down the road.

"I'd be happy to call your parents to pick you up," he offered, straight-faced.

"Screw that," announced the nineteen-year-old owner of the Jeep. "I'm driving."

"If I start giving Breathalyzer tests for OUIs, it's going to be a long night," Caleb said evenly. "Especially when I impound your vehicle."

"You can't do that," Stowe said.

Caleb leveled a look at him.

"Come on, Robbie." The other girl tugged his arm. "We can go to my place."

Caleb watched them gather their gear and stumble across the sand.

"I can't find my sweatshirt."

"Who cares? It's ugly."

"You're ugly."

"Come on."

Their voices drifted through the dusk. Caleb waited for them to make a move toward their cars, but something—his threat to tell their parents, maybe, or his shiny new shield or his checkpoint glare—had convinced them to abandon their vehicles for the night.

He dragged his hand over his forehead, dismayed to notice both were sweating.

That was okay.

He was okay.

He was fine, damn it.

He stood with the sound of the surf in his ears, breathing in the fresh salt air, until his skin cooled and his heartbeat slowed. When he couldn't feel the twitch between his shoulder blades anymore, he hefted the cooler and lumbered to the Jeep. His knee shifted and adjusted to take his weight on the soft sand. He'd passed the 1.5-mile run required by the State of Maine to prove his fitness for duty. But that had been on a level track, not struggling to stabilize on uneven ground in the dark.

He stowed the evidence in back, slammed the hatch, and glanced toward the beach.

A woman shone at the water's edge, wrapped in twilight and a towel. The sea foamed around her bare, pale feet. Her long, dark hair lifted in the breeze. Her face was pale and perfect as the moon.

For one second, the sight caught him like a wave smack in the chest, robbing him of speech. Of breath. Yearning rushed through his soul like the wind over the water, stirring him to the depths. His hands curled into fists at his sides.

Not okay. He throttled back his roaring imagination. She was just a kid. A girl. An underage girl in an oversize sweatshirt with—his gaze dipped again, briefly—a really nice rack.

And he was a cop. Time to think like a cop. Mystery Girl hadn't been with the group around the fire. So where had she been hiding?

Caleb stomped back through the trees. The girl stood with her bare feet planted in the sand, watching him approach. At least he didn't have to chase her.

He stopped a few yards away. "Your friends are gone. You missed them."

She tilted her head, regarding him with large, dark, wide-set eyes. "They are not my friends."

"Guess not," he agreed. "Since they left without you."

She smiled. Her lips were soft and full, her teeth white and slightly pointed. "I meant I do not know them. They are very . . . young, are they not?"

He narrowed his gaze on her face, mentally reassessing her age. Her skin was baby fine, smooth and well cared for. No makeup. No visible piercings or tattoos. Not even a tan.

"How old are you?"

Her smile broadened. "Older than I look."

He resisted the urge to smile back. She could be over the legal drinking age—not jailbait, after all. Those eyes held a purely adult awareness, and her smile was knowing. But he'd pounded Portland's pavements long enough to know the kind of trouble a cop invited giving a pretty woman a break. "Can I see your license, please?"

She blinked slowly. "My . . ."

"ID," he snapped. "Do you have it?"

"Ah. No. I did not realize I would need any."

He took in her damp hair, the towel tucked around her waist. If she'd come down to the beach to swim . . . Okay, nobody swam in May but fools or tourists. But even if she was simply taking a walk, her story made sense. "You staying near here?"

Her dark gaze traveled over him. She nodded. "Yes, I believe I will. Am," she corrected.

He was sweating again, and not from nerves. His emotions had been on ice a long time, but he still recognized the slow burn of desire.

"Address?" he asked harshly.

"I don't remember." She smiled again, charmingly, looking him full in the eyes. "I only recently arrived."

He refused to be charmed. But he couldn't deny the tug of attraction, deep in his belly. "Name?"

"Margred."

Mar-gred. Sounded foreign. He kind of liked it.

He raised his brows. "Just Margred?"

"Margaret, I think you would say."

"Last name?"

She took a step closer, making everything under the sweatshirt sway. *Hell-o, breasts.* "Do you need one?"

He couldn't think. He couldn't remember being this distracted and turned on since he'd sat behind Susanna Colburn in seventh-grade English and spent most of second period with a hard-on. Something about her voice . . . Her eyes . . . It was weird.

"In case I need to get in touch with you," he explained.

"That would be nice."

He was staring at her mouth. Her wide, wet, full-lipped mouth. "What?"

"If you got in touch with me. I want you to touch me."

He jerked himself back. "What?"

She looked surprised. "Isn't that what you want?"

Yes.

"No."

Fuck.

Caleb was frustrated, savagely disappointed with himself and with her. He knew plenty of women—badge bunnies—went for cops. Some figured sex would get them out of trouble or a ticket. Some were simply into uniforms or guns or handcuffs.

He hadn't taken her for one of them.

"Oh." She regarded him thoughtfully.

His stomach muscles tightened.

And then she smiled. "You are lying," she said.

Yeah, he was.

He shrugged. "Just because I'm"—*horny, hot, hard*—"attracted doesn't mean I have to act on it."

She tilted her head. "Why not?"

He exhaled, a gust between a laugh and a groan. "For starters, I'm a cop."

"Cops don't have sex?"

He couldn't believe they were having this discussion. "Not on duty."

Which was mostly true. True for him anyway. He hadn't seen any horizontal action since . . . God, since the last time he was home on leave, over eighteen months ago. His brief marriage hadn't survived his first deployment, and nobody since had cared enough to be waiting when he got out.

"When are you not on duty?" she asked.

He shook his head. "What, you want a date?"

Even sarcasm didn't throw this chick. "I would meet you again, yes. I am . . . attracted, too."

She wanted him.

Not that it mattered.

He cleared his throat. "I'm never off duty. I'm the only cop on the island."

"I don't live on your island. I am only . . ." Again with the pause, like English was her second language or something. "Visiting," she concluded with a smile.

Like fucking a tourist would be perfectly okay.

Well, wouldn't it?

The thought popped unbidden into his head. It wasn't like he was arresting her. He didn't even suspect her of anything except wanting to have sex with him, and he wasn't a big enough hypocrite to hold that against her.

But he didn't understand this alleged attraction she felt. He felt.

And Caleb did not trust what he did not understand.

"Where are you staying?" he asked. "I'll walk you home."

"Are you trying to get rid of me?"

"I'm trying to keep you safe."

"That's very kind of you. And quite unnecessary."

He stuck his hands in his pockets, rocking back on his heels. "You getting rid of me now?"

She smiled, her teeth white in the moonlight. "No."

"So?"

She turned away, her footprints creating small, reflective pools in the sand. "So I will see you."

He was oddly reluctant to let her go. "Where?"

"Around. On the beach. I walk on the beach in the evening." She looked at him over her shoulder. "Come find me sometime . . . when you're not on duty."

2

~∞~

THE FOUR O'CLOCK FERRY WHISTLE CUT THROUGH the bright air like an ambulance siren, piercing the quiet of Caleb's office.

He set his coffee mug on the desk blotter with a steady hand.

Only six weeks, and the rising wail no longer made him tense and wait for the inevitable second explosion that took out civilians and rescuers alike. He'd grown up with that whistle; he'd ridden that ferry home from high school; and part of him, at least, accepted he was home. Slowly, the familiar sounds and rhythms of the island were settling into his consciousness, awakening reassuring echoes in his blood. The cry of the gulls, the tide's ebb and flow, the lobster boats chugging out every morning, soothed him like a mother's rocking.

Progress, he thought wryly. Maybe in another two months he'd be able to walk down the street without his jaw and neck clenching, without scanning the doorways and rooftops for snipers. Maybe he'd start sleeping through the nights again.

An image of Margred—Margaret—wavered in his mind, her cloudy dark hair, her round breasts under a loose sweatshirt. *Come find me sometime . . . when you're not on duty.*

Okay, bad idea. After the mess he'd made of his marriage, Caleb knew better than to fall into another relationship based on loneliness and convenience.

But at least for those few minutes on the beach last night, he'd felt alive again.

A tap sounded on his door. Edith Paine, the town clerk, stuck her smooth gray bob into Caleb's office. Edith had been running town hall since before the current building's construction. She handled the town's billing and permits, scheduled appointments for the mayor, and served as the island's dispatcher during the day. Caleb never walked past her desk in the outer office without feeling like he ought to wipe his shoes first.

She sniffed. "Bruce Whittaker to see you."

Edith hadn't taken Whittaker's complaint last night—after-hours calls to the police were bounced to Caleb's cell phone. She wouldn't like being out of the loop.

Or maybe, Caleb thought, she just didn't like Whittaker.

"Thanks. Tell him to come in."

"You'll need to let him out," she warned. "I get off at four."

"Can't miss *Oprah*," Caleb joked.

Edith looked down her nose at him. "I have a four thirty kickboxing class at the community center." Turning her head, she spoke over her shoulder. "You can go in now. He's not doing anything."

Nothing that couldn't wait. Caleb tossed away a catalog advertising high-tech SWAT equipment and glanced up.

White male, six feet, wiry build, Bruce Whittaker wore his brown hair short and his shirt sleeves rolled. Caleb put his age in the mid-forties and his income considerably higher.

"Mr. Whittaker. What can I do for you?"

"You can do something about those trespassers on my beach."

The point was public land, but the question wasn't worth disputing.

Caleb raised his eyebrows. "They're back?"

"They came back this morning to pick up their vehicles."

"Then what's the problem?"

"You should have arrested them."

Caleb relaxed his hands on his desk blotter. "I wrote them up. And Stowe will have to appear in court."

"I want to see him in jail," Whittaker said.

Caleb nodded toward the steel and glass doorway that separated the chief's office from the island's two small holding cells. "We don't have the space or the manpower for me to play Barney Fife. I lock somebody up, we're both spending the night in jail. I don't mind sleeping on a cot if somebody's committed a serious crime. But I don't give up my bed because some kid bought beer for his buddies."

"They were trespassing," Whittaker insisted. "My beach rights extend to the low water mark."

Lawyer, Caleb thought.

"Within your property lines, yes," he said. "These kids were just outside, on public beach."

"They were still violating the law."

"Yeah, they were," Caleb agreed. "But I'd bet they won't now they know you've got a nice view of the party. I can drive by the next couple of nights, see if they show up again."

Or if she did. The woman. Margred.

Caleb shook his head. He'd already tried to track her down. Edith had never heard of her. Nobody at Island Realty had any record or recollection of a dark-haired Margaret, last name unknown. As chief of police, he had better things to do with his time than chase after some fantasy woman on the beach. But the lack of information about her aroused his professional curiosity.

Along with other things.

"Let me know if you see anyone," Whittaker said. "You catch them lighting fires again, I'll take care of them."

"You let me take care of them," Caleb said. "I'm not calling an open season on tourists or kids."

"An uncontrolled burn could destroy the ecosystem of this island."

The son of a lobsterman, Caleb understood how fragile the island's environment was . . . and how shaky its economy. The islanders, the real islanders, depended on both the sea and tourism to survive. Something a newcomer like Whittaker would never understand.

He saw him out and began his evening swing through town.

A tumbled line of weathered gray shops and houses divided the hard, bright blue of the sky from the deeper, wilder blue of the sea. A half-dozen high school kids straggled up from the ferry, the boys in boots and flannel shirts, the girls in flip-flops and midriff-baring jeans. Gulls wheeled and cried after the boats in the harbor. Everything appeared clear, bright, and remote, like the view through the wrong end of a pair of binoculars.

Or a rifle scope.

Caleb drew a deep breath and started down the hill, past Sea View Bed-and-Breakfast and Wiley's Market. The Barlow house was an art gallery now, the old Thompson cottage had been spruced up into a tourist center, but the narrow streets and struggling gardens hadn't changed in fifteen years. In fifty.

This is what he needed, he told himself. A sense of community, a shot at stability. Here he could assemble the pieces of a normal life to make himself whole again.

But today the snug, square houses, the quiet harbor, felt as pretty and flat as one of those postcards in the gift shop. Dissatisfaction lodged in his chest like unexploded ordnance, heavy and deadly. For a moment he couldn't breathe.

He forced himself along the uneven sidewalk, his gaze lingering between the buildings. Like insurgents were going to pop from behind the Lighthouse Gift Shop and start shooting.

Caleb kept walking. *Positive coping actions,* the shrink had counseled. Exercise. Work. Positive thinking.

Sex.

Which made him think again of the woman on the beach, her big, dark eyes, her wide, lush mouth. Her breasts.

Intimate relationships assist with relaxation and provide practical and emotional support, the Army doc had said.

Okay, so seeking out a foreign tourist with a thing for uniforms probably wasn't what the shrink had in mind, but a guy had to start somewhere. At least when Caleb was with her, he hadn't remembered Mosul. Hell, he'd barely remembered his name. And there had been an instant, gazing into those fathomless eyes, when he'd actually felt . . . more than desire.

Connection.

The well-lit windows and red awning of Antonia's Ristorante (PIZZA! BAKERY! SUBS! the sign proclaimed) spilled a welcome onto the sidewalk. The bell jangled as Caleb pushed open the door.

Regina Barone was working behind the counter, wearing a wide, white apron and a slight, distracted frown, her dark hair strained back from her thin face.

At the sound of the bell, she looked up, the frown dissolving. "Hi, Cal."

He smiled. "Reggie."

They'd known each other forever. He remembered her as a skinny, abrasive, ambitious girl, desperate to get off the island and out from under her mother's thumb. He'd heard she'd landed the job of sous chef in some fancy big-city restaurant, New York or Boston. She had a tattoo now, on her wrist, and a small gold crucifix around her neck.

But here she was, back on World's End, working in the family restaurant. Here they both were.

Why didn't he want sex with her?

Regina's eight-year-old son, Nick, hunched in a red vinyl booth in the corner, scribbling.

"How's the homework going?" Caleb asked.

Nick shrugged. He was a cute kid, with his mother's thin build and expressive Italian eyes.

"Fractions," Regina explained. "He hates them."

Nick's chin thrust out. "I don't see why I have to learn them, that's all. Not if I'm going to help Nonna in the restaurant."

Regina's mouth tightened.

"Got to learn your fractions," Caleb said. "How else can you make a half-mushroom, half-pepperoni pizza?"

Regina threw him a grateful look. "That's right," she told Nick. "You work in the kitchen, you need fractions. Half a cup. Three quarters of a teaspoon."

"I guess," Nick said. He bent back over his homework.

Regina smiled at Caleb. "So, what can I do for you?"

Invitation lurked under her words, wary yet unmistakable. She was a good woman, with a great kid and just enough baggage to balance his load. He tried to summon something, a spark, a tug, and felt . . . numb.

"What have you got to go tonight?" he asked.

"Besides pizza?" Shrugging, Regina wiped her hands on her apron and nodded toward the refrigerator case. "Lobster roll, clam chowder, lemon garlic chicken, shrimp-and-tortellini salad."

"Nice," Caleb said. "Your mother know you're catering to the yacht set now?"

Regina's eyes cooled. "We talked about it. What'll you have?"

Something there, Caleb thought. But unless the Barones took after each other with kitchen knives, it was none of his business. "How about two of the lobster rolls and the, uh . . . a double of salad."

"Coming up."

"Almost done," Nick announced.

Caleb glanced at the booth. "Good for you."

"When I finish, can I see your gun?"

"Dominick Barone—"

"It's okay, Reggie. I can't show you my gun," Caleb

explained to Nick. "A police officer can't draw his weapon in public unless he's prepared to use it. But you can look at my handcuffs."

Nick's eyes widened. "Can I? Cool."

Caleb demonstrated and then watched, amused, as the kid cuffed himself to a table leg.

"Cool," Regina echoed. She set the take-out bag on the table. "How about drinks?"

"Drinks," Caleb repeated cautiously.

Her mouth quirked. "To go with your dinner."

He wasn't a drinking man. No matter how much trouble he had sleeping, no matter how much he had to forget, he would not repeat his father's mistakes. But this time the gesture outweighed the principle.

"You got a wine would go with that?" he asked.

"A midpriced pinot grigio?"

"That would be good. Thanks."

Regina bagged the wine, adding two clear plastic cups to the top.

Caleb noticed Nick struggling to fit the key into the slot on the cuffs and grinned. "Let me give you a hand there," he said, unlocking them.

Nick rubbed his thin wrists. "Can I take them with me to school tomorrow?"

"Better let me hold on to them. I might need them."

"Hot date tonight?" Regina teased.

He cleared his throat. "Too soon to tell."

"Uh-huh. You be careful, Chief. You've been gone long enough to be interesting. Nick's not the only one on the island anxious to check out your equipment."

He actually felt himself flush. He dug for his wallet. "Yeah, well, whatever you heard, Edith hasn't actually chased me around the desk yet."

Regina laughed and rang up his order. He thanked her, paid, and left.

The late afternoon sun set the boats in the harbor ablaze, red, yellow, and white.

Had he fooled her? Or was he just kidding himself?

* * *

Picnic blanket. Cooler. Corkscrew. Condom.

Like an eager Boy Scout, Caleb was prepared for any-thing. His gaze swept the empty beach, the quiet, sparkling sea. The only thing missing was the girl.

I walk on the beach in the evening, she had said.

Maybe he was early. The sun wouldn't set for another hour.

Maybe she wasn't coming. Her purred invitation last night could have been a joke at his expense.

Maybe he should go home.

I want to touch you.

He glanced left, where the beach climbed toward Fisher-man's Wharf, and right, where it broke into a tumble of rocks and mud. A little exercise wouldn't hurt him.

He hefted the cooler and turned right.

On the other side of the point, the rocks got bigger and the going got tougher. Trees crowded the shore, forcing him along the water. The cooler knocked against his legs, pushing him off balance. His steps were uneven. His left knee ached.

Of all the lamebrained, dumb-ass ideas . . .

And then he saw her—Margred—her legs long and bare under a fluttering sarong-style skirt, her round breasts pressing against the tiny blue triangles of a bikini top, her wild, streaked mane lifting in the wind like some goddess rising from the sea. She stunned his heart. She stopped his breath. And the sight of her transformed him from a suspi-cious island cop to a sweaty teenager gaping at his first *Sports Illustrated* swimsuit model.

He waited for enough blood to return to his brain to form words. "You're here."

Her full lips curved. "I've been waiting for you."

"You must be freezing." That outfit she had on—*full breasts, firm thighs, pale, pale skin, God*—was more suited to a cruise deck in the Bahamas than the coast of Maine. Shrugging out of his jacket, Caleb draped it around her shoulders, trying not to grab. "Here."

"That's not necessary," she said. "I don't get cold."

He looked down at her cleavage and the pale swell of her belly and the rush went to his head and he felt dizzy. He stepped away from her before he forgot he was a mature officer of the law and fell on her like a horny twenty-year-old soldier after a nine-month deployment.

"We could move into the trees," he said. "It would cut the wind some." And be more private.

She glanced up the bank and then back at his face. "All right."

He followed her under the cool, dark shadow of the trees. Weathered picnic tables stood at angles on the uneven ground.

Caleb looked from the jacket hanging open around her shoulders to the stone pit with its rusty iron grill and said, "I could build a fire."

Yeah, because that would help him cool off.

She perched on one of the tables, and the sarong thing she was wearing fell away, exposing the long, lovely line of her thigh. Her eyes glinted. "If that's what you really want. What shall I do while you are building your fire?"

A real Sharon Stone moment, he thought, his blood pumping and his teeth on edge. The perfect fuck, and then you die.

He couldn't put his life back together that way. He wanted more than a one-night stand. Dinner, wine, conversation . . . all the trappings of a normal date. A normal life.

Then sex.

To please her, to tease her, to test himself, he flattened his hands on the picnic table, trapping her between his arms. She was so close. Warm and close. Hell, she was hot, and he was getting hotter by the second. He leaned in, sucked in by her closeness and her warmth, by those huge, dark, hungry eyes, and heard a rushing in his ears like the sound of the sea.

He was drowning.

He drew away. "You could unpack the cooler."

Margred pulled back sharply and met his eyes. "What?"

Caleb turned away to crouch by the open stone fireplace, ignoring the twinge in his reconstructed leg. "I brought dinner. In the cooler. You could unpack it while I start the fire."

*   *   *

Margred stared at the long, strong line of his back, frustrated. Amused. Affronted. Sex had never been this much trouble before. Humans were always in rut. Any other male would have had her flat on her back on the table and be pounding away between her thighs.

"I don't need you to *feed* me," she said.

Fire leaped in the grate. Straightening, he turned to face her, humor curving his mouth. "You don't get cold. You don't get hungry either?"

She narrowed her eyes at him. "Not for food."

He laughed. He had a nice laugh, deep and wry, but his eyes remained steady and sad. "I thought women liked to be courted."

She didn't know anything about what women, human women, liked. "It's not necessary," she repeated.

"Not for you, maybe. I thought we could spend some time getting to know one another."

He was serious.

"Why?" she asked.

His gaze held hers. His eyes were green, the color of the sea on a cloudy day. "Because you're a very attractive woman."

His compliment caught her off guard, melting her irritation. Surely she could give him something in return?

She blew out her breath. "What do you want to know?"

A corner of his mouth turned up. "We could start with an exchange of basic information. Marital status. Health history. Country of origin. I don't even know your name."

"I told you, it's Margred. Margaret."

"What do people call you? Meg? Maggie? Peggy?"

"Not Peggy." She tilted her head to one side, considering. "I like Maggie."

"Maggie," he repeated softly.

His deep voice shivered through her. She felt a tug under her breastbone.

Oh, this would not do, she thought, dismayed. She had not come for this.

"Are you married, Maggie?" he asked in that warm, mesmerizing voice.

Mated, he meant. She shook her head to rid it of memories. "I was. He died."

"I'm sorry."

His sympathy slid under her skin like a knife. "It was a long time ago." More than two score years. Long enough that she had given up hope her murdered mate would ever be reborn to find her again. Deliberately, she crossed her legs, flashed her most sultry smile. "What happens now is more important to me."

The man watched her with his sober green eyes. "And what happens now?"

"This," she said, and reached for him.

3

~~~

HER EYES WERE HUGE AND DARK, DEEP ENOUGH to drown him, wide enough to swallow him whole. She wrapped her arms around Caleb's neck, pulled him between her smooth, bare thighs, and kissed him.

Her mouth was silky hot, wet, and hungry. She tasted like one of those girly umbrella drinks, sweet with a raw kick underneath that slammed you in the head.

He was instantly hot. Incredibly turned on.

Closing his eyes, Caleb drank her in, the smell of her hair, the salt tang of her skin, the hot, wild sweetness of her mouth. Her breasts—she had amazing breasts—squashed against him. Her hands slipped from around his neck and slithered down his chest. She started unbuckling his belt.

He sucked in his breath. *Un-fucking-believable.*

Like a letter to *Penthouse*. Like one of Private Ziggy Fell's stories, "How I Spent My Time in the Green Zone." Like a frigging dream.

Except since Mosul, Caleb's dreams hadn't been this good.

Nothing had ever felt this good.

She cupped him, shaped him through his jeans, making this little hum of satisfaction in her throat, and he nearly swallowed his tongue. He was *so* screwed. Or he would be soon if he didn't do something about it.

Her hand explored, setting him on fire, threatening to send his careful plans up in smoke.

He speared his fingers into her hair, tugging back her head so he could see her face. She met his gaze boldly, those wide eyes dark with knowledge and desire, a tiny smile curving that slick, red mouth.

Why would he want to do anything to derail what could be the best fantasy sex of his life?

She wasn't an insurgent or a victim, a Third World prostitute or his ex-wife. She wasn't like anyone he had ever known. He could do whatever he wanted with her. Whatever she wanted.

His blood hammered through his body, thundered in his ears. And for whatever reason, she wanted . . . him.

Cradling the back of her head, he took her mouth with his. *Hot.* Her kiss was sweet and hot, her skin warm and damp with desire. Her hands left him to reach behind her own back. He fought his disappointment. But then the tiny triangles of her swimsuit tumbled to her lap, freeing her breasts to his gaze. To his touch. He covered them with his palms, testing their shape, their weight, their mind-blowing softness.

She tugged at his buckle, fumbled briefly with his zipper. He pushed her hands aside to help, standing between her legs as she perched on the picnic table.

His own hands trembled. *A little overeager there, Ace.* Would she notice? Or would she be too distracted, too revolted, by the purple waffle weave of scar tissue on his thigh to care about his reactions?

But she didn't comment on his scars. She shoved down his jeans and his briefs, freeing his bobbing erection, and squeezed his bare ass. Like she wanted this. Wanted him, scars and all.

Incredible.

He had just enough brains left to dig in his sagging pocket for his wallet.

Margred frowned as he pulled out the condom. "We don't need that."

He glanced down at his dark erection, thrusting against the shadowed curve of her belly, and fought to keep his tone light. "Looks to me like we will soon."

She laughed, and his tension eased.

"I meant, I have no diseases," she explained.

"Me either," he said. The Army poked and prodded, tested and treated for everything. And since his discharge there had been no one.

With one finger she traced from the coarse hair at his groin all along his length to the blunt, sensitive tip. A different tension gripped him. "Yes, you look . . . healthy."

Except for the jagged purple scar running up his thigh, the pins and plates holding him together, he was fine.

The sight of her slender, stroking finger almost drove the words from his head. "You could still get pregnant."

"No," she said, and stooped, and replaced her hand with her mouth.

His body jolted as if he'd been struck by lightning. Her hair tumbled over his thigh, brushed his belly, as she took him deep. The hot, wet suction shut down his brain. Heat built in the back of his head, in the base of his balls. He was losing it. He was losing control.

Pushing her flat on the picnic table, he gripped her knees. He needed to be with her. In her. Closer. Now.

"Wait," she gasped.

He froze.

She slid her arms out of his jacket sleeves and then wriggled out of her bikini bottoms. He stared. She had no tan lines. No tan at all. She was all smooth muscles and full curves, her small, pink nipples and thick, dark bush in startling contrast to her creamy skin.

She lay back and smiled at him. "Now."

Yes.

His barriers crashed. His control crumbled. He spread her thighs wide. She was ready. Wet.

Good.

He wanted to make it good for her. He wanted to make it last.

But she gripped him with her sweet, feminine heat and small, strong hands, and her hips rose to take him, all of him, and the need that drove him surged and broke. She moved with him and under him with grunts and little cries, her breasts swaying as he thrust into her. Her thighs tightened around his waist. Her bare heels rode his buttocks. He clutched her like a drowning man, his head spinning, his chest heaving. Sweat slicked them both. He was shuddering, shaking, falling apart. He felt her crest take her, felt her arch and flow around him, and in the wake of her release he let go, he gave it up, he gave everything up to her.

He bowed his head, his mind emptied. His body, emptied. *At peace.*

The sound of the surf drummed in his ears like the echo of his heartbeat. A sea breeze snuck through the trees and tickled his bare ass. His pants were crumpled around his knees.

He raised his head.

She lay quietly, her sleek, pale body spread out like some exotic picnic against the weathered wood, watching him with gleaming eyes in the firelight.

He wanted to give her . . . something. Tell her something. Thank her. He didn't know how. He didn't know her.

"Caleb," he said.

Her level dark brows arched. "What?"

"My name," he told her. "It's Caleb."

* * *

Margred did not need to know his name. She did not want to know anything about him. She chose human males for sex because they had short lives and even shorter attention spans.

But this one . . .

He regarded her with his sad, steady eyes, his hard, scarred body still lodged within hers, and something inside her softened and opened like a sea anemone in the tide.

He had worked her well. Her muscles felt loose and relaxed. The prickle in her blood was satisfied. She could give him at least a pretense of interest in return.

"Caleb," she repeated, testing his name. Tasting it, as she had tasted him.

He smiled faintly. "Caleb Michael Hunter."

Michael, the demon scourge. And *hunter* . . . Unease tweaked her. She ignored it.

"Those are warrior names," she observed politely.

"I guess." He shrugged. "I was in the Guard."

"You were a soldier?" That would explain the scars, she thought. And the wounded, wary look in those eyes.

"In Iraq."

She nodded as if she understood. "Do you want to talk about it?"

His mouth set. "No."

"Good." She wiggled under him. "Neither do I."

Humor lit his face, banishing the shadows from his eyes. "Well, we've got to find something to do for the next twenty minutes, Maggie girl. You destroyed me."

She had not.

She could. She could make him respond to her, force him to service her, empty him out like a clamshell. But his humor pleased her, and his wry self-deprecation.

Releasing him, she stretched and sat up. "You brought food, you said?"

He stood unmoving, with his pants around his knees, as she combed her fingers through her hair. The firelight slid over his strong, man's body: broad, hairy chest; flat, ridged abdomen; heavy genitals. Quite lovely, really.

"Sandwiches," he said. "And a bottle of wine."

"Well, then." She smiled at him.

He laughed and shook his head, hitching his pants over his hips. "I thought you weren't hungry."

"Maybe you've given me an appetite."

And for more than food.

She did not seek the company of her own kind. She and her mate had lived apart. Most selkies, like the harbor seals they resembled, were solitary. Even on land, in human form, they rarely touched except to mate. As their numbers dwindled and their ocean territories expanded, they barely interacted outside of Sanctuary, where the king's son kept court.

But this mortal male—*My name is Caleb,* he had said— attracted her like a fire on the beach. She was drawn to the deep sea green of his eyes, tempted to linger by the timbre of his voice.

I thought we could spend some time getting to know one another.

Impossible. The less he knew, the happier he would be. The safer she would be.

And yet . . .

He poked the fire, sending sparks shooting into the dark, and added another log. He'd brought a blanket, which he draped over the table.

"I should have done this before," he said.

"Why?"

"You don't have splinters?"

She laughed. "No. My . . . skirt protected me."

He was a careful man, she thought, watching him lay their dinner like an offering against the plaid blanket. Deliberate. Thorough. Good qualities in a lover, although his attention to detail could prove inconvenient. If he guessed . . . If he suspected . . .

But he wouldn't. Even the legends of her kind were fading from human memory. Centuries ago, every unwed village girl with an unplanned baby on the way, every sailor hauled up on shore after a storm, blamed or blessed the selkies for their situation—rightly or not. But in this new world, in this new time, the old explanations would never be believed.

Caleb set a sandwich in front of her. She bit into it, savor-

ing the textures and tastes on her tongue. Lobster, well . . .
She could always get lobster. But bread was a delicacy.
"This is delicious. You made this for me?"

"I bought it. From Antonia's." He popped the lid from a
plastic container and held it out to her. "You ever eat there?"

Her heart picked up a beat. He might not accept the truth,
but he was definitely seeking some explanation. "No."

"You should. If you're planning on staying."

She pretended not to hear the question in his voice.
"What is this? Shrimp?"

"Tortellini salad." But Caleb was not so easily deflected.
"Where do you live, Maggie?"

She hooked a shrimp from the container and licked her
fingers. His gaze narrowed on her mouth. Either he remembered her lips, her tongue on his body, or she should have
used a fork.

"Not so far away. Though I was born in Scotland," she
said. That should satisfy him. It was even mostly true.

"Scotland," he repeated, pouring something into her
glass. Wine, she guessed, from the bottle and the scent:
fruity, tangy, smelling of earth and yet not unpleasant.

"The Orkney Islands. Off the north coast." She lifted her
chin, daring him to disbelieve her. "I like to travel."

"How long are you staying here?"

But she wasn't trapped so easily. "I haven't decided."

He grinned unexpectedly, the lightning expression at
odds with his serious eyes. A knot hitched in her belly. Desire, yes, but something more, something . . . else. "Maybe I
can help you make up your mind," he said.

Oh, this was a dangerous game they were playing. She
liked it.

She sipped her wine, tilted her head. "Help me stay? Or
help me go?"

Their gazes locked. Without speaking, he stood and
moved around the table. Removing the glass from her hand,
he set it on the blanket, lowered himself to the bench beside
her, and pressed his mouth to hers. He smelled of wood

smoke, soap, and sex, and tasted like the wine, cool and earthy. She opened her mouth wider to take more of him in, frustrated when he broke their kiss to press warm lips to the arch of her eyebrow, the curve of her cheekbone, the hollow of her jaw. Could he feel her pulse under his lips?

"Stay," he murmured.

She flushed, flooded with the familiar awareness of her own feminine power and the novel thrill of his seduction.

Of course she would not stay.

Her kind never did, unless they were tricked or taken, stripped of their pelts and their power to return to the sea.

But it was sweet to be wanted so.

His mouth cruised her neck and shoulder, leaving her nerve endings alive and shivering in its wake. She tipped her head to give him better access, and he pulled her close, half hauling, half lifting her onto his lap. His chest was muscled, solid against her shoulder, his flesh hard and eager against her hip. He ran his hands over her, learning her, exploring breast and belly and thigh, as she lay sprawled across him like kelp over the rocks, warmed by the sun, moving in the tide. She was all open to him, naked and open, and he was tucked away, zipped behind stiff denim.

He spread her with his fingers, pressing down, pushing in. Quick as a fish, she twisted to straddle him, balancing on her knees on the narrow bench. She reached between their bodies, prepared to wrestle with his clothing, to wrest control, to snatch her satisfaction from him. But he was prepared for her. His pants gaped open. She felt the rough scrape of fabric against her thighs, the cold bite of his zipper, and then the warm thrust of his flesh, there, just there. Aah.

She sank her teeth into her lower lip, closing her eyes to take him in, to take it all in, to absorb the sensations inside and out. His thickness filled her. The fire was warm against her back. The moon rode high above the trees, its call cold and sweet on the air like the notes of a trumpet.

"Open your eyes, Maggie. Look at me."

Startled, she obeyed. Caleb was watching her, watching her face, his jaw clenched, his gaze penetrating. She was joined to him, connected with him. She felt the shock of it like lightning striking the sea.

He pressed up into her as hard, as far as he could go. She surrounded him, rising and falling as if she rode the waves to shore, rocking herself against him, everything in her pulling down, flowing down, rushing to the place where they were joined. Her nipples tightened. Her womb contracted.

She lost tempo, her movements becoming frantic, erratic. Her head dropped to his shoulder. His hands gripped her hips, steadying her, moving her to his rhythm.

Almost there, almost . . .

His fingers bit into her flesh. "*Look* at me."

But she was lost, liquid, gone, spinning away from him. Everything in her tightened and spiraled down. She shuddered, crying out, and felt him thrust up to meet her as he released hotly at her center.

Long moments passed before she drifted back to herself.

Perspiration glued their bodies together. His chest rose and fell. Her own breath flowed easily, but her heart beat as if she'd just surfaced from a long dive.

"Not twenty minutes, after all." He laughed softly, a quiet exhalation against her throat. "You're a miracle, Maggie."

Oh, no. Not a miracle. Angels dealt in miracles.

Selkies dealt in . . . Well, as a general rule, they did not deal in miracles. Or humans either. She had not visited him as an angel would, to bring tidings or a sign, to help or heal, to comfort or interfere in any way.

She had come ashore for sex. And now that her craving had been satisfied, she would return to the sea.

She slid her arms from around his neck, feeling him slip from her body with an odd sense of loss.

He grunted as she wriggled from his lap. "Where are you going?"

"I need . . ." She glanced toward the beach, her mind a blank. What could she claim to need? He had warmed her, fed her, serviced her—not once, but twice.

"Right." He grimaced, stretching his scarred leg in front of him. "Don't go too far. You need a flashlight?"

"No," she said truthfully. "I can see well enough."

Even in human form, her eyes were better adapted to the dark than his.

Caleb caught at her hand as she turned away. She looked back at him, trying and failing to resent his hold on her.

He smiled. "Hurry back."

She did not, could not, answer. But she owed him . . . something. Stooping, she kissed him one last time. His lips were dry and steady. Sweet.

She straightened, her heart drumming in her ears.

As she picked her way through the trees to the shore, she felt his gaze like a touch on her back.

*   *   *

Caleb watched her go, fighting the urge to call her back. After two rounds of vigorous sex, the girl probably needed to powder her nose or catch her breath or wash up or something. Although he didn't know anybody crazy enough to brave the water in May without a wetsuit.

But then, he'd never known anybody like Maggie.

It wasn't her willingness to have sex with a near stranger that made her unique.

Hell, that was how he'd met his ex-wife, in a smoky bar in Biloxi, Mississippi. The Last Call was a hunting ground for lonely soldiers from Fort Shelby in search of pool and pussy—not necessarily in that order—and local girls trolling for free drinks and husbands.

Sherilee, with her tailored slacks and expensive perfume, had seemed a cut above the regular clientele, a bank teller out slumming for the night with her girlfriends. Back then, she'd thought Caleb's uniform was cute and his taciturn Yankee silence sexy. He'd thought . . . Who was he kidding? He'd been far from home, estranged from his family, and staring down an eighteen-month deployment in the desert. They hadn't done much thinking. Or talking either. They'd gotten married right before he shipped out, and he was pretty sure Sherilee had regretted her decision before she'd even finished spending his imminent danger pay.

He knew better now than to imagine one night of sex was a good basis for commitment or even compatibility.

But this was different. Maggie was different, lush and full of life, uninhibited, uncalculating, generous in her love-making.

Caleb shook his head, disbelieving and flat-out grateful at the memory of what she'd done. What they'd done together.

But he was different, too. This time, he was determined to have an actual relationship with all the trimmings of a normal life, phone calls and flowers and family visits.

He winced, thinking of his father hunched over the scarred kitchen table, scowling into the bottom of a whiskey glass. Okay, a visit with *his* family might be pushing things. But at least he could take Maggie out, spring for dinner and a movie.

Make love to her in a bed.

Caleb rubbed his knee, glanced toward the tree line. When she came back, he had to get her phone number.

The fire hissed and popped. The sparks rode the updraft into the dark.

It was a long time before he accepted she wasn't coming back.

4

❦

WAVES BOILED OVER THE ROCKS AT THE SELKIES'
island Sanctuary. White veils of spray caught the afternoon
sun. Drops glittered in the air like diamonds. Farther out,
long lines of whitecaps rolled, their crests curling over the
deep blue green—the horses of Llyr, running before the
wind.

Standing alone in a tower room in Caer Subai, Margred
listened to the crash and roar of the tide. The mingled scents
of land and sea, life and decay, climbed to her window like
the rose vines in a fairy tale.

She stared down at the foaming sea, a discontent inside
her as cold and sharp as the wind blowing through the un-
paned windows.

She pulled her velvet robe, a relic of a fifteenth-century
queen, around her. Not for warmth, but for the comfort of its
rich texture. She had hoped being here in Sanctuary, among
her own kind, would still the restlessness that had roiled her
these past three weeks.

She had been wrong. Even the smooth fabric against her
skin failed to soothe the itch inside her.

She did not belong here, in the court of the sea king's son, where considerations of pair bonds and politics lurked behind every smile and ambushed every conversation. She did not seek another mate. She did not care about court intrigue. Better to have stayed in the isolation of the sea, in the independence of her own territory.

Hurry back, the man had said.

The thought disturbed her.

She turned from the window.

No rug covered the smoothly fitted flagstones under her feet. No fire burned beneath the massive mantle. The chandelier suspended from the beamed and painted ceiling held no candles. Unlike the children of the earth, selkies did not mine or make, grow or spin. Caer Subai was furnished with the salvage of centuries of wrecks: Viking gold and Cornish iron, silk hangings from France and wooden chests from Spain. The platters and goblets on the table were all of gold, and the high stone walls were covered with tapestry scenes of the Creation: a stylized wave, the dark, the deep, a dove, their bright silks preserved by the magic that seeped from the ancient stones like mist and lay like shadows in the corners of the room.

The children of the sea did not interfere with the ships that traveled over their ocean. But everything that fell beneath the waves was forfeit, human lives and human possessions both. Selkies plucked mortals from the wreckage when it pleased them, delivering the survivors safe to shore. Whatever else pleased them, they brought here, or stored in sea caves in their own territories.

On past visits, Margred had delighted in the treasures of Caer Subai. Her gaze rested on the fireplace, fancifully carved with sea monsters and mermaids, its whimsical design a testament to the artistry of its maker . . . and the odd humor of the prince. But now everything seemed faded. Spoiled. Tarnished. Flat. She should return to the sea.

No. The thought formed like a fog, unsubstantial and enveloping. *She should go back to the man. Caleb.*

Footsteps sounded on the tower stairs. "Margred?"

She shivered at the deep-timbred voice. It almost sounded like . . .

"Are you alone?" A tall, male form appeared in the arched doorway. He was dressed in rough fisherman's clothing, canvas pants and a shirt, that did nothing to disguise his extraordinary beauty.

Dylan.

The younger selkie had claimed a territory adjoining hers a score of years ago. She tolerated him because of his youth and bitter humor. Well, and because he was very good to look at, in a fierce and fine-honed way. Once she had even considered . . .

She half smiled and shook her head. He took himself too seriously to suit her.

He had spoken in English, so she answered in the same tongue. "As you see."

Dylan crossed the tower room, leaning his elbows on the window ledge beside her. Posing, she thought.

The wind ruffled his dark hair. "Perhaps you are alone too much," he said.

She shot him an amused look. "Do you speak for yourself? Or the prince?"

"Conn is concerned for you, of course."

"I don't see why."

"He wants you to be happy here."

"He wants me to whelp selkie babies, you mean."

"The prince is disturbed by the decline in our numbers," Dylan said in a careful tone. "At last count there were fewer than two thousand of our people left."

Margred arched her eyebrows. "At last count? Does Conn really believe the king and the others living beneath the wave"—the polite term for those selkies who rarely or never took human form—"would present themselves for his census?"

"You can't deny there are fewer of us born each year."

She did not deny anything. Her inability to bear her mate a child had been a source of real, if secret, grief to her four or five decades past.

She shrugged, feigning indifference. "A low birth rate is the price our people pay for immortality. The seas would be overrun with us else."

"Instead of which, our numbers are dropping. Our population may have been in balance once, but now too many of us are dying."

"And are reborn again in the sea," Margred said. "As we always have been."

As she had been herself, seven centuries ago.

"*Not* always. Selkies who die without their sealskins are not reborn. They cease to exist."

Memory welled like fresh blood from an old scar. "My mate was killed by poachers. I do not need you to explain to me what happens to a selkie who dies without his pelt."

Dylan watched her closely. "I have offended you."

But she would not give him even that much. "It is what it is. Mayhap his fate is one he would have chosen. Endless existence has its own . . . burdens."

"You are dissatisfied?"

Dissatisfied, restless, empty, alone . . .

She lifted her chin. "I am bored."

His gaze sharpened on her face. "I hear you've been amusing yourself ashore."

"And this interests you because . . . ?"

"Perhaps you would be better served if you redirected your energy toward your own kind."

She tilted her head. "Pimping for the prince, Dylan?"

"Merely delivering a friendly warning. There are dangers to becoming involved with humans."

"You are half human, are you not?"

His mouth compressed. "It's impossible to be half anything. You are selkie, or you are not. You live in the sea, or you die on land. I am selkie, like my mother."

So she had touched a nerve. She poked at it again, the way children on shore thrust sticks at jellyfish to watch them twitch. "But your father was human."

"I do not speak of my father."

"Tell me about your mother, then."

"She drowned. In a fisherman's net." The cry of the gulls carried upward on the wind. Dylan turned his head and held Margred's gaze. "Because she ventured too close to shore."

"Another warning?" Margred asked softly. "Have a care, Dylan. I do not take cautions well. Or instruction either."

"Something is happening," Dylan argued. "Something affecting the balance of power. Conn fears it. We all feel it. There's a disturbance in the demon realm."

Margred shivered. She did not want to think there was more to her recent restlessness than frustrated lust. An actual attachment to a human would be bad. An upset in the balance that existed between elementals, between the children of the sea and the children of the fire, would be much worse.

"Demons are always disturbed," she said. "What does that have to do with us? With me? The sea folk are neutral in Hell's war on humankind. We always have been."

"Hardly neutral," Dylan said, "if you're fucking one."

The barb shot home. She flinched and then aimed her smile like a knife. "The way your mother did?"

"My mother *married* my father."

Margred blinked, diverted. "Really? Why?"

Dylan's lips peeled back. "Why do you think? He took her pelt."

Ah. Selkies could not return to the sea without their sealskins. A mortal man could keep a selkie wife . . . as long as he kept her sealskin hidden. Because the children of such unions were rare—and usually human—the marriages even worked out. Sometimes.

"After I hit the Change, I found her sealskin," Dylan explained. "She took me back to sea with her."

Margred tried and failed to imagine entering the land beneath the wave for the first time at— How old must he have been? Twelve? Thirteen? Almost grown, floundering in an unfamiliar body and an utterly new world.

"That must have been . . . upsetting," she ventured.

Dylan inclined his head. "Awkward, at least. Stick to

your own kind," he advised. "Easier that way on everybody."

He was right.

Of course he was right.

She sympathized with his story. And yet . . . She glanced at his throat. He did not wear the triskelion, the wardens' mark, the sign of the prince's elite. But Dylan was still the prince's protégé, as much the prince's creature as Conn's hound. Had he issued his warning out of genuine concern? Or to further some agenda of his own?

She left him, making her way down the tower steps to the sea caves under the castle. Chinks of light pierced the thick stone walls. Margred's eyes adjusted to the gloom. The smell of the ocean rose from below like the smoke from a human fire.

As she circled down the stairs, another selkie climbed up: Gwyneth of Hiort. Her bare feet left damp splotches on the stone. A red robe trimmed with sable wrapped her naked shoulders. The black fur contrasted pleasingly with her milky skin and blond curls, but the choice of garment was still somewhat shocking. The children of the sea generally wore no pelts but their own.

Margred nodded politely. "Good hunting, Gwyneth."

Gwyneth smiled, revealing sharp white teeth between soft pink lips. "So it was. I went for fish and caught a fisherman—a trawler off Cape Savage."

"A handsome fisherman, I hope."

"Well enough. No staying power. Fortunately his mates supplied the stamina he lacked."

Margred raised her brows, amused. "You did the whole crew?"

Gwyneth shrugged, making the red robe slip on her shoulders. "It was a small vessel. Besides, one man between your legs is the same as another."

Memory stirred.

My name, the man had said, watching her with those sea green eyes. *It's Caleb.*

I thought we could spend some time getting to know one another.

Margred flushed. But she was no hypocrite, to rebuke Gwyneth for saying what she had thought herself.

The other selkie's gaze turned speculative. "I hear you've had good hunting yourself. In . . . Maine, is it?"

Feeling burst in Margred's chest—possessive, protective. "You hear a lot at Caer Subai," she said coolly. "And little worth listening to."

Gwyneth ran her tongue over her teeth. "I only say, if you found something tasty, you would not grudge a friend a bite."

Margred's eyes narrowed. Caleb was *hers*. "Unless I were still hungry."

Gwyneth's smile broadened. "Now you intrigue me."

"That was not my intention. Do not poach on my territory, little sister. Or I will bite you myself."

Gwyneth's laughter followed Margred down the stairs.

But the joke, she thought, was on her.

Somehow the human Caleb had snared her, tangled her up like an unwary swimmer caught in a net. Why else would she decide to go back? Fleetingly, she thought of Dylan's mother, who had drowned.

Dylan's warning rang in her ears: *Because she ventured too close to shore.*

The sea boomed and echoed as Margred descended. Moisture gleamed on the old stone walls. The way widened to a tunnel. The stairs ended in a smooth slab of rock. Light penetrated from the cave mouth, revealing a series of high-ceilinged chambers, one opening into another, wider, deeper, each lined with chests and scattered with treasures.

She picked her way to a sea chest bound and riveted in iron set on a ledge in the rock. Carvings of grain and apples chased around the rim. Shimmying out of her robe, she threw back the lid.

Her pelt lay inside, silver brown and brindled in a pattern of fine dark spots, uniquely hers. She scooped it up, cradling the fur skin against her bare breasts with one arm as she bundled the velvet robe away.

A fresh breeze teased her hair and ruffled the pelt in her arms. She raised her head to sniff the wind, shivering delicately.

Dropping the lid of the chest, she followed the air current to the mouth of the cave. Light bounced from the sea and glittered on the rocks. The sea cliffs towered at her back. Waves hissed and rushed at her pale, thin, human feet. She stood with the water foaming around her ankles as birds wheeled and cried over the ocean.

She raised the heavy pelt over her head. Its weight caressed her back and settled over her shoulders. She felt it wrap to embrace her as the Change took her, as her neck and forearms shortened, as her torso thickened, as her thighs fused and shrank. Color and sound dimmed. Brightness assaulted her expanding pupils. The cry of the birds sounded thin and far away. And oh, the smells! They poured over her, a thick, rich sea brew of kelp, cod, mussels, and plankton, carried to her on the breeze.

She inhaled deeply, lifting her sleek, bullet-shaped head to the wind. Her whiskers quivered. She humped her body forward over the rocks, propelling herself awkwardly with her stubby flippers and strong abdominal muscles. A wave surged to greet her. She let it lift and roll her, let it seize and take her, let herself glide, surrounded and immersed in pure sensation.

Sunlight struck through the darkening waves, through swaying forests of kelp and rocks teeming with life, with barnacles and limpets, seaweed and anemones. Here was grace. Here was freedom.

Here was home.

She plunged through the cool, dark water, leaving thought behind. Her worries streamed up and away like a chain of silver bubbles.

* * *

She could do this, first-year teacher Lucy Hunter assured herself at the end-of-year assembly. She could survive another summer on the island. She had before. Twenty-two of them, for God's sake.

She smiled encouragement at Hannah Bly, fidgeting with the rest of the island school chorus on a platform stage under the basketball goal. Students and parents packed the community center. Folding chairs squeaked on the wooden floor. The scent of coffee brewing in the lobby overlaid the gym smells of dust and sweat.

The important thing was to keep busy. She could run every morning and do lesson plans in the afternoon. The garden project she supervised met twice a week. She volunteered at the church and the library. With a little juggling, a little luck, she could stay out of the house and avoid the beach entirely until school began again.

"Takes you back, doesn't it?" her brother Caleb murmured low behind her.

Startled, Lucy turned her head. She had glimpsed him before the program started, surrounded by men eager to shake the hand of the island's returning war hero. But as soon as the children launched into their closing song, she figured Caleb would slip out to the parking lot to direct traffic.

She felt a glow of pleasure he would seek her out instead.

"It's nice to have you here."

"For a change."

Caleb had raised her since . . . well, since she was in diapers. After their mother disappeared, taking their thirteen-year-old brother with her, there hadn't been anyone else to do the job. Certainly not their father, who had responded to his wife's desertion by retreating to his boat and the bottle.

Caleb had left for college the year Lucy started third grade. But she remembered him standing at the back of the room for her end-of-year assemblies—her tall, kind, impossibly cool, remarkably tolerant older brother.

"You came as often as you could."

"Not often enough." Caleb stared out at the rows of folding chairs filled with parents and grandparents. The entire Hopkins family had turned out to recognize son Matt's graduation from the high school on the mainland. Regina Barone, in black pencil jeans and a chic white blouse, sat beside her mother, Antonia, in a purple velour track suit to see Nick advance a grade. "I missed your college graduation."

"You were busy."

He was in Iraq. Something else they never talked about. Lucy tried again. "Anyway, Dad came."

"Yeah. You told me in your e-mail. How'd that go?"

Not so well. Bart Hunter scowled through the ceremony and drank through dinner, uncomfortable in a tie and ill at ease in the busy, trendy restaurant she had picked out. Not even the clatter from the kitchen and the laughter from other tables could cover the silence between them.

"Fine," Lucy said. "I loved the flowers you sent."

His eyes narrowed. Well, she hadn't expected he'd be as easy to divert as one of her five-year-olds.

"And the check," she added hastily. "That was incredibly generous."

"I figured you could use it to move into an apartment someplace. Augusta, maybe, or Portland."

Lucy opened her mouth. Shut it.

"Why did you come back, Lucy?" Caleb asked.

It was a reasonable question. But then, her brother was always reasonable.

Which was why she could never explain to him why she had chosen to return. Back to the dark, cold house where they grew up, to the drafty rooms haunted by the shell of their father, the ghosts of their mother and brother.

Back to the island, where—for better *and* worse— everybody knew their name and their business.

Back to the sea she feared and could not live away from.

She had tried. Once. Ran away, hitched a ride from Port Clyde as far as Richmond and wound up on the dirty floor of a gas station restroom, puking her guts into the toilet. The memory still made her sick to her stomach.

Flu, the doctor on the island concluded, after Caleb had found her and brought her home.

Stress, the physician's assistant at the college infirmary told her when she collapsed on a visit to Dartmouth, where she'd been offered a scholarship.

Lucy didn't know or understand the reasons. But through cautious experimentation, she learned never to travel more than twenty miles from the ocean. She attended state college in Machias, within walking distance of the bay.

She licked her lips. "Why did you?"

Caleb raised one eyebrow. "I have a job here."

"So do I."

"How about a life?"

She stuck out her chin. "This is my life. Anyway, you're here."

"I'm thirty-three," Caleb said. Reasonable, as always. "You're twenty-three. You should be getting out more."

Lucy didn't point out that the ten-year difference in their ages didn't give him the right to dictate to her. He meant well. He always had.

"So should you."

His face shuttered. "Not a priority right now."

She shouldn't push. Open communication wasn't their family's style. Lucy hadn't even met Caleb's ex-wife—aka *the bitch*—before their wedding, and she didn't know any of the juicy details of their divorce. But prying into her brother's personal life seemed safer than discussing hers.

"What about that woman you were asking about a couple weeks ago? Margaret somebody?"

"What about her?"

"Are you going to see her again?"

"No. She left," he added, before Lucy could ask why not.

"Oh." *Oops.* This was why her family didn't talk. Too many awkward moments. She searched for something positive to say. "Well, maybe she'll come back. Like, to visit."

"No," Caleb said again in that *Drop it, Lucy* tone. "She's not coming back."

* * *

She wasn't coming back.

Caleb's hands tightened on the Jeep's steering wheel. Well, fine. He was trying to build a life here. Pursuing another Woman-Who-Would-Not-Stick, even one who looked like an angel and fucked like a dream, was not in his plan.

Which didn't explain what he was doing at nine o'clock at night driving along Old North Road toward the point.

Maggie's voice whispered in his brain. *I walk on the beach in the evening.*

Not for the last three weeks she hadn't.

She was a tourist. A one-night stand. An aberration. A mistake.

And he was an idiot, because he wanted her again.

Caleb scowled at the darkness beyond his windshield. It wasn't like he didn't have better demands on his time, more urgent claims on his attention.

The warmer weather brought out tourists like a rash. Brightly striped towels dotted the docks and hung from lines behind the rental cottages. Boats—and sometimes boaters—hit the water. Vacationers locked themselves out of their homes and cars, lost their dogs, their way, or their tempers. In the past week, Caleb had dealt with two kayak accidents and one fender bender, a petty theft at the Inn, and a handful of drunk and disorderlies. He'd spent his "free" hours trying to instill some respect for the speed limit in town and the ban against driving on the beach.

Whittaker had stood up at the last council meeting to argue for extending the ban to *walking* on the beach, which had created some hard feelings between the eel-grass lovers and the merchants who depended on the summer season to get them through the year. Caleb's offer to increase beach patrols and fine anybody caught littering had quieted things down some. But the extra hours away from his desk taxed his leg and left him with a backlog of paperwork.

Another reason why he should go home, ice his knee, and try to plow through his pile of trade journals.

He stared out at the night, an ache in his chest that rivaled the pain in his knee.

His sister's innocent question ate away at his defenses. *What about that woman . . . Margaret somebody? Are you going to see her again?*

He'd just make one more patrol swing, Caleb told himself. A lot of people were on the road tonight after the end-of-year assembly. Once he was sure they'd all made it home safely, he could . . .

Fire.

On the point. The glow struck through the scattered tree trunks lining the road.

He felt the slow, heavy thud of his heart and shook his head in disgust. Who was he kidding? She wasn't there. Maggie. She hadn't been back any time these past three weeks. No chance in hell she had changed her mind the one night he'd stayed away.

It was only kids again or clambakers. Still, Caleb had a responsibility to check it out. Fires were allowed only in the camping and picnic areas and by permit. He grimaced. Not to mention that if Whittaker spotted the flames, the lawyer would raise holy hell.

The Jeep's tires bumped off the road into sand and gravel. The shoulder was deserted, the sky clear, the moon full and bright.

Caleb frowned at the empty shadows under the pines. There should be other cars. Unless the party on the beach had come by boat?

He left his lights on and his motor running. In Portland, every police car came equipped with a camcorder mounted on the dash. Not on World's End. Chief Roy Miller hadn't bothered to keep up with technology, and so far the town council had resisted springing for a piece of fancy, new-fangled equipment simply on the new chief's say-so.

And maybe they had a point, Caleb acknowledged. He hardly needed video of a clambake.

He eased out of the vehicle, feeling the muscles in his tired right leg cramp and adjust as it took his weight. Something acrid tickled the back of his throat. Something burning.

Burning, on the beach.

Not the clean fire of driftwood either, or the sea salt smell of a clambake. This smell was awful, fuel and flesh, like the charred remains of a Sunday roast or the smoldering wreck of his Humvee on the sun-blasted road to Baghdad.

Caleb broke out in a sweat triggered by smoke and memory. That was okay, he was okay, he was riding beach patrol on World's End, not providing convoy security along the death corridor.

He reached for his gun anyway. Sucking in a very careful breath, he entered the shadow of the trees.

Fire roared from a skeleton of blackened timbers: shafts of white heat, tongues of orange flame. Red smoke boiled against a black backdrop of sea and sky.

No beer cans. No blankets. No kids. No people at all.

There. Wavering against the glare, outlined by angry flames, a figure—a man?—tall and thin and oddly fluid, stooped to drag another stick from the heap at his feet.

The heap shifted. Caleb's heart accelerated. Not sticks, then. In fact, that almost looked like ... He'd swear it looked like ...

Jesus.

He brought his gun up, instinct and training taking over from his brain. "Police! Don't move."

The figure froze above the crumpled bundle at his feet.

Sweat slicked the grip of Caleb's gun. Okay. So ... okay. He focused on the crouching guy, not daring to drop his gaze to the silent heap at the edge of the fire. Smoke carried the stink of burning across the sand.

He breathed through his mouth. "Stand up. Slowly. Hands in the air, where I can see 'em."

The tall, dark figure wavered against the flames, hands creeping over his head. Empty hands, Caleb noted with relief. He took a step forward.

And watched in horror as the figure whirled and leaped into the fire.

Caleb yelled and lunged forward. His injured leg buckled on the soft sand. He fell to his knees, and the night exploded in stars and sparks and pain.

Breathe. Crawl.

He couldn't see, he couldn't hear the guy. *The guy who jumped into the fire.* But he could smell him burn. The stench seared his nostrils and the back of his throat like swallowed acid.

He lurched to his feet, his heart drumming in his ears. Heat beat on his exposed face and hands as he ran toward the bonfire, close enough to recognize the heap on the ground as a body, a woman's naked body fallen forward on the sand, her skin orange in the lurid light. The image of her—round, glowing, naked—burned his retinas.

His heart stopped.

Maggie.

5

❧

CALEB PLUNGED TOWARD THE FIRE.

Maggie.

He reached for her. Heat scorched his hands and face. Pain seared his knee. Grabbing her bare ankle, he dragged her away from the hungry flames.

Her hair smoldered. *Shit.*

He hauled her into his arms. Her head lolled against his shoulder. He hoped like hell she hadn't broken her neck. In the bright moonlight, she looked like the phantom of the frigging opera, half of her face a silver mask, the other half blackened with blood.

Staggering to his feet, Caleb ran with her toward the water, pain stabbing with every step. It didn't matter, not with Maggie solid and warm in his arms. Warm and . . . alive? He fumbled for a pulse. There, just there beneath her jaw, he felt her life flicker against his fingertips. *Thank you, Jesus.*

The tide was out. He lowered her to the hard, damp sand, a sound escaping his clenched teeth as his bad leg took their combined weight. Methodically, he smothered the sparks in her hair with his hands. The small pricks burned his palms.

Airway? Clear.

Breathing ragged.

Circulation . . . The gash above her left eyebrow opened like a sullen mouth. The blood didn't bother him. Head wounds always bled. But her loss of consciousness worried him. That bastard must have hit her hard.

He stripped off his jacket to wrap around her. The sea whispered across the sand, soaking his pant legs, rushing over her bare white toes and calves. Caleb swore.

But the cold water revived her. She moaned.

"It's okay," he reassured her, even though it wasn't, even though she was naked and bleeding and whoever the fuck did this had jumped into the fire. "You're okay."

He reached for his cell phone.

She bolted upright and rolled away from him toward the fire.

"Hey!"

He threw himself on top of her before she burned herself. She fought him like a wild thing in a trap, writhing and clawing under him. He restrained her with his weight, trying not to squash her, trying not to hurt her, trying to maintain calm.

"Easy," he panted in her ear. "It's me. It's Caleb. Just take it easy."

She turned her head and bit him.

Jesus.

He clamped her jaw in his hand and squeezed. Not hard enough to bruise—he hoped—but hard enough to get her attention.

"Knock it off," he ordered.

And just like that, the fight went out of her. She lay under him, stiff as a ten-dollar whore. As a corpse. Fresh blood oozed from the gash on her forehead.

"Maggie—"

"Fire." She squeezed the word through her teeth. "In . . . the fire."

He'd thought she had missed her assailant's dramatic

leap into the blaze. But maybe not. Maybe she was even worried about the guy.

Doubt wriggled, a nasty worm under the anger and the fear. She *was* naked. Maybe . . .

"I'm going to look," Caleb said. "But you have to stay here."

She nodded—as much of a nod as she could manage with his hand still gripping her face.

Releasing her, he limped up the beach to assess the blaze. It shot into the dark night like a beacon, ten feet high and easily six feet across, raging on the edge of control. He was surprised nobody had called the fire department yet. Volunteers lived for shit like this. He scanned the beach. At least the surrounding sand and rock provided natural insulation, and the fire had been set far enough from the trees that escaping sparks wouldn't torch the whole island.

A log broke in the heart of the fire, releasing another gout of flame, another rush of heat. No way could anybody have survived a jump into or across that inferno.

So he should see a body, right? Remains. The human body didn't burn well. Too much water. Even cremation left large fragments of bone.

There should have been . . . something.

Instead, the fire burned clear and bright. He sniffed. Even the charred smell he'd noticed when he arrived was mostly gone.

So what the hell had he seen? What the fuck had happened?

The sand was disturbed in all directions.

He didn't have a prayer of processing the scene until morning.

And he had a naked, bleeding woman on his hands in need of medical attention.

He scanned the fire again, glanced toward the trees. If he was back in Portland, he'd have the combined resources of the city police, the fire department, and an EMS squad to call on. If he was back in Iraq, he'd have the support of his unit.

Or he could be pinned under a smoking wreck with his femur sticking out of his thigh, trying to return enemy fire with an M9 while the nineteen-year-old kid next to him bled out into the dirt.

Sometimes you had to work with what you had.

He reached again for his cell phone and felt Maggie's presence like a breath on the back of his neck.

Like he'd really expected her to stay put just because he'd told her to. (His last words to her three weeks ago— *Hurry back*—whispered in his head.)

He turned.

She stood on the beach behind him, her body shining like pearl through his open jacket, the blood on her forehead gleaming black, and her hair a wild glory in the moonlight. A wave of emotion—rage, desire, frustration—rushed him, cramping his gut.

"Why don't you tell me what happened," he invited quietly, his eyes on her face.

Her gaze flicked past him to the fire. "You said you would look," she accused.

Hostility was easier to handle than hysterics, but a part of him wished she would cry or cling to him or something— anything that would allow him to comfort her.

"I looked," he said. "I'll look again in the morning."

"The morning will be too late."

"Maggie . . ." He was jealous, he realized. And appalled that his personal reactions were intruding on what was now police business. "It's already too late for him."

Her lips drew back from her teeth. "Not *him*. You won't find him. I need what he took from me."

Caleb rubbed his smarting forearm thoughtfully. She had bitten him. Like an animal. She must really want . . . whatever it was.

"And what's that?"

"In the fire."

"What did he take, Maggie?"

She stared at him blankly.

Shock, he thought. He'd seen it before, in victims huddled at the side of the road after a car accident, in soldiers on stretchers after an enemy attack: the rapid breathing, the dilated pupils, the insistent repetition. She was in shock.

Or concussed.

He felt a quick lurch of concern. He couldn't rush her with questions like an overzealous rookie conducting his first interview. She needed time and medical attention before he could begin to make sense of what had happened.

What *had* happened? He had seen—Caleb could have sworn he'd seen—a man jump into a bonfire without leaving a trace behind. How the hell did you make sense of that?

He flipped open his phone.

"What are you doing?" Maggie asked.

"Calling Donna Tomah—our island doctor. You need somebody to check out that bump on your head."

And do a rape workup, he thought. Deadly anger coiled in his gut.

She put her hand to her head and looked at her fingers as if she'd never seen blood before. Her eyes were dark and dazed.

Caleb's jaw set. When he found out what had happened, when he found the bastard who did this to her, he'd heave him into the fire himself.

*   *   *

Her pelt was gone.

Stolen.

Burned.

Destroyed.

Fear welled thick and cold inside her, smothering her chest. Margred forced herself to breathe. She had survived, she reminded herself. Things could be worse.

She stared at her blood-smeared fingers. How could this be worse? Yes, she was alive now, but without her pelt she could never return to the sea. Never return to Sanctuary. Away from the enchantment of the island, she would age. She would live a span of human years and die, never to be reborn.

The fear spilled over, paralyzing her. Margred tried to force it down, but it was like trying to hold back the sea with her cupped hands.

Endless existence has its own . . . burdens, she had said to Dylan mere hours ago. But now . . . Now . . .

She closed her eyes in terror and despair. She was such a fool.

The device in Caleb's hand snapped shut. She opened her eyes and found him watching her, a terrible compassion in his eyes.

Her backbone straightened reflexively.

"Donna can meet you at the clinic," he said. "I'll get Ted Sherman to drive you. He's one of our volunteer firefighters."

A firefighter, she thought dully. Well, that made sense. She had caught a whiff of something—*demon*—right before the attack that knocked her unconscious. She had not supposed humans would have the knowledge to set a firefighter against a fire demon, but . . .

And then the rest of his meaning penetrated her numb consciousness.

"No," she said. "I can't leave the beach."

"Why not?"

She opened her mouth, but no words came out. She had no reason to stay. There was nothing for her here. No sealskin. No escape. No hope. The realization struck her soul, bleak as the dawn over mudflats. A howl built in the back of her throat.

The human watched her, his mouth kind and his eyes shrewd. "I'll join you," he said. "As soon as I've secured the scene."

He was leaving her?

He was leaving. Her.

Margred shivered with loss and indignation. Everything she knew was slipping away. She felt herself dissipating, escaping like water through her fingers. She wasn't about to let the one person she did know out of her grasp.

Caleb might be human, but at least he was familiar.

"I won't go. Not without you."

"Is there anybody I can call?" His voice was deep and very gentle. "To stay with you."

"No."

"A friend? Family member maybe."

Margred barely remembered the face of her mother, who had followed the sea king beneath the wave centuries before. She did not know the fate of her father. She had no mate, no child. She hunted, slept, lived alone.

She shook her head and then winced.

A crease appeared between Caleb's eyebrows. "No one?"

Her hands clenched beneath the long jacket cuffs. She did not relish his pity. She was selkie, one of the First Creation, a child of the sea.

Or she had been.

In the sea, in her own territory, her lack of connections had never troubled her. But in the human's world, maybe everyone was tangled and bound together.

He must not suspect she was not of his world.

She let herself sway on her feet, let the jacket fall open over her bare breasts. It was not so hard to pretend dizziness. Her head throbbed. Her legs trembled. The demon's attack had frightened her—weakened her—more than she wanted to admit. "I . . . can't think. I don't remember."

Caleb did not look at her breasts. Those clear green eyes remained fixed on her face with an intensity that made her uncomfortable. "All right," he said slowly. "You can wait in the Jeep until Ted gets here, and then I'll drive you to the doctor."

* * *

The inside of his vehicle—*Jeep,* Margred repeated silently to herself—was dark and warm and smelled of metal and oil and man. Land smells. Alien smells. In the quiet dark, reaction seeped in, corroding her fragile composure. The roof and frame pressed in on her like the iron bars of a cage. She shifted on the slick upholstery, her blood pounding in her head, staining her fingers through the folded white square he had given her.

She opened her mouth to breathe.

The driver's side door popped open and Caleb slid into the seat beside her, his big body looming out of the darkness. She managed not to jump.

"All set," he said. "You keeping pressure on that cut?"

She nodded carefully, as if her head might fall off.

His lips curved. "Atta girl. Still bleeding?"

Her fingers were warm and sticky. "Not as much."

"Good. That's good." He thrust a key into the side of the wheel, and the Jeep shuddered to life. He glanced at her. "Buckle up."

She blinked.

His mouth compressed before he reached for her. She inhaled once, sharply, as his shoulder flattened her back against her seat, as his hard arm brushed her breast. His hand was almost in her face. He drew a strap down across her body, securing it with a click beside her hip.

The pressure on her chest increased.

He leaned back. "There you go."

Her mouth was dry. She could not go anywhere. She was strapped in. Tied down. Trapped.

He twisted in his seat to pull a similar belt over his own broad body, grunting as his knee connected with the steering wheel. A little of her panic leaked away.

"You'll like Donna. Dr. Tomah," he added when Margred didn't say anything. "She retired to the island about five years ago before she decided retirement wasn't really her thing. Talked the town into building her a clinic, and now she handles pretty much everything that doesn't require a trip to the hospital in Rockport."

She forced herself to listen as if his words held some clue to her dilemma. As if she cared. She didn't. But there was something soothing, all the same, in his quiet manner and deep, easy voice.

He was talking now about the council budget and a new X-ray machine, soft, meaningless words that filled the silence and washed over her like water. She leaned her aching head against the cool glass and stared out at the darkness rushing beyond her window.

His voice stopped. The vehicle stopped.

Margred roused to find him watching her. "Did you do that on purpose?"

"Do what?" he asked, straight-faced.

"Bore me to sleep?"

Caleb smiled. She had the sense he was not a man who smiled often or easily. A trickle of warmth eased the ice in her belly. "All part of the job, ma'am."

She fingered his jacket over her shoulders. Studied the badge gleaming on his shirt pocket. "This is a job?"

"Sometimes." His gaze met hers. She felt it again, that curious melting in her stomach. "Sometimes it's personal."

* * *

It was personal now, Caleb thought. Whether he liked it or not.

Maggie sat upright on a padded table, her shoulders straight and her eyes wide and blind. She had exchanged his bloodied handkerchief for a clinic cold pack and his jacket for a cheap paper gown. Even though he understood the need to reduce swelling and preserve whatever evidence remained, he wanted to wrap her, warm her, take care of her somehow.

She hadn't clung to him or cried. But when Donna Tomah had questioned Caleb's presence in her examination room, Maggie had said flatly, "He is with me."

So now Caleb crowded the corner near the head of the table while the doctor sat at the foot. Despite his aching leg, he didn't sit. He couldn't sit. He'd pulled off the big reassuring act in the Jeep, but inside he was churning with the need for action, with pity and admiration and cold, deep rage.

Motionless, he watched as Maggie checked little boxes

on a medical form and handed the clipboard back to the doctor.

Donna's round face, unlined beneath her salt-and-pepper hair, creased in a frown. "You've left a lot of blanks."

Maggie's hands twitched in the paper drape across her lap. "I did not know what to write."

Donna pursed her lips. "Last name? Age? Address?"

Deliberately, Maggie loosed her grip on the drape and replaced the cold pack on her head. "I don't remember."

Caleb stirred in his corner.

"Did you lose consciousness?" Donna asked Maggie.

Caleb answered for her. "Yes."

"How long?"

Maggie hesitated.

"She was out when I arrived at the scene. Say, at least five minutes."

"Was this injury intentionally caused by another person?"

Maggie looked at Caleb.

"You're safe now," he said gently. "You don't have to protect him."

Her full lips pressed together. "I am not protecting anyone."

"So, intentional injury?" the doctor asked.

"I . . . think so."

"Somebody was standing over her when I got there," Caleb volunteered. "He may have hit her with a stick. Plenty of firewood on the beach."

"Is that what happened?" Donna asked.

Maggie shrugged. The paper gown shifted on her shoulders.

"Do you remember arriving at the beach?" Caleb asked.

A slight hesitation. Victims were often unreliable witnesses, too eager to please or afraid of reprisal. She could be unsure or in shock or struggling with the language. She could be confused.

Or lying.

"Not really," she said.

"Did you see anybody when you got there?" he persisted.

"I . . . no."

"Tell me what you saw."

"The fire."

"What else?"

She shook her head, in denial or frustration. "I don't remember."

Donna's gaze met his. "Trauma to the head," she murmured. "It's possible."

"Retrograde amnesia? Doesn't that usually only affect recent memory? Before and after the event?"

"Why don't you let me finish my examination before you make a diagnosis." The doctor glanced at the clipboard on her lap. "Are you on any medications? Prescriptions, over-the-counter drugs?"

"No, nothing like that."

"What about birth control?"

"No," Maggie said.

A memory exploded in Caleb's brain.

"You could still get pregnant," he had warned her.

"No," she'd said, and taken him in her mouth.

"There are things I can give you," Donna said. "If we determine pregnancy is a possibility."

He snapped back to the present.

"It's not," Maggie said.

The doctor cleared her throat. "We find in about five percent of rape cases—"

"I was not raped."

Caleb's instincts went on point. "You said you didn't remember."

"I do not need to remember," she said firmly. "I would know."

He wanted to believe her.

Reason enough, in his experience, to doubt. She was naked and unconscious when he found her. Anything could have been done to her. His stomach pitched. Anything.

She might not remember. Or she could be in denial.

"It's easy enough to confirm," he said.

A glint surfaced in those dark, deep eyes. "Easy for whom?"

He was silent.

Donna tapped her pen against the clipboard. "Just a few more questions."

Caleb kept his hands in his pockets and his gaze on Maggie's face as she answered the doctor's questions in a low, clear voice that told them . . . absolutely nothing.

She didn't know.

She couldn't remember.

She wouldn't say.

"Date of last menstrual cycle?" Frustration tinged the doctor's voice. Caleb sympathized.

"I'm not sure."

"Are you sexually active?"

A pause, while every muscle in his body tensed.

The doctor tried again. "Do you remember the last time you had intercourse?"

She remembered . . . something. He saw it in her eyes.

"It's all right," he said in the even tone he used to soothe new recruits. "No one is blaming or accusing you of anything. We just want to find out what happened so we can take care of you."

"The last time?" Donna prompted.

Maggie's face was pale and collected. A tiny pulse beat beneath her jaw. "Three weeks ago."

Three weeks . . .

His chest was tight. "What about tonight?"

"I don't understand."

"What were you doing on the beach tonight?"

Maggie's gaze collided with his, her eyes dark and unfathomable. "Looking for you."

6

DONNA GLANCED FROM MAGGIE TO CALEB, SPECU-
lation sparkling in her eyes. "You two know each other?"

Maggie was silent.

Caleb didn't blame her. Their relationship was none of
the doctor's damn business. Or wouldn't be under most circumstances. Too bad these weren't ordinary circumstances.
Maggie was Donna's patient. And Caleb . . . Well, he was
willing to tell the doctor whatever she needed to hear to provide Maggie with the best possible care.

So, okay, he didn't know Maggie's last name or her favorite color, her permanent address or her childhood pets.
But they'd had sex on a picnic table. Twice. That counted
for something.

Know her?

"Yes," he said.

"So . . ." Donna pursed her lips. "Any idea who I should
list as the responsible party?"

Victims Compensation would cover only part of the bill.

"Put my name," Caleb said. "At least until we locate
some family."

As simply as that, he claimed her.

There would be winks, he knew, and nudges and teasing comments when he patrolled the dock or dropped by Antonia's for his morning cup of coffee.

But as long as Maggie was tagged as the police chief's girl, she would be accepted and protected by the tight-knit island community. The news might even give the son of a bitch who attacked her a few anxious moments.

Caleb hoped so.

"Well, then." Donna set down her clipboard and smiled at Maggie. "Let's have a look at you."

Maggie stiffened, but she allowed the doctor to palpate her skull and shine a tiny penlight into her eyes.

Caleb caught himself leaning forward and settled back deliberately in his corner. For months now, he'd been trying to feel a part of things. Connected. Now he had to struggle for his professional detachment.

"Hmm," Donna said.

Fuck detached.

"What's wrong?" Caleb asked.

"Her pupils are enlarged."

"Is that bad?"

Donna made another noncommittal noise. "They are responsive to light. And the reaction is symmetric." She flashed, peered, flashed again. "It's just . . . odd."

Maggie blinked. "There is nothing wrong with my eyes."

"No blurring?" Caleb asked. "No double vision?"

"No," Maggie said.

Donna shot him an annoyed look.

He shut up, jamming his hands in his pockets, as the doctor continued her examination. Mouth. Throat. Wrists. Arms. Breasts. Thighs. Every part he had touched and taken and caressed . . . He looked up at the stained acoustic tile on the ceiling. Forced himself to look back at Maggie on the table.

The doctor had reached her feet. She spread her toes, as if checking for needle marks, and paused.

Maggie pulled her foot away.

Donna allowed that, making another note on the chart. "Good motor responses. Now I want you to scoot to the end of the table and lie down."

Caleb pulled in his lower abdomen, instinctively protecting his crotch. He knew what was coming. Hell, he'd provided the rape kit from his trunk.

Maggie looked at Caleb. "Why?"

He would rather have faced an alley full of blind windows than that dark, wary gaze.

"I need to do a vaginal exam," Donna explained.

"To assess your injuries," Caleb said.

Like that made the violation of her body and her privacy all right.

"This is to help me?"

He wanted to believe that. Had to believe it.

"To help you," he said evenly, "and to help me catch whoever did this to you."

Maggie tilted her head, keeping her gaze on his face. "You want this?"

No, he didn't. He didn't want anybody touching her. Nobody but him.

He fisted his hands in his pockets. "Yeah."

She lifted one shoulder in a shrug before lowering obediently to the table. The paper crinkled under her as she moved.

The rape kit was open on the counter, vials and slides in a neat row. Caleb had never been in the room during a pelvic before. His ex-wife, Sherilee, had never even discussed her appointments with him except to complain. *"Men have it easy,"* she'd said. *"You have no idea."*

She'd been right.

He had worked rape cases in Portland, always waiting outside the curtained cubical to take possession of the evidence and question the victims. Not that he didn't care about them. He did. But he'd never been forced to witness this second assault on their bodies and their dignity, to imagine how it must feel to lie on your back with your feet in metal stirrups while some stranger sat between your open thighs.

Increasingly uncomfortable, he watched as Donna swabbed and combed and probed. Maggie endured the exam in stoic silence, her eyes veiled.

Maybe he should have taken her to the hospital on the mainland, he thought now that it was too late. She was stabilized. There would have been somebody, a trained nurse, a victims' advocate, to comfort her. To hold her hand. To do all the things he couldn't do.

She inhaled sharply and grabbed his forearm.

Stunned, he stared at her grip on his arm, her slim, pale fingers, their nails short and shining as shells on the beach. Her wrist was mottled purple and red.

She had fought him, Caleb remembered. On the sand, writhing and clawing under him. He *had* to hold her down.

Guilt burned under his breastbone.

Cautiously, he covered her small hand with his much larger one. How could she bear for him to touch her? But she didn't pull away.

With his thumb, he gently stroked her bruise over and over.

"All right now." Donna turned from the sink holding the speculum. "I want you to try to relax."

Relax? Caleb's belly tightened again. *Jesus.*

Maggie took one look at the gleaming metal implement and bolted upright on the table. "No."

Hell, no, he agreed silently.

Which was stupid. He was thinking like a man—a man who cared about her—instead of like a cop.

"Would you feel better if Chief Hunter left the room?" the doctor asked.

"I would feel *better*"—Maggie bit the words out—"if *I* left."

So would Caleb. Unfortunately, even if Maggie refused the pelvic, they weren't finished yet.

He turned to Donna. "How much more do you need?"

The doctor frowned. "We don't have the equipment for a CT scan, but I should take X-rays. She needs stitches, of course. I have to draw a blood test for STDs and take more samples for the rape kit."

Maggie snarled. "I was not raped."

The possibility shook Caleb.

He reminded himself she could still be in shock. Or in denial. But faced with her fierce certainty, he allowed himself to doubt. To hope. If she wasn't raped . . .

"What about her external injuries?" he asked Donna.

"Aside from the head wound?" Donna pursed her lips. "Those abrasions on her wrists are certainly consistent with a struggle."

Caleb winced. Whatever she needed to hear to provide care, he reminded himself.

"I had to restrain her," he said.

The doctor's eyes cooled. "So you bruised her wrists?"

"I bit him," Maggie volunteered.

The temperature in the room dropped another twenty degrees.

"I really think it would be best if I spoke to Miss—to Maggie alone," Donna said.

"Why?" Maggie demanded.

"The doctor wants to be sure I'm not the one who hit you," Caleb said in a carefully neutral voice.

"That is stupid," Maggie said.

"No." Caleb spoke slowly, his gaze never leaving the doctor's. "It makes good sense. We've admitted to a relationship. I bring you in here injured, confused, with no recollection of your assailant. For all she knows, I raped you myself."

"Then she does not know you," Maggie said.

Her warm conviction filled a hole in Caleb's chest he hadn't realized was empty. Maybe he hadn't imagined that moment of connection three weeks ago.

He set his jaw. It couldn't be allowed to matter. He had his job to do. They both had their jobs to do.

"She's trying to protect you," he said.

Donna thawed slightly. "For what it's worth, there are no bruises or lacerations that would indicate rape. Of course, an internal exam might reveal more."

"But you don't think so," Caleb guessed.

The doctor shrugged. "It doesn't matter what I think. We both know hunches don't hold up in court."

Maggie folded her arms across her breasts. "What about what I think? Or is that also not allowed to matter?"

Caleb and Donna exchanged glances over her head.

"She has the right to revoke consent," the doctor said.

Hell, he knew that.

That didn't mean he couldn't intimidate her. Persuade her. He had enough experience as a cop and as a man to coax an unwilling woman. But to do so now, in the face of the doctor's doubts and Maggie's own fierce certainty, seemed itself a kind of rape, an incursion of her body and her self.

And for what? What was he trying to prove? That even though he'd let the guy who did this get away, he could help her somehow after all?

Frustration gnawed his gut.

"Seal the rape kit and do—whatever you have to. Whatever's medically necessary," he clarified, unsure if his decision made him a good guy or just a bad cop. "Is there a lock on your refrigerator?"

The doctor nodded.

"Good. I'll pick up the kit in the morning. I don't want any questions about chain of evidence." If they even had any evidence, which he was beginning to doubt.

"Photos?" Donna asked.

"I'll take them before you stitch her up."

Donna pursed her lips. "Is that all right with you?" she asked Maggie.

She held herself as still as a deer in the woods, frozen on the point of flight. "What if I said no?"

Easy, Caleb told himself. She had been poked and prodded and pressured enough.

He shrugged. "Then I'd skip the pictures, and you'd have a real interesting scar there on your forehead."

"Scars are a sign of strength. Of survival."

She wasn't serious. Or maybe she was. Memory stirred in his mind and in his heart. She hadn't freaked out at the sight of the purple waffle weave on his leg.

"Mostly scars are a sign you got caught in the wrong place at the wrong time," he said. "Let the doctor do her thing, and if you're good, maybe she'll give you a Wonder Woman Band-Aid."

Maggie narrowed her eyes. "Wonder Woman."

He smiled. "You want to hold out for SpongeBob, fine. But that's my final offer."

Donna sniffed. "If you two are done playing doctor, I'll finish here, and she'll be free to go."

"Right. Thanks," Caleb said.

Maggie pulled her paper gown tightly closed. "Go where?"

*   *   *

He woke on the floor of an empty room in front of a dead fire.

The smell of ashes drifted from the grate and coated his tongue. Pain pulsed in his temples and flashed in his head. His body felt pounded, pummeled, as if he'd been in a fight, as if his internal organs, lungs and liver and spleen, had been worked over, rearranged, pushed aside to accommodate something alien.

Like the mother of all hangovers.

He had been sitting staring into the flames, sipping a fifteen-year-old single malt Laphroaig. The smoky sweet aftertaste lingered, roiling his stomach and burning the back of his throat. He could see his empty shot glass on the carpet a few yards away.

He must have drunk more than he thought.

He pushed with his arms and levered himself to his knees. Spots danced, black and bright, before his eyes. His stomach lurched. He swayed on all fours, head hanging, taking deep breaths in and out. In. And out.

When he had control again, he crawled to the glass. Mustn't leave it on the floor. Mustn't let anyone see. He reached for it, his hand shaking. Stared, puzzled, at the dark smear on his cuff. Too dark for whiskey, too deep for soot . . .

Blood?

Shock cleared his brain.

Had he hurt himself when he fell? Was that why his memory was fuzzy, his head throbbed?

He staggered to his feet, heart tripping in panic.

The harsh light of the bathroom made him reel. Gripping the cool porcelain sink for support, he inspected himself in the mirror. He looked . . . fine. All right, not fine. His eyes were red-rimmed and bloodshot, his face the color of the ashes in the grate. But he wasn't injured. The blood—if it was blood—wasn't his.

He held his shaking hand under the faucet. Water soaked his cuff and ran red into the sink. The stain spread, pink against white.

Oh, God.

What had happened? Why couldn't he remember?

His throat was dry. He swallowed two Excedrin with a glass of water. Two glasses of water. Despite the churning in his stomach, he was almost unbearably thirsty. Dehydrated. He splashed his face with trembling hands. Water dripped on his shirt as he stared at his reflection. His eyes . . .

Something lurked at the edges of his vision or in the corners of his eyes. Like flames licking a hole through paper. Like a face flickering at the window of an empty house.

The hair rose on his arms.

He cursed. He was *fine*.

He snapped off the light, plunging the bathroom into darkness.

Stripping off his clothes, he stumbled to bed.

* * *

Margred leaned her head against the back of her seat and closed her eyes. Caleb had left her in the Jeep outside the Inn with the instruction to wait for him. She might as well obey. She didn't think she could move if she tried.

It wasn't that she didn't care what happened to her anymore. She cared desperately. But like a sea bird tangled in fishing line, she did not see any way to affect the outcome. Her struggles merely exhausted her. Sapped by fatigue and shock, she was reaching the limits of her puny human strength, increasingly, blessedly numb.

Or almost numb. When Caleb opened the door on the driver's side, she felt a warming little flicker of . . . relief? Recognition?

He frowned. "Are you all right?"

He meant to be kind, she reminded herself. "Just tired."

Tired of his questions. Tired of being urged to remember what she pretended to forget. Preferred to forget.

The smell, the demon smell, neither human nor mer nor angel nor sidhe.

The hunger.

The pain.

She wanted to forget. But the blurring of memory she accepted as a mercy, Caleb regarded as an obstacle. He wanted the truth.

Only she knew he could not handle it.

He cleared his throat. "Yeah, about that . . . We've run into a little problem."

Her poor, weary heart jumped into her throat.

A *little* problem?

Smaller than, say, being attacked out of the dark by a demon? Than having her identity and immortality stripped from her with her pelt? Than being hit over the head and left to age and die?

"What kind of a problem?" she asked.

"There's no room at the Inn."

She stared at him, uncomprehending.

"They're full up," he explained. "I was afraid they might be. They only have nine guest rooms, and with the season starting . . ."

She struggled to process what he was saying. "I need a place to shelter. At least for the night."

Her caves . . . But she could not reach her caves in her current condition. In her human shape.

"Not a problem," Caleb said. "I'll take you home—to my father's house. My sister can put you up for the night. You shouldn't be alone anyway."

"I won't be alone. I can stay with you."

His mouth tightened. "That's not a good idea."

"Why not?"

"I only have one bedroom."

She did not see the problem. "You have a bed."

"I won't take advantage of you that way. I can bunk on the couch for a couple of nights, but it's not a solution. Not a long-term solution."

"I cannot think about long-term right now," Margred snapped.

Silence.

"You'll like my sister Lucy," Caleb said at last. "Everybody does. And she could loan you some clothes."

The clothes decided her.

Or maybe it was his unassailable kindness. His determination to do the right thing.

Margred glanced at the covering the doctor had provided, a loose turquoise smock and pants decorated all over with pink dancing bears. "As long as they don't have bears on them."

Caleb's face relaxed. "No bears," he promised, and started the Jeep.

*   *   *

Lucy was dreaming when the phone rang. Not the usual dreams of drowning or being chased by red-eyed monsters. She dreamed about her mother. Her mother, singing. And her mother's songs whispered and echoed in her head like the ebbing tide.

Lucy didn't remember her mother. She hadn't dreamed about her for a long time, even though when she was little— six or seven—those were her favorite dreams, the ones she pulled out and played with during the day. They were all pretty much the same. One night the phone would ring or a knock would sound on the door, and when Lucy woke the next morning, her mother would be in the kitchen cooking breakfast, pancakes with blueberry syrup like Jennifer Logan's mom or muffins studded with walnuts and cranberries like Mrs. Barone.

She never told anyone about the dreams. Not Caleb, who always left her cereal in a bowl and a note on the counter before he took the ferry to school. Not her father, who left the house hours earlier to haul his traps and set his lines. Bart Hunter never wanted to hear his daughter's dreams. Or a word about her mother.

By the time Lucy started college, the dreams stopped. But sometimes at night when the phone rang, she felt her heart leap and then hurry in a childish, hopeful beat: *What-if, what-if, what-if . . .*

Usually, the caller had simply dialed the wrong number. Tonight, though, Caleb was on the other end of the line, and he wanted her help. Or rather, one of his cases did, some poor woman, homeless and hurt, who had been assaulted on the beach.

Caleb had always been chivalrous, kind to underdogs and strays.

"I hate to bother you," he said. "You still keep a key on the porch?"

"Under the lobster buoy, same as always. But I don't mind getting up to let you in." She was flattered that for once Caleb was asking for her help instead of riding to her rescue. Flattered and happy.

Or she would be if she weren't so groggy.

She scrambled out of bed, pulling her University of Maine at Machias sweatshirt on over her LIVE, LAUGH,

LOVE, TEACH T-shirt. By the time Caleb's Jeep crunched onto the gravel drive, she had fresh sheets on one of the upstairs beds and the tea kettle whistling on the stove. Turning down the gas, she hurried to the door.

Caleb climbed the three steps to the porch, moving slowly, as if he'd had a long day. Or his leg hurt him. "I appreciate this, Lu."

She flushed, unused to thanks. "Don't be silly. This is your house, too."

Caleb grunted. "Dad still up?"

"No, he . . . he was sleeping in his chair when I got home." She glanced over her shoulder at the empty living room. "He must have taken himself up to bed."

"Drunk?" Caleb asked.

"Sleeping," Lucy repeated firmly. She didn't want to make trouble, any more trouble, between her father and her brother.

"He could have come tonight. To your end-of-year program."

"I didn't expect him to."

Caleb snorted. "You should. He—"

The Jeep door opened and a woman stepped down onto the gravel. A young woman—well, youngish—and medium tall, with wide, dark eyes and waving dark hair and skin as pale and perfect as the inside of a shell.

Lucy's jaw dropped. *This* was Caleb's stray?

She glided toward the house with a graceful assurance that fit her better than the wrinkled pediatric scrubs she wore. Despite the police windbreaker around her shoulders and the stark white bandage on her head, she looked sophisticated, confident, exotic. Like a movie star in Africa.

"This is Maggie," Caleb said matter-of-factly. Lucy wondered if her brother was even aware of the warmth in his eyes, the subtle possessiveness of his hand at the woman's waist as he guided her up the last step. "Maggie, my sister, Lucy."

Lucy met that wide, dark gaze and heard a roaring in her ears like the sound of the sea. Everything inside her expanded, squeezing the air from her lungs. She opened her mouth to breathe.

Confusion flitted across the woman's face. "Your sister? But . . ."

Caleb's expression sharpened. "What is it? Do you recognize each other?"

The pressure in Lucy's chest increased. It wasn't recognition. More like heartburn. She dragged in a breath and held it the way she had taught herself to do, until everything inside her was forced back into its proper place.

"N-no," the woman said slowly. "I just— For a moment, I thought . . . It's nothing."

Lucy breathed again. "Would you like some tea?"

"No. I am tired. I would like to sleep."

She could have said thank you, Lucy thought. "I'll show you to your room, then."

"I'll do it." Caleb touched her arm briefly. "You go make us tea. I'll join you in the kitchen after I get Maggie settled."

Lucy smiled with amusement and a touch of wistfulness. Settled? What was her brother planning to do? Read her a story and kiss her good night?

But of course, she didn't tease him.

"The bed's already made up," she said. "Good night."

*   *   *

The humans' house was dark and cramped and smelled of earth and must, of cooked food and worked metal. It was both alien and ordinary, with no hint or sign of the amazing burst of power that had punched Margred on the threshold.

"What was that about?" Caleb asked as he followed her down the hall.

"I'm not sure." Margred struggled for an explanation that would satisfy them both. "Perhaps, as you said, I have met your sister before."

"And both of you have forgotten all about it," Caleb said dryly.

She turned to face him. "Do you remember everyone you have met?"

"Pretty much. Yeah. All part of the job."

All part of the man. Margred gave herself a moment to admire him, the thoughtful green eyes, the long, strong jaw, the sensitive mouth. He was dogged and concerned, observant and conscientious.

Easy to use, she thought, but difficult to deceive.

She changed the subject. "Where am I sleeping?"

"In here." He opened a door for her.

Margred glimpsed the pair of neat beds with plain brown spreads, one turned down invitingly to reveal crisp white linens, and arched one eyebrow. "Two beds?"

Had he decided to stay with her after all?

"This was my room," Caleb explained without a blink. "Mine and my brother's."

"And where is he sleeping?"

"No idea. He moved out when I was ten."

She stood in the center of the worn beige carpet to survey the small paneled room. Bare walls with a king's ransom in books crammed casually on one shelf. No pictures. No decorations. Only some shiny statuettes holding laurel wreaths and a few photographs tacked over a desk. She identified a row of unsmiling young men as an athletic team and the child with the baby on his lap as Caleb holding Lucy. The boy standing beside them was a few years older.

"This is your brother?"

Caleb hitched his thumbs into his back pockets. "Yeah."

She bent to look. Something about those brooding black eyes, that tumbled dark hair, that slightly sullen mouth . . .

Her heart beat faster. Would that explain . . . ? No. Yes. *No.*

"What is his name?" she asked.

But she knew. In her heart, she knew.

"Dylan."

7

CALEB WATCHED LUCY BUSTLE AROUND THE kitchen, touched and more than a little amused by her attempts to mother him. Like they were four and fourteen again, and she'd coaxed him to one of her teddy bear tea parties.

"Ice." She plunked a plastic bag on the table in front of him. "For your leg."

"My leg is fine," he lied. He balanced the ice on his knee.

"Tea?" she offered next, brandishing the kettle.

He needed coffee. Or a Scotch.

But he still had a long night ahead, and he never drank in front of his sister. In her eyes, at least, he wanted to be different from their father.

"Tea would be great. Thanks."

She dropped two tea bags into mugs and then hesitated, her hand hovering over the canister. "Do you think Maggie would like a cup?"

"Not yet," Caleb said. "She wanted to wash up. I got her some towels and showed her the bathroom."

"You are very kind," Maggie had said as he turned on the taps and adjusted the water temperature.

Kind, hell.

He wanted to see her naked. He wanted to undress and bathe her himself, to touch her pretty breasts with their pale pink nipples, her smooth, amazing skin.

No, he wasn't kind. But he wasn't a total jerk either. So he told her to call if she needed anything and he'd left, unable to trust his own control.

Lucy nibbled her lower lip. "Do you think that's a good idea? She could faint. Slip."

"The door's open." Visions of Maggie, naked, wet, and vulnerable, invaded his brain. He cleared his throat. "I told her to use your soap and stuff."

"Of course."

He watched his sister's face, trying to see if she minded having her sleep interrupted and her home invaded. When she was a big-eyed little kid, he'd known what made her laugh. What made her cry. What made her tick. Now . . . He didn't know. Hadn't made the effort to know, for too many years. "I'm sorry to dump this on you."

"You're not dumping."

Truth? Or just the desire to please? Except for a few anxious occasions when Lucy was in her teens, she'd never liked to make trouble, never wanted to call attention to herself.

"But she must have family somewhere who will be worried about her. Friends." Lucy set his tea in front of him and added sugar and milk to her cup, not meeting his eyes. "A husband."

"She's not married," came out of his mouth.

Lucy laid down her spoon. "How do you know?"

How did he? Did he? His ignorance chafed him.

"She told me."

"But . . . on the phone you said she couldn't remember anything."

Tension crept into his shoulders. "She told me before," he said evenly. "When we had dinner."

"Cal!" His sister's eyes brightened. "Is Maggie the one? The one you said wasn't coming . . ."

"Back," he finished for her. "Yeah."

"That's fan—" Lucy's brow pleated. "Wait. You had dinner, and you don't know her last name?"

Worse. They'd had sex, and he didn't know her last name.

Which had to be on the Top Ten List of Things You Don't Say to Your Sister. Hell, it was something Caleb hated admitting to himself.

"We had dinner," he repeated. "We didn't swap life stories."

Just bodily fluids.

Shit.

"So, how will you find her family?" Lucy asked.

"I'll call the sheriff's office on the mainland in the morning." Caleb sipped his tea. Too hot. "He'll run her description through the NCIC database, see if he can find a match in missing persons."

"How long will that take?"

"Depends on what he turns up. If I have to chase down partial matches in several states, it could be days."

Lucy twisted her napkin in her lap. "Can't you, I don't know, take her fingerprints or something?"

Caleb was used to working in a department, as part of a unit, a team. He'd had female partners—good ones. But he wasn't used to kicking cases around with his baby sister, or discussing his love life. "You sure ask a lot of questions."

Lucy shook out her napkin. Grinned. "I teach six-year-olds. They respond well to simple, direct questioning."

"I'll remember that the next time I interview one," Caleb said.

"They also like to change the subject."

He smiled, acknowledging her point. She had changed. He admired the competent, good-humored young woman sitting across from him, but a part of him was wistful for the kid he remembered. Or maybe he missed being the brother she could look up to. The guy with all the answers. "Her fingerprints won't be in the system. Not unless she has a criminal history."

Which he didn't believe.

He pushed back from the table. "Thanks for the tea. D'you mind keeping an eye on Maggie tonight?"

"Of course not. Should I sit up with her?"

"You don't have to do that. Wake her every two or three hours and ask Maggie her name. As long as she can answer and she isn't vomiting or having seizures, she should be all right. If she develops bruising around her eyes or her headache gets worse, I want you to call me."

Lucy nodded, her expression solemn again. "Anything else?"

"I've got the instruction sheet from the doctor. I'll leave it with you." He hesitated. He was asking a lot of the little girl he remembered, this sister he barely knew. He couldn't do his job without first ensuring Maggie was somewhere safe and taken care of. But . . . "You sure you're okay with this? Getting up every couple of hours?"

"School's out. I don't have to wake up early."

"She'll still be here in the morning."

"So, I'll have company."

He hadn't realized how nice it would feel to be able to depend on a member of his family.

"Great. Thanks. Well." He stood. "I should get going."

"You should get some sleep, too," Lucy said.

"I've got to get back. I can't count on a bunch of volunteer firefighters to preserve the scene indefinitely. As soon as it's daylight, I'll search the area."

Lucy carried their mugs to the sink. "You mean, for her clothes?"

Caleb shrugged. "Clothes, purse, keys."

A body.

Nobody jumped into a bonfire and simply disappeared. There had to be traces, either of a survivor or a body.

He would find them.

"You won't find him," Maggie had said, curling her lip in scorn. *"I need what he took from me."*

"And what's that?"

"In the fire."

"What did he take, Maggie?"

She hadn't answered him. Distress or distrust had kept her from speaking. Her silence cut him like a broken bottle.

"I'm going upstairs," he said. "To say good night."

His sister gave him a dubious look, but she didn't question him. Which was good, because he couldn't explain even to himself this restless need he had to see Maggie, to get things straight between them. By talking, if she'd talk.

Or by any other means.

He climbed the narrow stairs, rubbing absently at the bite on his arm. What did Maggie know? What did she remember? How could he protect her unless he knew?

He stopped in the darkness on the stairs. In the shadows of his own mind, he saw again the tall, thin figure waver against the flames before it whirled and leaped into the fire.

And disappeared.

Sweat crawled down his back. He hadn't had a flashback in weeks. His nightmares were getting better. But he had to face the possibility that Maggie's danger had triggered some kind of stress reaction, a hallucination or something.

No wonder she didn't trust him.

He couldn't trust himself.

*   *   *

Brothers, Margred thought dazedly.

If the blow to her head hadn't already made her temples throb, this new revelation would have done it.

Caleb was Dylan's brother, the son of a human father and a selkie mother. Did that make him half selkie, then?

Dylan's words echoed in her memory. *"It's impossible to be half anything. You are selkie, or you are not. You live in the sea, or you die on land."*

You die.

As she was dying. Drying up.

Margred huddled in the tub, her flesh shrinking from the strange shining pipes and cold, slick surfaces. Outside of Sanctuary, away from the magic of Caer Subai, selkies in human form aged at almost the rate that mortals did—one reason the very old, like the king, chose to live "beneath the wave," rarely assuming human shape.

Margred imagined the threat of aging, more than the fear of death, would have driven Caleb's mother to leave her husband and two children behind.

Thirteen years on land?

The prospect made her shiver.

No wonder when the Change had come on Dylan, his mother had seized her chance to return with her firstborn son to the sea. Caleb would still have been a child then. Lucy must have been an infant.

But . . . Margred frowned, unsettled. How could their mother have known that the Change would not come upon them, too?

How could she have left them, not knowing?

Maybe . . . Margred spread her toes beneath the water, swishing them idly back and forth. Maybe their mother had intended to return? Dylan said his mother had died, drowned in a fisherman's net. So the selkie woman had never seen her younger children come to adulthood.

Most children born of mer-and-mortal unions were human, Margred reminded herself. Caleb might have the sea in his blood, but he was solidly of earth, as firmly grounded as an oak tree.

As for his sister, Lucy, well . . . Margred sank deeper into the tub. She could not dismiss the punch of power that had greeted her arrival or wash away the niggling suspicion there was more to Caleb's sister than her shy welcome and anxious eyes.

How much more?

You are selkie, or you are not, Dylan had said.

If either Caleb or Lucy were selkie, if they had ever experienced the Change, Margred would know. It did not take any great magic to sense the aura of another elemental. She could smell it. Neither Caleb nor Lucy had betrayed any awareness of who they were.

Any recognition of what Margred was.

She felt a queer twist of heart. What was she now? Now that her pelt was gone.

She fought a flutter of panic. The children of the sea lived in the moment. She was not used to having to think, to weigh and calculate and discard her options.

But she could not lie here like a pup on an ice floe waiting for the hunter's club. She had to plan. To act.

Was there any way to restore what had been taken from her?

Conn would know, she thought. The king's son had made a study of magic, or at least had studied as much as any of the sea folk. Margred herself had learned to read, despite a scarcity of books. Sea water was not kind to pulp and print. Conn maintained some sort of library at Caer Subai, but generally knowledge among the mer was passed on parent to child and mind to mind.

When it was passed on at all. For along with their birth rate, the selkies' aptitude for magic had been declining for years. Centuries.

The sea king's son warned about the slow wane of the selkies' power, but his preoccupation with his people's fate was not a popular topic. The children of the sea counted themselves among the First Creation, elemental, immortal, inviolate in their primacy. What need did creatures of magic have for spells and enchantments?

Well, she needed something now, Margred thought.

She needed . . . help. Not human help, although she was grateful to Caleb for sheltering her.

She had to contact Dylan to find out what, if anything at all, Caleb and Lucy knew about their heritage.

And she needed to get word of her plight to the prince. Tomorrow she would go down to the sea to summon a messenger. Conn would tell her what to do.

If anything could be done. The whisper licked along her nerves like flame.

She sat up in the tub, water sluicing from her bare shoulders. She would not think that way. She was enough of a fatalist to accept that what would be, would be.

And enough of a survivor to take her pleasures in the meantime.

Reaching a hand for one of the pretty colored bottles along the edge of the tub, she unscrewed the cap and sniffed.

*   *   *

Caleb was climbing the stairs when the smell smacked him like a wet towel.

A cloud of scent and steam rolled from the bathroom and enveloped him. Cucumber, melon, apricot, strawberry, mixed and mingled together.

His head swam. Like a fricking bomb had gone off at a farmers' market.

He cleared his throat. "Maggie?"

"In here." Her throaty voice purred through the open bathroom door.

Hell, he knew she was in there. Wet. Naked.

Vulnerable, he reminded himself.

"Do you, uh, need anything?"

"Yes."

He waited.

Nothing.

He released his breath. Okay. He'd seen her naked before. Recently. Just because she sounded like a wet dream and smelled like a whole roll of Lifesavers was no reason to lose his mind or his cool.

He shoved his hands in his pockets, as if he was approaching a crime scene. *Don't touch.* "Right. Coming."

The door stood open. He walked in and there she was, naked in the bathtub, her dark hair damp on her bare shoulders and her breasts just below the bubble line.

"Well." He focused on her face with an effort. "You look better."

Her cheeks were flushed. Her knees rose from the sea of foam like little pink islands.

"I feel better." She stretched her shoulders, and her breasts bobbed briefly above the scented bubbles.

He felt like an idiot, stiff and awkward. Aroused. "What did you want?"

"I need to go back to the beach," she said. "Will you take me?"

He shook his head, caution penetrating his fruit-flavored, lust-induced fog. "It's too late."

"Likely in more ways than one." Her full lips quirked and then firmed. "Nevertheless, I must go."

"Why?"

Her eyes challenged his. "Does it matter?"

"It might." He remembered her wild struggle to reach the fire. She didn't trust him. He needed her to trust him. "What's on the beach, Maggie?"

"Nothing now."

"Then—"

She stood. Bubbles streamed down her body, parted over breast and thigh, slid over that gorgeous length of leg. "Will you hand me a towel?"

His tongue was suddenly too large for his mouth. His pants were too tight. Wordless, he grabbed a towel off the edge of the sink and extended it toward her.

Maggie wrapped her body, tucking the edge of the towel between her breasts. "If you won't take me, I will find my own way."

He narrowed his eyes. "I'll take you."

No reason not to, he reasoned, after he had processed the scene. Maybe returning to the place she'd been attacked would jog her memory.

She smiled faintly. "Thank you."

"You did that on purpose."

Her smile broadened. "Do you care?"

"Not if I get to see you naked," he answered frankly, and was rewarded by her laugh.

"Then we both are satisfied."

"Not by a long shot." Edgy and restless, he prowled the short distance to the sink and back, his hands still safely anchored in his pockets. "I'll pick you up tomorrow. After lunch."

She tilted her head, regarding him. "Not in the morning?"

"I'm busy."

"Ah." She shrugged, making the towel move in interesting ways. "Until tomorrow, then."

He'd expected her to object, to acknowledge that she wanted him. Needed him, even if it was only for this. He had to find some way to reforge the connection between them, to remind her she was his.

Unable to resist, he bent to kiss her, a brief, frustrated meeting of mouths.

And left with the taste of her on his lips.

8

WHEN THE SUN ROSE, BLEEDING PINK BETWEEN the gray sky and the iron ocean, Caleb gained the light but lost four of the men he had assigned to protect the crime scene.

Red sky at night, sailor's delight.
Red sky at morning, sailor take warning.

Last night, he'd called out the island's volunteer fire department, posting guards at the access road, the hiking trail, and both ends of the beach. Most of the firefighters were willing to sacrifice sleep for the novelty of playing policeman. But working men couldn't ignore their jobs to stand around outside the yellow tape, smoking and speculating. Howard and Manuel had left with the lobster boats at 5:00 A.M.; Dick and Earl had taken the 7:00 ferry to the mainland.

Caleb recorded their exits in the log book, aware of his team slipping away. His time, slipping away. His chances, slipping away. At 10:00 A.M., the ferry would return, carrying the state evidence team he had requested to process the crime scene.

Too late, he thought.

The wind snatched at his notebook. He anchored the pages with one hand, glancing from his diagram of the scene to the heavy clouds above.

Some small-town police chiefs were too proud or too dumb or too damn territorial to call in the State Criminal Division for anything less than homicide. Mainers liked to do for themselves, and cops used to dealing with petty thefts and traffic violations didn't always realize how quickly a case could be lost by a single missed or mishandled piece of evidence.

Caleb knew. But there wasn't a damn thing he could do about it. Rain and tide threatened the point. If he didn't conduct a detailed search soon, his crime scene would be irretrievably contaminated, the evidence swept or washed or blown away.

I need what he took from me, Maggie had said.

He wanted to find it.

Whatever it was.

* * *

Five hours later, Caleb sat at his desk with a mug of bitter coffee, working his way through the paperwork required by the state lab as methodically as he'd worked his way across the beach.

His eyes were gritty with sand and ash and lack of sleep. His leg throbbed. His stomach growled. He hadn't stopped for breakfast. Sliding open his desk drawer, he groped under the files and procedure manuals for the brown prescription bottle that held his painkillers.

The doctor had said Maggie wasn't supposed to take aspirin because of the risk of bleeding into the brain. Had Lucy remembered?

He reached for the phone with his other hand, punching in the number from memory. His sister answered on the second ring.

"How is everybody?" he asked.

"Maggie's fine. We're both fine. We're about to have lunch. Where are you?"

"No nausea? Headaches?"

Muffled voices carried over the line.

"She has a bit of a headache," his sister reported moments later. "I gave her some Tylenol."

"Good," Caleb said, feeling foolish. "That's good."

"Maggie wants to know when you're going to take her to the beach."

"Later." He glanced at the window, where a cold, gray rain lashed the glass. "It's raining."

"Do you want to talk to her?"

He tapped the plastic bottle on the desk. He shouldn't feel like a damn fifteen-year-old calling a girl and then hanging up because he had nothing to say.

But he had nothing to offer her. Not yet. He looked from the piles of crap on his desk to the piles of crap on the floor.

"I'll call back," he said, and hung up.

Cradling the pills in his hand, he squinted at the bright warning labels: *Do not take on an empty stomach. May cause drowsiness. Do not drive or operate heavy machinery.*

His hand clenched in frustration before he dropped the bottle back into the drawer.

He needed Vicodin and about twelve hours of sleep. He'd settle for a shower and a cigarette. Instead, he took another sip of cooling coffee. He'd managed to give up smoking in the hospital, and no amount of frustration was driving him to go through that again.

He rubbed his eyes. What he really needed was a body. Or a weapon. Clothing. Hell, even footprints or tire tracks. But the wind and the tide had destroyed any obvious marks, and the beach had been disconcertingly, discouragingly bare. Not even a cigarette butt. Well, except for the firefighters', carefully restricted outside the perimeter.

Caleb was—had been—a good investigator. He'd combed and sifted the scene, photographed and preserved everything, however apparently insignificant. But he'd found nothing to identify Maggie.

Or her attacker.

A rap sounded on his office door.

"Come in."

Edith poked her head inside, curiosity flashing behind her glasses. "Detective Sam Reynolds."

Caleb seriously considered not getting to his feet—his leg hurt like a son of a bitch—and then did it anyway. "Detective."

Reynolds had smooth brown hair, quick eyes, and neat whiskers. A field rat, rather than a lab rat.

"Sam. CID."

Like Caleb needed to be told. He raised his eyebrows. "You're it? You're my Evidence Response Team?"

The investigator smiled, revealing large white teeth. "Somebody die that I don't know about?"

"Nope."

"Then I'm it." He sat in the molded plastic chair that was all the town of World's End could afford for its visitors. "What've you got for me?"

"Food wrappers, beer cans, one rubber flip-flop, a couple fishhooks, and a load of fire debris." Caleb didn't need the look on the other man's face to tell him he had squat. He nodded to the sealed cartons on the floor behind him. "It's all in there. Taped, dated, and labeled. Agency number, item number, description, and source."

"You've done this before."

"Major crime division," Caleb explained briefly. "Portland."

"Good for you. Makes my job easier. Paperwork?"

"All but the case synopsis. I can fax it to you this afternoon."

The whiskers twitched. "Meaning you want me to take your boxes and get out of your hair."

"I'd appreciate it if you'd save me the trip," Caleb answered carefully. "I'm on my own here."

"You call the sheriff's office?"

In a one-man jurisdiction, the county sheriff's department was your best resource. Which still put Caleb's nearest backup forty minutes away by boat.

"Yeah. He's accessing the NCIC missing persons database for me."

"I thought you said the victim was still alive."

Caleb massaged his leg absently under the desk. "She is. She's not talking."

"Uncooperative?"

"She doesn't remember the attack. Or anything else."

Except him. She remembered him.

"What were you doing on the beach last night?"

"Looking for you."

Reynolds scratched his mustache. "Not a crime to lose your memory."

"No."

"If she really did lose her memory."

Their eyes met a moment in perfect understanding. Female victims of domestic disputes often lied or claimed loss of memory to protect themselves or their abusers. If Maggie knew her attacker . . .

Caleb shook his head. He wanted to trust her. More, he wanted her to trust him.

"The doctor suspects concussion," he said. "She may never remember. Which is why I'd really appreciate your help."

Reynolds shrugged. "I'm here. I'll transport your boxes for you. But I can't promise we'll find anything."

They hauled cartons in the rain, in and out of Caleb's Jeep, down the dock and onto the ferry. By the time they were done, Caleb was sweating under his yellow police slicker and his leg felt as though he'd gone three rounds with Vlad the Physical Therapist. But it was worth the pain to save half a day traveling to the crime lab in Augusta.

Caleb signed off on the evidence log and drove the two blocks back to town hall.

"Edith." He greeted her as he passed her desk.

The town clerk looked up from her filing. "Antonia Barone is waiting for you."

Caleb stopped. "In my office?"

Edith looked down her nose at him. "She's not out here, is she?"

"Right. Thanks."

Shit.

At least Edith had warned him. Caleb had been a cop for nine years, a detective for six of them. He knew community relations were as much a part of the job as public safety. But when he was a kid, Regina's mother, Antonia, had scared the shit out of him. Even now, she was intimidating.

She was also his boss.

He limped to his office and found her fidgeting in front of his desk, wearing an oversized jacket and a red slash of lipstick.

"Mayor." He greeted her cautiously.

She snorted. "Let's cut the mayor crap now. The only reason I took this job was because Peter Quincy wouldn't serve a fourth term and the council couldn't find anybody else to put up against that asshole Whittaker."

Caleb's lips twitched. "Yes, ma'am." He pulled out the ugly molded chair and gestured for her to sit. "What can I do for you?"

She plopped down, fixing him with hard, dark eyes. "You can tell me what the hell is going on. Every idiot who's dropped by the shop for a cup of coffee is saying some woman from Away got herself raped up at the point last night."

Caleb clamped his jaw. "There was an assault, yes. The nature of the woman's injuries hasn't been determined yet."

Antonia scowled, clearly unsatisfied.

"Summer girl?"

The island population consisted of year-rounders; summer people, who came back to the island year after year; and tourists. Time and community service sometimes blurred the divisions, but they were still felt among the island natives.

"First-timer," Caleb said.

Antonia nodded once.

"Well, that's something."

Caleb swallowed his anger. Antonia didn't know Maggie, he reminded himself. An attack on a tourist struck at the islanders' sense of safety and their wallets; an attack on one of their own struck at their hearts.

"But it still doesn't make us look good," Antonia continued darkly. "It doesn't make us look *safe*."

And public safety, her tone suggested, was his responsibility.

He happened to agree with her.

"I'm working on it," Caleb said.

"Hm. I heard you shut down half the island."

Caleb leaned back in his chair, refusing to be baited. "I limited access on Ocean View and Old Wharf Roads and the north hiking trail. Hardly half the island."

"I had some tourists from the ferry in the shop this morning complaining they couldn't picnic on the point."

He raised his eyebrows. "It's pouring rain. Sell them some breakfast and send them to the gift shop until it clears."

Antonia barked with laughter. "Already did."

He stood again. "Then, if that's all—"

Antonia didn't budge. "I like you," she said unexpectedly. "Didn't think I would. I don't like your father, and I never had much use for that mother of yours. But at least you understand how we do things around here."

"I understand," Caleb said dryly. Too well to take offense anymore at comments about his parents. "That doesn't mean I'll let it interfere with how I do my job."

"Fair enough. What are you going to do next?"

Was she asking as mayor of World's End, trying to stay apprised of a troublesome investigation? Or was she merely curious?

"I need to canvass the houses in the area, ask if anybody saw or heard anything on the point last night."

"Last night everybody was at the school assembly."

Not everybody. Not Maggie.

Not the son of a bitch who had attacked her either.

"You could help me out," Caleb suggested. "Make a list of who was there that you remember."

Antonia studied him. "I guess I could do that. You should come by the restaurant later. Talk to Regina."

He intended to. He intended to talk to a lot of people. "Did she see something? Say something?"

Antonia snorted. "You think that girl talks to me?"

"Then—"

Antonia's face turned an uncharacteristic red. "I just thought maybe you'd like to see her."

Was she matchmaking? The possibility left him amused and maybe a little flattered. Embarrassed.

"I do need to talk to her. To one of you," he amended. "Are you still hiring for the summer?"

"We're always hiring. Kids around here can make more money fishing for lobster, and the ones from Away don't know how to work. Lucy looking for a job now that school's out?"

"Not Lucy, Maggie. The woman who was attacked last night," Caleb explained. "She might need something to tide her over for a while."

"She have any experience?"

"I don't know," he admitted.

He knew too damn little about her.

"Hm." Antonia got to her feet, gathering her jacket around her. "Well, bring her by. Reggie can talk to her."

Caleb wasn't sure if Antonia was pushing off the new hire as a way of throwing him together with Regina or as a form of punishment. Antonia had never forgiven her only daughter for leaving the island and the restaurant. Or maybe she hadn't forgiven her for coming back unmarried with a two-month-old son in tow. Either way, Maggie had a job interview. "Thanks."

"Don't thank me, it's business. Speaking of which, I need to get back to my kitchen."

"I'll see you out," Caleb said.

Antonia waved him off. "Don't bother. It's raining."

"I'm going out anyway. Those calls," he reminded her.

At least the rain would keep people home, where he could find them.

"You'll get soaked," Antonia predicted with dour anticipation.

Caleb locked his office door. "I don't mind a little rain."

In Iraq, he'd lived with dust. Dust and heat. From May to September, the *shamal* blew from the northwest, kicking up clouds of sand that found their way through every chink into every crease and canteen. Each day he'd felt his soul dehydrating, bits of himself withering and blowing away like dust. At night he had dreamed of the rain. Of the rain and the sea.

Caleb grimaced as he descended the town hall steps. So pulling twenty-four-hour shifts hadn't been part of his dreams. He was back, wasn't he? He was home, doing the job he was trained to do in the community he was sworn to protect.

He just hoped it was enough.

* * *

He wasn't coming.

Margred ran her hands over her hips, chafed by the elastic of her unfamiliar undergarment and an even more unfamiliar disappointment.

He was coming *later*. Because it was *raining*. She sneered at her image in the mirror. As if a little rain would make him melt.

"Don't you like it?" Lucy asked beside her.

"It" was the dress Lucy had pulled from her closet for Margred to try on.

Margred smoothed the blue material over her thighs, inspecting her reflection in the glass above the bedroom dresser. She had washed the blood and sand out of her hair last night. Her face was pale, her eyes looked bruised, and the swollen purple bump on her head was bisected by a line of ugly stitches.

Still, if she must wear clothing, this garment was certainly more flattering than the oversized shirt she had worn all morning.

She offered the girl a smile. "It fits. The other—those jeans—made me look like a haggis."

Lucy picked up the discarded jeans from the floor and folded them. "That's because I'm tall and skinny and you're, um . . . you're—"

Margred narrowed her eyes. "Short and fat?" she inquired sweetly.

Lucy exhaled on a laugh. "No! God, no. It's just that you have, you know, a figure. Curves. Anyway, you look great in that dress. A lot better than I do."

Very likely. On the hanger, the simple sleeveless dress had resembled a sack. It probably hung from Lucy's angular shoulders the same way.

Margred eyed her consideringly. "You are attractive. You look . . . strong."

This time, Lucy's laughter bubbled out. "Yeah, that's what I always wanted to hear. I ran track in college," she volunteered.

"Ah," Margred said, as if she had the faintest idea what the girl was talking about.

She turned back to the mirror. The blue fabric poured over her curves like water over rocks. Only the elastic cutting into her hip spoiled the flowing line. Reaching under the skirt, she tugged the panties down her legs.

"Much better," she pronounced.

Lucy goggled. "Yes, but—"

"What?"

"Don't you feel a little, um . . ."

"Comfortable?"

"Naked."

Margred looked in the mirror again. She didn't see the problem. All the parts that humans kept covered were covered. "No."

"Well . . ." Lucy's grin transformed her face. "Caleb's going to swallow his tongue when he sees you."

Margred tossed her head and then winced. "If he ever gets here."

She was not accustomed to waiting, for Caleb or any other man. She was not used to depending on others for clothes, for food, for transportation.

For survival.

"It's not like you could go to the beach now anyway," Lucy pointed out in a reasonable tone that made Margred's hackles rise. "Not in this rain."

"I do not mind the rain."

Water was her element. She could turn the current and control the waves. She could warm the surface of the sea to create fog or cool the air to make the rain fall. She could . . . The possibility bloomed and quivered inside her like a pink sea coral.

She could make it stop raining.

Or not.

What else had she lost, along with her pelt?

Her head throbbed.

"Are you all right?" Lucy asked.

"I . . . yes," she said slowly. *Maybe.*

Tentatively, she sought the glimmer deep within her, sinking down through levels of awareness like a shell tumbling to the ocean floor, gold to blue to green to gray. Her breathing slowed. Pressure built in her chest. Maybe there . . .

Or there, a buried gleam gone too quickly to identify.

She opened her eyes to find Lucy staring at her with worried gray-green eyes.

Caleb's eyes, Margred thought. Her breath hitched. "I need to be outside."

"I don't think so," Lucy said. "It's raining. And your head—"

"My head is fine," Margred said firmly.

Her pulse pounded behind her eyeballs. She dismissed the pain. Her head was probably going to hurt a lot worse before she was done.

She descended the narrow stairs, one hand on the banister for balance.

Lucy trailed behind her, complaining. "My brother told me to take care of you."

"Your brother is not here."

That was the problem. Part of the problem.

One she intended to remedy.

Margred had never been much of a weather shaper, any more than she was a magic handler. Why bother? As she had told Lucy, she did not mind a little rain. And messing with the water cycle was generally not a good idea.

But if she could . . . Her heart beat faster.

She had to try. Not simply because Caleb refused to take her to the beach, but because she needed to know her own limits.

Downstairs, the house felt even darker and more cramped. Unlike the tourist boxes built along the beach with wide windows to admit the view, this cottage had been constructed and positioned to withstand the worst that winter and the sea could throw at it. The darkness did not bother Margred. Even in human form, her eyes adjusted easily to the gloom. But she could feel the upper floor pressing down on her, the surrounding pines closing in.

Caleb's mother had lived *here*?

For thirteen years.

Margred shivered and walked to the front of the house.

"Where are you going?" Lucy demanded.

"I need air," Margred said and swung the door wide.

The wind poured in, wet with rain and the smell of earth and pine and, faint and faraway, the scent of the sea. Margred breathed in.

"You're getting the floor wet," Lucy said.

Margred ignored her.

Holding the sea air deep inside her lungs, she began to cast again, her seeking thought like a golden hook spiraling down and down. The rain misted her face and dampened her bare arms. She held them up to the clouds, reaching beyond the fat, wet drops and freshening breeze to where the rain swam on the currents of air like a shoal of bright fish. This was only a small, localized storm. Well within her power.

If she had power.

If she were still selkie.

If her head didn't hurt quite so much.

Frowning in concentration, she tested the flow of the air, the gathering condensation. She felt power gather heavy in her loins until she was pregnant with it, until it rippled in her stomach and pushed at her lungs, until it surged and filled her. She opened her mouth, panting.

Water was her element, she reminded herself. The rain streamed down her face and saturated her gown. All it would take was a push here, a breath there, a tiny adjustment in temperature . . .

Ah.

Something gave, in her chest and in her loins and high in the air overhead. The power rushed to fill the breach, spilled from her into the sky. *There. Now.*

Ow, ow, ow.

Pain—flashing, slashing—shattered her head and left her empty. Aching. Margred swayed, grabbing the door jamb for balance.

Lucy rushed to her side. "Come on. Come inside. Sit down."

Margred allowed herself to lean on Lucy's shoulder; allowed Lucy to support her, hollowed, limp and dripping, to a chair. Had she . . . ?

"You're all wet," Lucy scolded as if she were addressing a child. "What were you thinking? It's raining."

Margred blinked. Her head pounded. But through the fog in her brain, she could feel the change in the skies overhead, the shift in pressure, the flow of water vapor.

The alluvium of magic.

Half blind with pain and triumph, she raised her face and smiled. "Not for long," she said.

9

CALEB'S CELL PHONE VIBRATED ON HIS BELT. HE
reached for it, one hand on the wheel and his attention on
the wet road.

Edith, calling to report some minor trespass that required
the chief's attention?

Or Antonia, with another complaint?

He glanced at the display and recognized the number on
the tiny screen. His pulse quickened.

Lucy, he thought.

And then, with another surge of adrenaline, *Maggie.*

Visions of brain bleeds and abusive ex-boyfriends
flashed through his head.

He thumbed the speaker button. "What's wrong?" he
barked.

"Nothing's wrong," Lucy said hesitantly. "I just, um . . ."

Nothing was wrong. He loosened his grip on the wheel.

As a detective, he knew better than to jump to conclu-
sions. Or to jump down his sister's throat. His lack of sleep
must be getting to him.

No, Maggie was getting to him.

"Sorry," he said to his sister. "What's up?"

"I, um— It's stopped raining."

He looked through the rain-spotted windshield to the east, where the clouds were beginning to break. "I can see that."

"Yes. Well. Maggie wants to know when you're going to the beach."

He couldn't let his personal life interfere with his investigation. Although a little beach trip could serve both. Maybe a return to the crime scene would trigger memories of Maggie's assailant. God knew he didn't have anything else to go on at this point.

"Soon," he said. "How are you both holding up?"

"I'm okay. Maggie's head still hurts. I made her go lie down while I put her dress in the dryer."

"What?"

His sister sighed. "It's complicated."

"Right. Later, then," he said, and ended the call.

He didn't need complicated. He'd come home to World's End in search of a simple, normal life, to put down roots, or return to them.

Maggie was a stranger without ties to the island. Without home ties at all. She didn't even remember her past.

Or maybe she was running from it. He couldn't dismiss the possibility that she knew the man who attacked her.

Either angle was a complication Caleb hadn't bargained for.

And yet she drew him.

He had always been a sucker for strays. Lost dogs, feral cats, even sea creatures stranded by the tide . . . Not that his father had ever allowed him to keep the baby birds that fell from their nests, the dogs that followed him home.

He wanted to keep Maggie.

But even dazed and bloodied, homeless and naked, Maggie was more than a victim. She was stubborn, courageous, and vibrantly, vitally alive. He admired her. Wanted her.

Which meant things were about to get a lot more complicated.

Bruce Whittaker's house perched on a hill above the point like an island cottage on steroids. Caleb parked at the bottom of the driveway, noting the late-model Lexus SUV in the carport, the half-closed blinds in the middle of the afternoon.

Most of what he needed to know to police his town he could pick up over a morning cup of coffee at Antonia's or a beer at the Inn after the boats came in. Amazing what people would confide in a casual setting to their local cop: bad feelings at home or a kid in trouble at school, a mailbox or a dog gone missing, items lifted from the gift shop, tourists' cars blocking residents' driveways. Caleb nodded and listened and filed it all away.

It sure beat the hell out of canvassing the projects. Or waiting on unreliable Intel from terrified Iraqis.

The downside of the island grapevine was that his pool of potential witnesses had shrunk to a mere puddle. In the city, a canvass of the neighborhood involved thousands of windows, hundreds of doors, dozens of passers-by and man-hours.

Caleb had covered the entire point area in three hours. Stiffly, he climbed from the Jeep and approached the porch. *More damn steps.*

And so far he had nothing.

The houses here were few and set back from the ocean. Islanders didn't build on the point. Anyway, most of them had spent the evening at the school assembly. The tourists wouldn't recognize unusual activity on the beach at night if it bit them on the ass. Whittaker, with his view of the point and his constant complaints, was Caleb's last, best hope.

The lawyer hadn't answered his door or his phone the first time Caleb came around. The shiny vehicle beside the house didn't mean anybody was home. The island was small enough that folks could walk most anywhere.

In the rain?

Caleb knocked again.

A shadow moved beyond the leaded glass.

Out of habit, Caleb stepped to the side of the door, his elbow pressing the butt of his gun.

The door opened. Whittaker, pale-faced and clean-shaven, stood framed in the shadows.

"Sorry to bother you," Caleb said easily. "Do you have a moment?"

Whittaker blinked, as if the light pained him. "Is someone hurt?"

Something clicked in Caleb's head like the safety release on a gun. "Why do you ask?"

"Well, I— Isn't that what anyone asks when the police show up on their doorstep at . . ." Whittaker winced. "I'm sorry, it's hardly the wee hours of the morning now, is it?"

"Three o'clock," Caleb said. "Can I come in?"

"Of course." Whittaker stepped back, opening the door wide. "Make yourself at home."

Not likely. Outside, at least, the gray shingles and crisp white trim made some concession to the New England setting and the neighbors' sensibilities. But the open floor plan inside didn't look like any home Caleb had ever lived in. A massive stone fireplace dominated one end of the great room. A six-foot-long aquarium full of fish occupied the other. In between, wide plate glass windows overlooked the point.

Caleb hooked his thumbs into his front pockets. "Nice view," he commented.

"I like it."

"Unless it's raining."

"What are you talking about?"

"Your blinds are down." Caleb touched the blind cord, raising one eyebrow. "May I?"

Caleb opened the blinds on a clearing silver sky. From where he stood, he could see trees and rocks give way to a curve of sand and shale. Tumbling gray waves rolled into shore. The rain had beaten out all trace of his activity on the beach that morning. The fire debris was gone, along with the yellow crime scene tape.

But a blackened smudge still stained the sand where the fire had burned last night.

He turned from the window. "Seems a shame to block this out."

"I have—had—a bit of a headache this morning. The light bothers my eyes."

"Sorry to hear that. Your head hurt last night, too?"

"As a matter of fact, it did. What's this about, Chief? I hardly think you dropped by to inquire after my health."

"I was wondering if you noticed any unusual activity on the beach last night."

"Three weeks ago, you told me dealing with kids and tourists was *your* job. Or have you changed your mind?"

Public relations, Caleb reminded himself. "Why don't we sit down?"

Whittaker shrugged. "Be my guest."

He led the way to the room's two massive leather sofas.

Caleb sank down with a sigh of relief, stretching his leg in front of him. The cushions of the couch released a pleasant tang of wood smoke and whiskey. "So you didn't see the fire?"

"I have no idea what you're talking about."

"Maybe you could just talk me through your evening. Do you mind if I take notes?"

"I can't imagine why you need a record of our conversation, but if it will help . . . I fixed dinner around six, six thirty. Grilled fish and polenta, if you're interested. I washed up and then settled down with a book and a drink until I went to bed."

Both the answer—and the attitude—were pretty much what Caleb was expecting. "Alone?"

"Unfortunately."

"And what time was that?"

"I really didn't notice. Early. I told you, I had a headache. Now, if you're finished—"

"You didn't look out the window? Take out the garbage? Check the locks before you turned in?"

Whittaker's face pinched. "I may have done."

"Which?"

"I probably checked the door."

"Front door?"

"Yes. Is there some reason you are questioning me like a common criminal?"

"A woman was attacked on the beach last night. It's possible you saw or heard something that could help me identify her attacker."

"Not with a migraine. And not in the dark."

Right. Like you needed daylight to spot a bonfire.

"Do you remember turning on a porch light?" Caleb asked.

"I told you, I was alone. I don't turn on the outside lights unless I'm expecting company." Whittaker stood. "Look, Chief Hunter, I appreciate your diligence, but it's too late. If you hadn't let those kids go a few weeks ago, perhaps last night's incident would never have happened."

Asshole.

"There's a big leap between underage drinking and assault," Caleb said, keeping his tone even. "Unless there are some steps in the middle you can share with me."

"You're the one who mentioned fire. I naturally *assumed*—"

Caleb's cell vibrated. He checked the caller ID. *Lucy.* Again.

"I have to take this," he said to Whittaker.

The lawyer shrugged. "Go right ahead. As far as I'm concerned, our conversation is finished."

"Could be," Caleb said. He turned, facing the clearing sky beyond the windows. "Lucy. What's up?"

"Caleb, I'm so *sorry.*"

Tension gripped the base of his neck. "What's wrong? How's Maggie?"

"She— I . . . I was only gone a little while, fifteen minutes, I swear, I—"

"Take a deep breath," he advised, though his own pulse was pounding in his ears. "Tell me what happened."

Lucy gulped. "I had to go out. Just for a few minutes.

Maggie said she'd be fine. But when I got back, she was . . ."

His heart lurched. *Oh, Christ.* She was what?

Dizzy?

Unconscious?

Dead?

"Gone," Lucy finished miserably.

"Gone where?" Caleb snapped.

"I don't know, I—"

A flutter of blue on the beach below caught his attention. A woman's dress. Caleb's gaze narrowed. A dark-haired woman in a blue dress, strolling across the wet sand. He clenched the phone. Something about the way she moved . . .

"It's all right," he cut across his sister's babbled explanations. "I found her. I'll call you later."

He strode toward the door. "I'll be in touch," he tossed to Whittaker.

"I hardly see the need—"

Caleb shot him a look that shut him up fast. Public relations be damned. He had to get to the beach. He had to get to Maggie before she . . .

What the hell did she think she was doing?

He lost sight of her as he plunged down the porch steps, ignoring his pain in his need to get a better look. Glimpsed her again from the top of the narrow track that plummeted down the cliff face to the shore. Definitely Maggie, he thought, studying her pale, bare arms, her wavy dark hair.

He yelled her name.

The wind snatched his voice. It buffeted his face, kicking up whitecaps out at sea and stirring the slippery clumps of grass dotting the slope. Caleb scowled. He could drive a quarter mile down the road to the nearest beach access. Or he could risk his footing, his dignity, and his neck on the path.

He started the climb down.

Patches of loose shale and roots like trip wires booby-trapped the trail. Every step, every jolt, jarred the screws and plates of his reconstructed leg until he felt like the freaking Tin Man slowly shaking apart. Halfway down, his boot slid out from under him. His leg twisted. His knee gave. He slid, half on his ass, as his hands scraped gravel. He grabbed at a scrub spruce to save himself and hung on a moment, getting his breath and his bearings.

Maggie never looked up.

As he watched, she pulled the blue dress over her head and shed it on the sand.

His jaw dropped.

Underneath the gown, she was naked. Totally, completely, gloriously exposed. He stared, a seething stew of worry and fury and lust boiling inside him as bare-assed—bare everything—she sauntered to the sea.

He worked enough spit into his mouth to swallow. Didn't she realize anybody could be watching? Not to mention that after this morning's rain, the water must be freezing. She could get hypothermia, damn it. She could get dizzy and drown.

He slid a few steps toward her.

She didn't seem to care. She waded into the churning surf, as naked and relaxed as she'd been in the bathtub last night.

Caleb was ready to strangle her. He wanted her safe. He wanted her home. Was it too much to expect her to wait a couple of hours while he did his best to catch the bastard who'd attacked her?

Apparently it was.

The white caps curled and foamed around her calves. Around her thighs, waist, breasts. Caleb caught his breath as a bigger wave rushed in. Maggie staggered, spread her arms, and disappeared under the surface of the water.

Cursing, he flung himself down the path. He stumbled around bushes and over rocks and onto sand.

And froze, transfixed by the sight that met him at the bottom of the cliff.

Maggie stood breast deep and bare shouldered in the sea. The sun broke through the clouds, sparkling on the crests of the waves, the slow, green roll of the water. Waves danced all around. She laughed and held out her arms, her dark hair sleek against her head, her face shining with water and sunlight.

The ground shifted under him. His knees gave out like they had on the path, even though the sand here was soft and level. Because leaping, playing, arcing through the waves, their gray bodies smooth and powerful, dolphins circled her, two or six or ten of them, close, so close his heart stopped in fear for her, and wonder.

What the fuck . . . ?

*   *   *

Margred stroked the dolphins' broad, flat sides, soothed by their strength. And by their chatter. The *muc mara* had responded swiftly and joyfully to her call, readily accepting her charge to carry her plea to the prince.

Of course, she could not be sure how much of her message, exactly, would reach Conn. Dolphins were intelligent and kind, less deliberate than whales, less bloodthirsty than sharks, less easily distracted than birds or fish. But they did not live in time as humans did, or even as the selkie. They flowed as the sea flowed, and what they understood no one, perhaps not even Conn or Llyr himself, knew.

She watched their leaping passage, her throat closing with gladness and a terrible despair. They had come to her and comforted her. But she could not follow them into the green coolness of the sea, into the rolling waves, into the gold-veined darkness.

Her loss dragged at her like waterlogged clothing. With heavy steps, she turned to make her way to shore.

Caleb stood at the water's edge. The sight of him, solid and still, lifted her spirits so that for a moment she forgot both caution and sorrow.

He shook his head. "I never saw anything like that."

Caution returned in a rush. She tilted her head. "Have I

made so little impression, then, you do not remember me naked?"

He smiled, as she intended. But he was a hard man to distract. "I meant the dolphins."

"You must have seen dolphins before."

"Not come into shore like that, so close to a swimmer. Once, when I was a kid, my mother . . ." He stopped.

His *mother*? Margred felt a spurt of excitement. His mother was selkie. If he knew, if he remembered, perhaps she could confide in him.

"When you were a child . . ." she prompted.

He hesitated; shrugged. "It was a long time ago. I was four. Five, maybe. She brought me to the beach. She didn't very often. Dylan, sometimes, but— Anyway, she was swimming in the deep water, where I wasn't allowed to go, when the dolphins came." His sea green eyes were deep and lost. "All these years, I thought I'd made it up. You know, the way kids do, when they're bored or lonely."

Her childhood was shrouded in time. She could not remember feeling bored. But she understood lonely.

She touched his arm. "Tell me about your mother."

He looked away, a muscle bunching in his jaw. "Nothing much to tell. She left us when I was ten. You should put some clothes on."

Who is distracting whom now? she wondered, amused and a little put out. "Why?"

A glint appeared in his eyes. "Public indecency in the state of Maine carries a maximum penalty of six months or five hundred dollars. You don't want me to arrest you."

She tossed her head. "You might as well. You locked me up in a house all morning."

"I left you with my sister. Who was worried about you, by the way. Why the hell didn't you tell her where you were going?"

"She was not there."

"You could have left a note."

She had never thought of it. "I am not used to accounting for my comings and goings."

"Better get used to it."

Startled, she met his gaze. The glint had deepened. Become hotter. More personal.

Her breath caught. *Well.*

She sauntered past him, aware his eyes followed her. Whatever other powers she had lost, she could still compel a man's gaze. She bent, giving him another eyeful, and retrieved her dress, crumpled on the sand.

Behind her, Caleb cleared his throat. "What were you doing?"

For one mad moment, she actually considered telling him. But he was half human, with no apparent awareness of his selkie side. Humans could not encounter anything strange without attempting to understand it. Master it. Control it.

"Swimming," she said.

"Naked." His tone made it not-quite-a-question.

"Your sister does not like me to get her dress wet."

"You shouldn't get your stitches wet."

"Sea water heals." She eased the dress over her head, pulling and patting the material over her damp skin before she turned to face him. "What do you think of the dress?"

"It's a little tight on you."

She glared.

His eyes crinkled. "You shouldn't have come down here alone."

"I was tired of waiting."

"Which doesn't explain why you were on the beach in the first place."

Dangerous waters, she thought. "I told you last night. I was looking for you."

His gaze sharpened. "So you remember some things."

She touched her finger to his cheek and trailed it down his throat. "I could hardly forget you."

He caught her hand in a hard grip, imprisoning it against his chest. "No games, Maggie. What else do you remember?"

So serious.

And so sincere in his concern, in his desire to help her. The sincerity moved her more than threats could have.

"What more do you need to know?"

"Why don't we start with your name?"

That one was easy. "Margred."

"Last name."

She shook her head.

His mouth tightened. "Address?"

She stared at him blankly.

"You had to come from somewhere. You were born in Scotland, you said."

She was foolishly pleased that he remembered. "That's right."

"Do you have friends there? Family?"

"No family."

"Anybody likely to come looking for you?"

She thought of Conn. "I . . . It's possible."

"Who?" The word cracked like an ice floe.

She recoiled. "I don't remember."

Caleb drew in a quick, frustrated breath, and released it on a sigh. "Look, Maggie, I can protect you. I want to protect you. But you need to trust me."

"I do," she protested. *To a point.*

She pressed her fingers to her aching head. In truth, the attack last night had come out of the dark, a blaze of hunger and pain, too quick to defend against or identify. But she had not imagined that whiff of demon. Expecting a mortal to take her side against an elemental was insanity.

Caleb could not protect her.

And she was oddly reluctant to see him fall, a human casualty of a skirmish between Fire and Water.

He captured her other hand and held it against his chest. "Then let's make a deal. From now on, I won't badger you for answers. And you cut the sex-and-games crap and tell me when you honestly don't remember something and when you're just not going to say."

His offer was so unexpected she gaped at him, her mind whirling. It could be days before the dolphins carried her message to Conn, days before the prince responded. Until then, she was on her own.

Or not entirely on her own. She could feel the beat of Caleb's heart against her fingertips.

She lifted her chin. "We could try that."

Caleb's lips curved. He leaned down to brush her mouth with his, a hint of pressure, a whisper of heat, promising, tantalizing. Her toes curled into the damp sand in anticipation.

And then . . . nothing.

She opened her eyes. "What was that?"

He was still smiling down at her, all heavy-lidded, satisfied and sexy. "A kiss. To seal the deal."

She slid her fingers between the buttons of his shirt, pulling him closer. Seeking pleasure. Seeking to forget. "This," she told him, "is a kiss."

His lips were warm and firm. She bit them, wanting more of him, his textures, his flavors. He opened for her, and then his hands were in her hair and his tongue was in her mouth and she was gasping, reaching for him, the whisper of heat sparking and spreading, warming her from the inside out. She wanted to crawl inside him and be warm all over, forever.

His hand fisted in her hair, making her wince. "I want—"

"Yes," she said, ignoring the pain.

He kissed her again, harder this time. She wiggled closer, fitting their bodies together. He grunted—in pleasure? in pain?—and staggered. Through her wet dress, she could feel everything, the bite of his buttons, the cold edge of his buckle. Him. She could feel him, hot and hard against her. She wriggled again in pure delight, twining her arms around his neck.

He half dragged, half stumbled with her a few yards up the beach to the privacy of the rocks. Crowding her into a recess in the cliff wall, he covered her with his broad, hard body, his warm, urgent mouth.

The rush was like diving—the plunge into sensation, the

immersion in feeling. Her hands gripped his shoulders. She could have this. She could have him.

"Touch me," she demanded.

He yanked up her dress. She was already wet and ready for him. He made a sound, or she did, as she arched to meet his hand, as her head dropped back against the rock with an audible thump.

She saw stars.

"*Jesus.* Are you o—"

She grabbed his wrist, bringing his hand between her legs. *"Don't stop."*

He didn't stop. But he cupped the back of her head with one hand, protecting her from the rock, and stroked her with the other, his fingers parting her, rubbing her, making her breath catch and quicken, making her writhe and rise on tiptoe, almost there, almost . . .

Ah. Relief came like a burst of tiny bubbles rising quickly to the surface, releasing in her blood.

"Well." Caleb's voice was strained with lust and laughter. "That was quick."

Margred opened her eyes, smiling languidly. "I told you I was tired of waiting."

10

CALEB LAUGHED AND WRAPPED HIS ARMS AROUND her. His erection lodged against her belly.

It was surprisingly sweet to be held so, Margred mused, supported by his strength, surrounded by his warmth, his scent. She nuzzled his shirt.

He pressed his lips to her hairline—gently—before tipping back her head to study her face. Her heart expanded uncomfortably. "What am I going to do with you, Maggie girl?"

Her hand wandered down his uniform slacks. "I would have thought that was obvious."

His eyes half closed in pleasure. He swelled against her hand. But then he drew back. "If I try to take you now, standing, I'll dump us both in the sand. Not to mention lose the use of my legs for a week."

She arched her eyebrows. "So?"

His rare grin flashed. "So, we still have to haul ass up the cliff to get to the Jeep."

Margred frowned. She had never cared particularly

about the sexual satisfaction of her partners. Still, she was piqued Caleb could deny himself, and her, so readily.

He stroked a strand of hair back from her forehead, the gesture so tender her heart gave another quick, inconvenient lurch. "Besides, the next time I make love to you, it will be on a bed. And I'm taking off my pants."

"You could take your pants off here."

"Not unless I'm willing to pay five hundred dollars for public indecency."

She arched her eyebrows. "I did not realize your naked-ness came at such a price."

"Honey, you can see me anytime for free. But not here." He set her at arm's length. "Where are your shoes?"

"I do not have any."

"Lucy didn't loan you a pair of sneakers?"

"She tried." The memory made Margred smile. "Your sister has big feet."

"She grew into them. How about flip-flops?"

They rubbed the webbing between her toes. Margred shrugged.

"Right, then." Caleb tucked in his shirt, glancing from her bare feet to the rocky path. "I'll go up, drive around, and meet you."

Taking care of her again.

She was grateful . . . and unexpectedly annoyed.

"I can walk. I walked here."

"Uh-huh." He didn't sound impressed. "Show me your feet."

When she didn't move, he reached for her ankle and raised it himself. Margred curled her foot to hide her toes. Caleb didn't appear to notice, focusing instead on the bat-tered sole. Human legs were built for walking. Human feet . . . Well, the walk from the cottage had put Margred forcibly in mind of the human story about the mermaid, the one who wished to become a mortal woman and then felt as if she were dancing on knives.

Caleb studied her bruised and bloodied foot, his face expressionless. "I'll pick you up at the beach access. We can drive to Wiley's, get you a few things you need."

Buy her things, he meant.

"I have no money," Margred said.

His mouth compressed. "I'll make you a loan."

"And how will I pay you back?"

He released her foot, brushing the sand from his hands. "I've been thinking about that."

"I'm sure you have. You think of everything."

His gaze pinned hers. "What's that supposed to mean?"

"Just that . . . you live very much in your head. You are always considering consequences—what is logical, what is next, what is the right thing to do. I do not live that way."

"And you think it's wrong."

"Not wrong," she corrected. "But it makes us . . ." She raised her hands, let them fall. "Different."

He stood very still, his eyes steady on hers. "Maybe it makes us a good match."

Maybe. The possibility curled around her heart. But there were other differences between them, differences he could not guess at.

Differences that made any lasting relationship between them impossible.

* * *

Antonia Barone slammed a tray on the steel counter and glared at her daughter. "I don't need you to tell me how to make lasagna. I've been making lasagna since before you were born."

Regina's frustration bubbled like the pots on the stove. Usually she could keep the lid on. Not today. Not when they were short-staffed and Antonia had waltzed out in the middle of the lunch rush, leaving Regina to deal with a horde of wet and disgruntled tourists on her own.

"I'm not telling you how to do anything. I'm just saying if we used fresh mozzarella instead of that preshredded crap you buy—"

"—the people who come in here wouldn't know the difference," Antonia finished triumphantly.

"Yes, they would. People recognize quality when you put it in front of them. If you educate their palates—"

Antonia snorted. "Educate! I'm running a restaurant, not a school."

The bell over the entrance jangled.

Antonia jerked her head toward the front of the shop. "Go see to our customers."

Customers. Sandy tourists demanding pizza. Unimaginative islanders who liked their salad dressing bottled and their clams fried. Maybe her mother was right.

Regina banged through the swinging door that led from the kitchen to the dining room.

And stopped dead at the sight of Police Chief Cal Hunter with his arm around a strange woman.

Regina gave herself a quick shake. What did she expect? Cal had never shown any real interest in her. Any romantic interest, she amended, recalling his kindness to Nick. Obviously, skinny, sharp-tongued single moms weren't his type.

No, Caleb's tastes ran more toward . . . Well, toward curvy, exotic women with full lips and lots of cleavage.

Like this one.

Regina watched as Caleb steered the woman forward with one hand at her waist. Somebody had banged her up good. But even the ugly stitches marching across her hair line only added a touch of vulnerability that probably appealed to a big, protective guy like Cal.

She was barefoot. The restaurant's policy—NO SHOES, NO SHIRT, NO SERVICE—was clearly printed on the sign in the window.

Regina wiped her hands on her apron. What was she going to do? Call the police? "Hi, Cal. Who's your friend?"

"This is Maggie. Maggie, Regina Barone."

The woman inclined her head without speaking.

"Nice to meet you." Regina looked at Cal. "You're a little early for dinner."

He did that attractive eye crinkle thing without actually smiling. "I wanted to beat the crowd."

"Be glad you weren't here at lunch time, then. We had a line out the door and nobody behind the counter. What can I get you?"

"I need money," the woman said.

Regina blinked. "Excuse me?"

Caleb cleared his throat. "Your mother mentioned you were a little shorthanded. I thought Maggie here might be able to help you out."

Ha. Like he was motivated by some desire to make her life easier. Regina looked over at Cleavage Barbie. "You got any experience?"

"What kind of experience?"

"Waiting tables, washing dishes, working the cash register. That kind of thing."

"No."

No, of course not.

Regina sighed. "You talked to my mother about this?" she asked Caleb.

"She said it was your decision."

Great. Her mother wouldn't even let Regina buy decent mozzarella, but as long as there was a chance of something going phenomenally, fantastically wrong, it was her decision.

"Okay. Well, let me get you some forms. We'll see how you work out."

The woman—Maggie—looked at Caleb. "Forms?"

"Give us a minute," he said.

She held his gaze for a long moment while Regina got the necessary paperwork. "Here you go."

With a shrug, the woman slid into a nearby booth with the forms and a pencil.

"You can't add her to regular payroll," Caleb said to Regina.

Regina raised one eyebrow. "You want me to pay her cash?"

"It wouldn't be the first time someone in a restaurant got paid under the table."

"And is that your recommendation as an officer of the law, Chief Hunter?"

"It's my request," Caleb said evenly. "As your friend."

"Well, shit," Regina said in disgust.

He smiled, and for a second she felt like Nick, acting out for a little male attention. "Not that it's any of my business," she asked, "but why?"

Caleb hesitated. "I was hoping you could keep an eye on her. Let me know if anybody gives her a hard time."

"You mean, besides my mother?"

Caleb's eyes crinkled again. "I was thinking more of a male somebody, six-two, six-four, around a hundred and ninety pounds."

"And would this tall, skinny male be the one who messed up her face?"

"Maybe."

Regina felt a flash of sympathy for the woman in the booth. Men could be real shits. But she had other people she needed to worry about.

"Are you expecting him to come back to finish the job?" she asked. "Because now that school's out, Nick is around a lot. I won't do anything that puts him in danger."

"I wouldn't ask you to," Caleb assured her. "I'm just working a hunch."

"A hunch." Regina glanced at Maggie. The woman had abandoned the forms in front of her and was coaxing Hercules from his customary perch in the front window. The cat, who normally disdained the restaurant's patrons, stretched out his neck to sniff her fingers. Regina considered that a point in Maggie's favor. "What does she think about this hunch of yours?"

"We haven't discussed it."

"Why not?"

"She says she doesn't remember the attack."

Was it Regina's imagination, or had he put the slightest emphasis on *says*?

"Do you believe her?"

"I believe," Caleb said deliberately, "she may not want to remember."

"Because she's protecting somebody," Regina guessed.

His expression was sober. "Or running away from something."

* * *

"Congratulations." Caleb eased down onto the bench opposite Margred, stretching his leg with a relieved sigh. "You have a job."

"Money," she said with satisfaction.

"Not until you actually start working, but yeah, that's the idea."

"When do I start?"

"Regina wants you on the lunch shift, maybe build your hours from there. I'll drop you off tomorrow on my way to work."

"Tomorrow," she repeated.

"Yeah. Tonight"—he took a breath, surprised by the jitter of nerves in his stomach—"I thought you could stay with me."

"In your bed."

His words on the beach lingered between them: *The next time I make love to you, it will be on a bed. And I'm taking off my pants.*

"Unless that's a problem for you," he said carefully.

"Why would it be a problem?"

He was a good cop, but he couldn't read her face, her voice. Was she amused? Or pissed at him?

"I want you to stay with me. But you're not obliged . . ." He stopped and tried again. "You don't owe me anything."

"You are in your head again," she observed.

"I don't know what you're talking about."

"You are worried if I stay with you, I will have sex with

you out of a feeling of obligation. That I will be dependent on you and resent you for it."

He'd gone almost thirty-six hours without sleep. He didn't have the energy—or the wits—for man-woman games. "Something like that."

Margred snapped her fingers, and the big cat, Hercules, strolled over to investigate. "You see this cat?"

"Yeah. So?"

"The people here feed it, do they not?"

"When Antonia's not looking."

"They let it come inside." Margred scratched the cat's chin. Purring, the feline rubbed against her fingers. "It suffers me to touch it, to pet it. But they do not own the cat." Her gaze met his. "Any more than you would own me if I choose to stay with you."

He rubbed his face with his hand. "That means you're sleeping with me, right?"

Her full lips curved. "Oh, yes."

"Fine." He was suddenly less tired. "Let's get something to eat and go home."

After they left Antonia's, however, he took her to buy the basics: T-shirts, toiletries, and shoes. The island shops didn't carry a wide selection of women's clothing, but on the racks of resort wear at Lighthouse Gifts, they found a flowing skirt and a pair of drawstring pants to get Maggie through the next few days.

Caleb carried their purchases to the cash register.

Jane Ivey rang them up, her brown perm practically quivering in excitement. She'd had the same tight brown curls—and maybe the same sweater—twenty years ago, when Caleb used to stop in her shop on his way home after school. This was what he'd come home for. This sense of continuity. Of community. Of connection.

"Terrible thing last night, Chief," she greeted him.

"Caleb, please."

"I don't know what's going to happen to business if people don't feel safe vacationing here."

He tried to reassure her. "I don't think you need to worry just yet."

"Most folks come to World's End to get away from all that."

"All that?"

"Violence." She shot him a glance. "Of course, I suppose you're used to it, coming from Portland."

She made the city across the bay sound like Las Vegas. Or Sodom or Gomorrah.

"People are pretty much the same wherever you go," Caleb said. "Crime, too."

"Still . . . we never had anything like this happen when Roy Miller was chief." Her hand lingered on a box of condoms. "You buying these?"

Sometimes community was a real pain in the ass.

"Yes, ma'am. I'm too old to swipe them from the shelves like I used to."

"You never," Jane said comfortably. "Is that her? The girl who was attacked?"

Caleb followed her glance to where Maggie wandered the aisle of MAINE key chains and shot glasses and shrink-wrapped shells from Florida.

She looked completely out of place, her perfect body imperfectly covered by his sister's blue dress, her pale beauty shining in the dingy store like the moon through clouds.

"Her name is Maggie," he said.

"Poor thing," Jane said. "Not from around here, is she?"

Maggie fingered a display of cheap shell necklaces, the kind teenagers bought themselves on vacation. Her eyes were lost.

They tore his heart.

"I'll take one of those," Caleb said. "A necklace."

"Which one?"

"It doesn't matter." Whatever would ease that wistful look in her eyes, the bleeding in his chest. "Whatever she wants. Charge it."

He paid for the clothes, the condoms, the necklace, before he joined Maggie standing in front of a wire cage of hermit crabs in gaudy shells.

He touched her gently on the arm. "See something you like?"

She turned, her face set, her lips trembling. "No. Why are those here? Why are they trapped like that?"

"They're for sale. For the tourists."

"They do not eat them?"

"No. They're . . . pets, I guess you could call them. Souvenirs."

"That is horrible. Their environment is too dry."

She sounded really upset.

"Uh . . . They're *land* crabs," Caleb said.

"I know what they are." Her voice rose. Jane glanced their way. "They are *dying*. You must stop this."

"Yeah." *Shit.* "The thing is, the store's not breaking any laws."

"They should be free."

As a matter of fact, he agreed with her. He regarded the skittering legs and beady little eyes of the creepy crawlies in the cage. But . . . "Even if I bought them all and set them free, they'd die. The climate here is too cold."

Maggie's stricken gaze met his. She bit her lip. "Yes. Yes, you are right. I did not think."

"I'm sorry," he said, although he didn't know what the hell he was apologizing for. "What can I do?"

"It would . . . They would be better if they had water. A sponge. Can you do that? Can you give them water on a sponge?"

"Yeah, sure."

Feeling like a fool, he went to convince Jane she needed to water her crabs.

*   *   *

Margred watched him walk away, broad-shouldered and logical.

He was right. She knew he was right.

It didn't matter. The stench of waste and decay wafted from the land crabs' cage, choking her. They were trapped. They were dying.

She was trapped and dying, too.

She couldn't stand it. While Caleb spoke to the woman behind the counter, Margred hurried from the shop. She needed to be outside, to feel the air on her face, to smell the wind blowing from the sea.

Water. She missed the water.

Pink streaked the sky above her head. At the bottom of the hill, beyond the clutter of boats in the harbor, the ocean rolled gray and welcoming.

Pressure built in her lungs. She stood on the sidewalk, struggling to breathe.

"Maggie." Caleb spoke behind her, his deep voice patient and kind.

He could not help her any more than he could help the poor, doomed crabs.

She turned to face him.

His green eyes were watchful. "Ready to go home?"

She could not go home. Not without her pelt. She was marooned in an alien landscape, and the constant vigilance she needed simply to survive wore on her nerves as much as the constant walking wore on her feet.

Her throat closed. She nodded.

"This way."

He escorted her along the sidewalk, one hand at her waist, possessive and protective as a bull seal with a new cow. She should have been amused. Annoyed. But there was comfort in that light touch, reassurance in the way he steered her steps and opened her door and disposed of her packages in back.

He settled into the seat beside her, his big, square knee thrusting into her space. His long-fingered hands were strong and gentle on the wheel.

Desire fizzled along her nerves, easing the pressure in her chest.

They rode to his house in silence.

Caleb lived on the east side—the ocean side—of the island, in a solidly constructed cabin tucked under the trees, at once solitary and completely a part of its environment. Pine needles released their fragrance underfoot as he guided her to the front door.

Inside, one big chair and a bigger couch faced a wide, flat, black screen. No pillows. No plants. Just dark, warm colors against pale, smooth wood, and a stack of magazines piled by a chair.

He showed her his bedroom, tidy and a little bare. Margred stood in the middle of the room, her gaze traveling from the neatly made bed to the window. Through the wooden blinds, over the tops of the trees, she glimpsed the sea, shining like a secret in the last light of evening.

Longing took her breath.

"You can lie in that bed and watch the sun rise over the ocean," Caleb said quietly behind her. "After Iraq, I . . ."

His silence tugged at her. "After Iraq, what?"

"Nothing." He deposited her bags on the bed and nodded toward an open door. "Bathroom's through there. You can shower, change, whatever. I'll be in the living room if you need me."

She understood he was giving her time to rest and regroup before he joined her. She appreciated his consideration.

"Well." He stuck his thumbs in his pockets. "Make yourself at home," he said, and left her.

She looked around the clean, organized space, the polished shoes set side by side beneath a chair, the coins stacked by size upon the dresser. A far cry from the magpie luxury of Caer Subai.

She sank down on the mattress, momentarily overwhelmed. What was she doing here? What was she doing?

Make yourself at home, Caleb had said.

Her gaze fell on the shopping bags. All right, then. She could do that. Opening the nearest one, she rummaged inside for shampoo and lotions.

Something glinted at the bottom of the bag. She reached down and closed her hand on it.

A necklace.

Her heartbeat quickened foolishly as she drew it out, a simple black ribbon with tiny chips of coral and sea glass between two round silver beads like pearls. She had admired it in the shop. In the middle, suspended like a charm, was a shell. A Scotch bonnet.

Her fingers curled around it.

Caleb must have seen— He must have known— He must have bought it for her.

She sat for a long time, the necklace in her hand and her gaze on the sea beyond the windows. Her heart felt strangely full. Heavy.

She was . . . touched, she decided. He had touched her with his gift.

That means you're sleeping with me, right?

Oh, yes.

Not from obligation, but because she wanted to.

Satisfied with her decision, she fastened the necklace around her throat, fumbling with the clasp.

Squinting, she regarded the shell against her chest. Pretty, she thought. A little hum started in her blood. Smiling in anticipation, she opened the door.

And found Caleb asleep on the couch.

Ah. Well.

Her heart stumbled in disappointment. Her lips pursed. She could wake him. She would wake him.

In a moment.

He looked so . . . not exactly peaceful, lying there. Even in sleep, tension dug lines between his brows and compressed his mouth. His short, thick lashes shielded his eyes. His beard lurked just beneath his skin. The heaviness in her moved from her heart to her loins. She wanted to test the texture of his jaw with her palm.

When had he last shaved?

When had he last slept?

She knew he had been on the beach last night and again

this morning. Searching the scene, Lucy had explained. Talking to people. Had he gone to bed at all?

As she watched, his open hand clenched on the cushions of the couch. He shivered, as if he were cold.

She was not used to denying herself. She did not like it. But Caleb was obviously exhausted.

With a sigh, Margred went back into the bedroom, pulled the blanket from his bed, and covered him.

11

HIS DREAM STANK OF CORDITE AND METAL, BLOOD and fear. Sweat ran under his helmet and soaked his armpits.

Caleb shouted. "Get in, get in!"

Specialist Mike Denuncio sprinted toward the Humvee and threw himself into the tiny foam-cushioned backseat. A flurry of pops followed him like a string of firecrackers on the Fourth of July.

"Go, go, go!" Caleb ordered.

The Humvee lurched. Panting and swearing, the driver—nineteen-year-old Specialist Danny Torres—engaged gears. The V-8 engine rattled and rolled. The radio shrieked and squealed. Shouting. Shots. More pops, louder. Closer.

From the turret, the 50-caliber machine gun sprayed the cabin with dust and noise. Mike was reloading, slamming rounds into the chamber of his M16. The radio squawked in English and Arabic. The Humvee dodged and weaved.

"Look right. Right! On the roof."

Heart pumping, Caleb returned fire. Through the bullet-pocked windshield, he saw the vehicle ahead bounce and shimmy as they roared out of ambush. The flat, featureless road ahead straightened out between a line of concrete bunkers. The Humvee picked up speed.

"Okay?" Caleb shouted.

"Okay."

Mike gave him a quick thumbs-up.

A green and white highway sign in Arabic loomed over-head. A horn blared. A vehicle wandered the median. *Rush hour, Iraqi style.* Caleb inhaled cautiously.

And the road erupted in a blast of smoke and pain.

He couldn't breathe.

He couldn't see.

He couldn't think.

He lay choking on dust while asphalt rained down on him, sharp as shrapnel. He covered his head. There, beneath his arm, was that a—? Boot. Just a boot, and a foot, and a boot tag stamped with somebody's blood type, somebody's social security number . . . His gunner. Jackson.

Jesus God.

The stench of blood and burning rolled over him. His legs . . . His left leg wasn't working. He started to crawl to Danny, crumpled a few yards away, his uniform torn and black with blood and grime. He had to help him. He had to save him. Crawl. Pain throbbed through him, robbing his strength, his breath. *Crawl.*

He put one hand on the boy's shoulder to roll him over and stared into Maggie's face.

Her head lolled. One side of her face was black with blood. It streaked her hair and ran into the ground. Despair filled him. He was too late, she was dead, he hadn't saved her . . .

She opened her eyes—blue eyes, *Danny's* eyes—and spoke.

"Wake up," she said.

*   *   *

Caleb woke with a start. His heart pounded. His leg was on fire.

Maggie bent over him, her eyes concerned—brown eyes, so deep and dark it was hard to tell pupil from iris.

She laid a hand along his cheek, cupping his jaw. "Wake up," she repeated. "You are dreaming."

"Yeah, I . . ." He struggled to sit, fighting his way through the remnants of his nightmare. "Sorry."

"You are exhausted. You should come to bed."

"Yeah." He got his feet under him and tried to stand. Fuck. "I, uh . . ."

He rubbed his face with his hand as if he could scrub away the image of Danny dying. Of Maggie, bleeding and naked at the base of the fire. "How long was I out?"

"Not long enough, obviously." She frowned. "You are in pain?"

"Kind of," he admitted. His leg felt as though somebody had whacked him with a baseball bat.

"Your sister gave me pills. You have pills?"

"In the bathroom."

"Good."

"No." He was already reeling from the dream and stupid from lack of sleep. He didn't need drugs. "They make me loopy."

She arched her eyebrows. "Loopy?"

"Tired. I can't do my job if I can't concentrate."

"You are hardly alert now. You need pills. And rest. Come." She butted her shoulder against his chest, dragged his arm around her neck. "I will help you."

"I can walk."

"Not well."

He could have protested. But the truth was, she felt really good under his arm, soft and warm and surprisingly strong. Her hair waved against his cheek.

"Come on." Her voice was breathless. He was too heavy for her. But she didn't sound annoyed.

He staggered with her to the bathroom and swallowed his pills. Swaying on his feet, he did his business, washed his hands, and brushed his teeth.

When he opened the door again, Maggie was standing there, so fucking beautiful his heart constricted in his chest.

"Come to bed," she said.

The last of his nightmare vanished, banished by the prospect of taking her to bed. His bed.

"I've been waiting my whole life to hear you say that."

Her lips curved. "We met only three weeks ago."

He leaned on her, nuzzling her, buzzed on Vicodin and the smell of her hair. "All my life," he repeated solemnly.

They shuffled the few steps to the bed, moving like kids at a high school dance.

"I'm going to do you slow this time," he promised. "I want to go down on you."

"Yes."

He lowered himself to the mattress, aware of her busy fingers tugging on the covers, on his shirt and belt. He lay back, watching her. Her T-shirt gaped as she wrestled with his shoelaces. He could see her breasts. So soft. So beautiful. So . . .

His head touched the pillow.

He slept.

*   *   *

Caleb drifted between wake and sleep, his mind floating and at ease, and his body uncomfortable. He could dismiss the familiar pain of his leg. The insistent pulse of his arousal was harder to ignore. Particularly with Maggie lying soft and warm beside him.

God, had he really fallen asleep on her last night?

He turned his head. She slept facing him, curled in on herself, her knees drawn up and one arm tucked under her pillow. Self-contained. Secret.

With one finger, he stroked a strand of hair back from her face, careful not to touch her stitches or the purpling bruise on her forehead. Despite her hurts, last night she had cared for him. Comforted him.

Undressed him.

The memory of her small warm hands tugging at him dried his mouth. Anticipation buzzed in his blood, pooled heavy in his groin. He rolled onto his side.

Her eyes opened, and her gaze fused with his.

He felt it again, that little shock of connection, that click inside, like two pieces of a puzzle snapping together in his brain, like a key sliding home in a lock.

"You're awake," he said softly. Foolishly.

"Mm." Her hand glided down his belly, brushing his erection. "You are, too."

He half closed his eyes at the intense pleasure of her touch. "I conked out on you last night."

She stroked him up and down, slowly. "You can make it up to me now."

He caught her wrist and pulled her hand away from his body. "I plan to."

She tugged against his hold, a tiny pleat appearing between her brows. "Then—"

"Ssh." He stopped her protest with his mouth.

She responded easily, eagerly, parting her lips and kissing him back. But when she would have taken the kiss deeper, when she sucked on his tongue and slid her thigh along his, he trapped her hands again.

"Let me," he whispered against her mouth.

"Let you what?"

"Let me . . . kiss you. Here." He pressed his lips to her warm, flushed cheek. "Here." He moved to the arch of her eyebrow. "Here." He nipped her chin.

She stopped struggling. Her mouth curved. "Anywhere else?"

"Everywhere," he said, and followed through, touching and kissing and licking his way down her lush, firm body, loving the way her breath caught and her muscles tightened under his hands.

Her nipples stood at attention. He pushed her breasts together, sucking and playing with them until she arched and offered more. He wanted more. He wanted everything. To taste her, take her, keep her . . . He clamped down on his

greed, stroking his tongue over her again. He wanted her to
know who she was with. To need him. Remember him.

He skimmed his lips over her smooth, curved belly,
pressed warm, wet kisses to the insides of her thighs. Her
hips lifted, inviting him, urging him on. He parted her with
his fingers, devoured her with his eyes. She was slick and
hot. Wet. Squirming. He lowered his head, inhaling her excitement, teasing her with his breath.

She raised her head from the pillow, her eyes dark with
arousal. Watching him. "Please."

He thrust two fingers inside her, feeling her clench
around him. "Please what?"

"Caleb!"

His name on her lips broke his control. He lowered his
head, loving the way she moved and shuddered, gasped and
moaned under him. Because of him.

He wanted to make this last forever.

Maggie had other ideas.

She grabbed his short hair and pulled hard enough to get
his attention. Her face was flushed, her eyes fierce. "Inside
me," she said. "Now."

He was flattered, moved . . . and incredibly turned on.
"Let me get a condom."

"Now."

But he was determined to protect her. They'd already
had sex once without a condom. Maybe she'd been on the
pill then. But she wasn't now. He needed to prove to her he
could be trusted to take care of her.

So he made her wait while he opened the box and covered himself and lay down again. His leg wouldn't support
him on top.

Maggie pushed him flat on his back and swarmed over
him, her naked breasts brushing his chest, her knees strad-
dling his thighs.

He grunted in pleasure and pain.

She levered herself up, pushing against his shoulders.
"Are you hurt?"

No.

Yes.

Who cared? Her new position pressed their lower bodies together. She was hot and wet and right where he wanted her.

He gritted his teeth. "No," he said, and grabbed her hips, thrusting up into her.

Magic.

He wanted—he'd intended—to take it slow this time. But she was on top, rocking him, riding him, taking him in a galloping rush of pleasure. Her breasts were in his face, her lips swollen and parted, her eyes dark and blind.

"Maggie."

She looked at him, really looked, so he could see the heat and the tenderness in her eyes. That was all it took. He came in a blinding rush that emptied his balls and his heart. And thought he heard, as she collapsed against his chest, her whisper his name.

*   *   *

Margred had missed the sunrise over the ocean. She'd missed Caleb's rising, too. At some point—after they had made love the second or third time—he had left their bed. She heard him moving about in the other room.

But he was right. You really could lie in this bed and watch the sea. The dance of the sunlight on the waves gladdened her heart.

She stretched between the sheets, enjoying the feel of the fine fabric against her bare skin. She had never slept with a lover before. It was strangely . . . satisfying. The possessive weight of Caleb's arm, the steady cadence of his breathing, his naked body beside hers all night long . . . His body temperature was several degrees cooler than hers. That, too, was surprisingly comfortable.

The mingled scents of sex and man clung to her skin and hung in the air of the room. She breathed them in, her body loose and relaxed.

And smelled something else. Something—cooking?— teasing her nostrils and her appetite.

Caleb was cooking her breakfast.

How . . . sweet.

She pulled his T-shirt over her head, being careful not to catch her stitches, and padded to find him.

He was in the kitchen, standing half-naked with his back to the doorway, attending to something on the stove. Her gaze skimmed over his smooth, powerful shoulders, down the strong, long line of his back to the waistband of his jeans. And below.

Another hunger stirred. Maybe breakfast should wait.

She came up behind him, slipping her arms around his waist. "Good morning."

He jerked, tensed, and then relaxed. "Good morning," he said, his voice rough with sleep.

She pressed a kiss between his shoulder blades, ruffling her fingers through the line of hair that bisected his muscled belly. He sucked in his breath. His muscles jumped under her hand before he turned in her arms. She could feel his arousal through his jeans, against her stomach.

She licked her lips. "What are you making?"

His gaze dropped to her mouth. "Eggs. Toast. I'm not much of a cook."

She had never cooked in her life. She rocked against him, loving the heaviness in his gaze, the hardness of his body. "It smells wonderful."

His smile broke, more dazzling than the sun on the sea. "Witch. That's the coffee."

She rubbed her nose against his bare chest. "Is that what it is?"

"Probably." He cleared his throat and reached beside the stove for a glass pot full of some clear brown liquid. "Want some?"

"Coffee?"

"It's fresh."

Margred had never begged for a lover. (And dismissed the memory of her own voice, saying *"Please."*) Perhaps he needed time to recuperate?

Anyway, she was hungry.

With a shrug, she released him. "All right. Thank you."

He poured her coffee while she sat at the table. She sipped from the cup and grimaced. It didn't taste nearly as good as it smelled.

"Do you take sugar?" he asked.

Did she? Why not?

"Yes."

He passed her a blue bowl full of fine white sand and a spoon. Tentatively, she added a heaping spoonful to her cup.

Ah. Better.

She added more. *Better still.*

She added a third spoonful, and closed her eyes in appreciation. *Heaven.*

Sighing with satisfaction, she set down her cup. "Thank you."

Caleb regarded her, a quizzical expression on his face. "Don't mention it."

He slid a plate of eggs and toast in front of her. Margred picked up her fork.

He poured himself coffee and sat down facing her. "We have to talk," he said.

She paused with her fork halfway to her lips. "You don't make that sound like a good thing."

A laugh escaped him. "Yeah. Well. If it helps you, it's a good thing."

A pause, while her breakfast cooled.

"You can trust me," he said.

He looked so dear. So earnest. So . . . safe, with his jutting jaw and serious green eyes.

"I do," she said.

As much as she was able, she amended to herself.

Caleb reached across the table and clasped her hand. His hand was firm and steady. The mer were sensual creatures, but they rarely touched outside of mating or nursing offspring. That warm, strong clasp was oddly . . . comforting. "Then I need you to tell me the truth."

"The truth," she repeated cautiously.

"Tell me what happened the other night."

"I don't remember."

The cool disappointment in his eyes was worse than a slap.

"No, really," she insisted. With an effort, she forced her mind to go back. Selkies lived immersed in the sensation of the moment. It was not their way to dwell on past unpleasantness. But for Caleb's sake, she would force herself to recall.

"I had just . . . arrived on the beach when I was attacked. Struck." Her lip curled in self-disgust. "I must have made it easy for him. I am not usually so unaware."

"Him."

"My attacker."

"You're sure it was a man, then."

She frowned. "I assumed . . . There was movement." She flapped her left hand in the air just behind her head to demonstrate. "Above and behind me. I thought . . . It would have to be a man. Or a very tall woman."

Who smelled like fire spawn.

Best not to tell him that.

"Okay, that's good," Caleb said. She blinked. When had he pulled out his notebook? "So, you never saw him. His face."

"No," she said definitely.

"But you can guess who it was."

What. Not who.

"No."

Caleb's eyes, green and steady, held hers. "You notice anything else? A sleeve, maybe. A shoe. Anything."

She shook her head. "I was stunned. I fell. I do remember—"

Caleb's attention sharpened. "What?"

"It's nothing."

"Tell me."

"A smell," she admitted reluctantly.

"A smell," he repeated. "Can you describe it?"

A demon smell. No, she couldn't say that. But she had

promised to tell the truth. "It was . . . very pungent. A burning smell. Like sulphur."

"The bonfire maybe," Caleb suggested.

She shrugged.

"What was he burning?"

"What?"

"The other night, you said . . ." Caleb flipped pages in his notebook. " 'I need what he took from me . . . in the fire.' What did he take from you, Maggie?"

"I don't—"

—*remember*.

But she couldn't say that, she had promised not to say that, they had a deal. "I can't say."

"You weren't wearing anything when I found you." Caleb's voice was gentle.

She bit her lip. "No."

"You want to tell me about that?"

She had stepped out of her pelt. She remembered folding it, hiding it in a recess in the cliff. Heart quickening in anticipation, she had approached the curve of the rock, when she heard—felt?—the attack explode out of the dark behind her, slamming her onto the rocks. Pain burst in her head. She crumpled. And felt the fierce, consuming will of another licking at her flesh, rolling over her like smoke. She fled its possession into unconsciousness.

Shuddering, she pressed her fingers to her head.

"Can I get you anything?" Caleb asked, his voice gentle. Inexorable. "More coffee. Water, maybe."

She swallowed. "No. No, I am fine."

"Your clothes," he prompted. "What happened to them?"

"I took them off."

"Why?"

"I was . . . swimming."

"You took your clothes off to go swimming," Caleb repeated without expression.

She raised her head. "Yes."

"Did you plan on swimming?"

She looked at him blankly.

"Is that why you went to the beach that night?" He rephrased the question. "You wanted to go swimming?"

"No, I told you. I wanted to see you."

"After three weeks, you suddenly decided—what? You had to see me?"

She felt the dangerous shift, like the warning tug of the tide, and reacted instinctively to protect herself. "Poor Caleb. Did you wait for me? Were your feelings hurt?"

"Maggie—"

"I was there. What more do you want me to say?"

His mouth set in a firm, flat line. "So, you arrived at the beach. What time?"

"The sun had just set," she offered. "The tide was almost at the full."

"I'll check the tide tables. You didn't happen to look at your watch?"

"I was not wearing a watch," she said with perfect truth.

"What time did you leave your house?"

She was silent.

"Maggie?"

She did not, could not, answer him.

Caleb sighed. "Okay, we'll let that go for now. How did you get there?"

"I don't understand."

"We didn't find a car. Did you walk?"

"I . . . may have."

"So, you came through the trees . . ." He paused expectantly.

"From around the rocks," she said. "Where we—where you climbed down the other day."

"Good. You came down the path?"

"No."

"How did you get to the beach, Maggie?"

You can trust me, he'd said.

He wanted the truth, he'd said.

So she gave it to him.

"I swam."

His palms slapped the table. "Damn it, Maggie, we have a deal. No games, no lies. Remember?"

Margred's indignation mingled with regret. So much for telling the truth. If he could not handle *"I swam,"* he was not likely to deal well with *"I am an immortal selkie trapped in mortal form—oh, and your mother was, too."*

She settled back in her chair, arching her eyebrows. "The deal I remember is, no games, no lies . . . and no badgering. Or have you forgotten that part?"

"I'm trying to help you," Caleb grated.

"Then respect that I might have reasons—good reasons—for what I say or do not say."

"I can't protect you if you won't talk to me."

He could not protect her in any case, Margred thought with a tear at her heart. But she knew him well enough now to realize he would never accept that answer.

12

≈

"THIS ISN'T *CSI: AUGUSTA*," SAM REYNOLDS told Caleb three days later. "These things take time. You know that. If you're looking for the presence of an accelerant—"

"I'm not." Caleb sat at his desk, Maggie's file open on the desk before him and the receiver tucked under his jaw. He needed the state's resources. He respected Reynolds's expertise. But this was still his case. His woman. "The evidence was recovered from a bonfire. The debris could be soaked in lighter fluid and it wouldn't tell me a thing about the assailant except he sucked at starting fires. I need a bio-chemical analysis of anything he could have used as a weapon."

"Basically, all your fire debris. Which, like I said, is going to take time."

Donna Tomah had said the same thing when Caleb saw her yesterday. *"Recovering memories takes time."*

Caleb stared down at Maggie's photo: the ugly gash on her forehead; the wide, exotic mouth; the dark, unfathomable eyes. How could he protect her when he didn't know who she was? Or what she was running from?

"What about the rape kit?" he asked Reynolds.

"Results won't do you any good without something to compare them to."

"You can run them through the criminal databases."

"Assuming her assailant has priors," Reynolds said.

"That's why I want results on the debris. If we can identify a weapon—"

"Or a suspect."

Frustration jabbed Caleb. "I don't have a suspect. I have jack shit."

"Sucks for you," Reynolds said. "Look, this case may be big news where you are, but it's not a priority here unless—"

"It's a homicide," Caleb finished grimly. "Got it. Thanks."

"At least your victim is still alive."

More alive than anyone he'd ever known. She burned with life like a fever. Even her body temperature was hot.

Caleb cleared his throat. "Yeah."

"She talking yet?"

"Nope."

"She's not a fugitive, is she?"

It was a reasonable question. Caleb had asked himself the same thing. "Not according to NCIC. Her fingerprints don't match anything on file."

"So, no criminal history. You check Missing Persons?"

"I'm telling you, she's not in the database. There's a sixteen-year-old girl went missing downstate twenty years ago, no fingerprints on record. But the profile doesn't match—wrong age, wrong eye color."

"You could put out a press release," Reynolds suggested. "Appeal to the public. You know, 'Police seek help identifying beautiful naked woman,' that kind of thing. You'd get a lot of responses."

"From every crackpot and crazy within five hundred miles. No, thanks."

"How do you know *she's* not crazy?"

Tension lodged at the base of Caleb's skull. He massaged the back of his neck with one hand, holding the phone in the other. "She's not."

"Just forgetful," Reynolds said dryly.

"She has a concussion."

"She bumped her head. Doesn't mean she's telling you the truth."

Suspicious bastard.

But he was right. Caleb didn't know what troubled him more—that Maggie could be lying to him or that he wanted so desperately to believe in her.

"I'm trying to talk her into seeing a neurologist on the mainland. Get a CT scan, do some memory retrieval techniques," he said.

"Right," Reynolds said. "Pump her with enough amobarbital, she might relax enough to answer a few questions."

"I was thinking hypnosis."

"Sure. If you want the DA to throw out her account in court."

Caleb's jaw tightened until his back teeth ground together. "You got any better ideas?"

"Not really. Have you considered maybe your Jane Doe—"

"Her name is Maggie."

"Right. Have you considered maybe she doesn't *want* to be identified?"

"Hiding from somebody."

"That, or somebody's already caught up with her, and she's protecting him."

Caleb had considered that, all right. Maggie was living with him. Sleeping with him. He knew she liked her coffee sweet and her sex fast and rough. But how well did he really know *her*?

He had a sudden, vivid memory of Maggie smiling and playing with the cat under the table. *"It suffers me to touch it, to pet it. But they do not own the cat."* Her gaze met his. *"Any more than you would own me if I choose to stay with you."*

"Just see what you can do to move things along on your end," he told Reynolds.

And he would do the same, Caleb thought, hanging up the phone.

Maybe Maggie didn't want to remember. That's what amnesia was all about, wasn't it? The mind protecting itself against things too terrible to recall.

He pushed away the memories of Iraq, of Jackson's boot, of Danny's face . . .

Hell, he'd like nothing better than to forget himself.

As long as Caleb was prepared to ignore his job, forget his responsibilities, he could play house and pretend. Pretend that his leg wasn't held together with screws and scar tissue, that he didn't withdraw into his work as surely as his old man had retreated into a bottle. Pretend Maggie was free to be with him, in his house. In his bed.

It wasn't just that she was available for sex. He'd had that with Sherilee, at least in the beginning.

Maggie enjoyed life. She savored every meal, every morning, every shift in the weather.

And sex. God, she loved sex. The things she did with her hands and with her mouth . . . Those noises she made in the back of her throat, like she loved what she was doing . . . what he was doing . . .

Yeah. That was different. She was different.

She never complained. Not about her head or her feet, the trauma of the attack or the strain of her new job. Not about the odd gaps in her knowledge that made Caleb wonder if her assailant had hit her a little bit too hard. Not about his scars or his nightmares or his lack of progress on her case.

Maybe she liked playing house, too.

Not that Maggie was what Caleb would call domestic. Regina reported she was almost useless in the kitchen.

But somehow his house felt more lived in with her there. He liked the way she opened the windows, security risk or not. He liked the way the bathroom smelled after her shower, the bottles she left on his sink, the sugar bowl open on the kitchen table.

Only three days, and already she was making a space for herself in his house. In his life.

His life, Caleb thought, his gut twisting. Not hers.

Before Maggie came to the island, she'd had another life. They had to deal with that, they had to get past that, before they could go on.

How else could he keep her safe?

How else could he be sure she wouldn't leave?

He opened the door to the outer office. "Edith."

"Chief." She swiveled around to hand him a note. "George Wiley says somebody took twenty-five pounds of ice from the cooler out front without paying."

Caleb raised his eyebrows. "Ice?"

"George is pretty upset about it."

Caleb rubbed the back of his neck. Community relations, he reminded himself. "Any leads?"

Edith cocked her head, as if listening to the island breeze. "I hear Bobby Kincaid is turning thirty tomorrow. Boys might be planning a party."

Caleb remembered Bobby. Shaggy hair, flannel shirt, about Regina's age. He used to sneak beers behind his father's garage in high school. "Fine. I'll talk to George, see if he'll take payment instead of pressing charges, before I drop by Bobby's. I'm headed that way anyway to meet the ferry."

Edith regarded him over the rim of her glasses. "Planning a trip?"

Caleb forced a smile. "I want to show Maggie's picture around."

Again.

He was grasping at straws. He knew it. But he was running out of options. Circulating Maggie's description and photograph to the sheriff's office and the state police had drawn a big fat zero.

"I thought you said the pilot didn't recognize her," Edith said.

The pilot hadn't. The crew didn't.

"Maybe somebody else will," Caleb said.

A tourist, a builder hauling lumber, a housewife back from the mainland with her weekly shopping.

Edith shrugged. "That reminds me. Paula Schutte from Island Realty called."

Caleb waited. He'd already combed through the realty's rental records. No Margred. No Margaret. No SWF booking an island getaway three weeks or three nights ago. Still, maybe Paula had had better luck.

"She has that list you wanted," Edith continued. "All the property owners who handle their own rentals?"

Not so lucky, after all. But still helpful. "Great. Tell her I said thanks."

"You don't need to thank her," Edith said tartly. "This is her hit list. That woman is going after every unlisted property on the island."

"That's her job," Caleb said. "You can't blame a person for doing her job."

Edith gave him another significant look over her glasses. "Some people don't know when to quit."

Caleb smiled wryly. "Guess not," he said, and went to meet the four o'clock ferry.

* * *

The birds came while Margred wiped tables after the lunchtime rush.

She straightened, damp rag in hand, to watch them wheel and dip in sudden numbers over the harbor, brilliant white against the blue. Her heart rose, carried with them on the wind.

She liked working the front of the restaurant. Not only for the view of the sea and to get away from the clatter of pans and Antonia barking in the kitchen. She liked watching Hercules bask on his window ledge like a seal in the sun and Nick, with his tongue between his teeth, coloring in a booth.

She had spent almost seven hundred years alone, living apart even from her mate. The humans' interactions fascinated her. Their lives were so short and so busy, so varied in their preoccupations and concerns. She liked the fishermen who clomped in, tanned and tired, smelling of sweat and the sea. She liked the older women, easing their soft, comfortable bodies onto the padded seats, and the families standing in line for bottled water and ice cream. She liked the young mothers, exchanging support and advice over salads and iced tea while their babies drooled on crackers and fists.

She watched them, the little ones, and felt a longing, an emptiness in her belly that had nothing to do with hunger or lust.

She had never carried a child. She had scarcely ever seen one in human form before.

Most selkies chose to whelp on the beach, living beneath the wave until their young matured to Change. Or at least were weaned and could survive on their own.

Babies were even more dependent than pups, Margred thought, watching a mother buckle her bundle into its carrier seat. Helpless. Useless, with their small, grasping starfish hands and clear, bright eyes and wide, toothless smiles.

How lowering to realize she wanted one. A small, curled weight against her heart with eyes as green as the sea . . . Her breasts felt heavy at the thought. Tender.

The mother picked up the plastic clamshell cradling her infant, calling to Regina behind the counter. "See you, Reggie."

Regina waved. The tiny cross of the murdered Christ glinted on her bosom. "Bye, Sarah."

The tall man waiting for his change shifted, crackling his paper take-out bag. Something about the sound whispered along Margred's nerves like smoke. The hair along her arms stood up.

But she was distracted by the baby and the woman struggling with the heavy door.

"You forgot your bag." Margred scooped up the cloth bag bulging with mysterious baby things and held it out.

"Oops." The girl bumped the door with her hip and transferred the carrier to her other arm. The baby kicked small, stockinged feet.

"I could carry it to the car for you," Margred offered.

Sarah smiled. "That would be great. Thanks."

Margred helped with the door and the bag. She watched from the sidewalk as the girl and her child drove away, an unaccountable feeling of loss tugging at her chest.

The silver road, a sprinkle of bright grass, and a line of steeply pitched roofs led to the harbor. Dark masts and white sails rose up from the deep blue swell of the sea. The wind carried the smell of the boats, fish and fuel, and the cries of the birds that followed their wake.

Too many to count, Margred thought, watching them circle the harbor. They rose and fell, spiraling on the wind. Calling back and forth, almost as if they were searching for something.

Her breath caught. Searching for someone.

For . . . her?

She hurried into the restaurant, tugging on the strings of her apron. "I am leaving."

Regina looked up from refilling the sugar dispenser. "You feel okay?"

"I am fine. I must go."

"You have twenty minutes left on your shift."

Margred blinked, taken aback as always by this human preoccupation with time. She wanted to go *now*.

And then it struck her. She had been waiting for a response from Conn for three days. What was another twenty minutes? When had she begun to divide her existence into measurable, even increments?

With shaking hands, she retied her apron.

"Twenty minutes," she said.

*   *   *

Maggie had a body any man would notice and no man could forget.

So why the hell had nobody seen her?

Caleb rubbed the back of his neck. Maybe he should have gone around the docks with a pinup photo instead of a head shot. But even in a grainy photograph, sporting a bruise and a line of stitches at her brow, Maggie's beauty was remarkable. Memorable.

"Recognize her? Sure." Henry Tibbetts pushed up his ball cap with his thumb and scratched his forehead. "That's Maggie, Antonia's new waitress. I thought you two were, like, tight."

"Yeah, she does look kind of familiar." Stan Chandler spat over the side of his boat, the *Nancy Dee*.

Caleb waited, stifling his impatience as Stan studied the photograph. Water slapped the pilings. Rusting ironwork stained the long, scrubbed deck like blood. Over the water, the gulls were going crazy, like extras in *The Birds*. Somebody must have thrown out a bucket of chum.

"Lara Croft," Stan announced triumphantly. "You know, the actress? Looks a lot like her."

But nobody remembered taking Maggie on as a passenger. Nobody admitted renting her a boat. Nobody recalled seeing her arrive on the island.

There were other days, Caleb told himself as he drove to pick up Maggie after her shift. There were private docks and beaches all around the island. Somebody had given her a lift or noticed her getting on or off a boat. She didn't—damn it, she didn't swim to the island, whatever she said.

He had been too easy on her. Too careful. He couldn't let . . . feelings . . . get in the way of doing his job.

He pulled into the narrow lot behind the restaurant. Antonia stood by the Dumpster, smoking a Lucky Strike.

She glared as he climbed from the Jeep. "You gonna tell me to quit?"

Caleb wanted a drag so bad he could taste it, sweet and

raw, sliding into his lungs. "I was going to ask you to blow some smoke my way."

"Ha." Antonia exhaled obligingly in his direction. "Regina's always bitching at me to take it outside."

"Secondhand smoke is a documented health hazard," Caleb said, straight-faced. He leaned in to take another hit. "You do operate a public space."

"It's my damn restaurant," Antonia grumbled.

"Which explains why you're out here by the garbage."

"It's the boy," Antonia admitted grudgingly. "Had asthma when he was a baby."

"And you don't want to set a bad example."

Antonia shrugged and ground her cigarette underfoot. "How's the search coming, Chief?"

Caleb accepted the change of subject. "It would go faster if I had some help. I'm looking into hiring another officer. Part-time," he added before she could say no.

"Roy Miller never asked for help."

"Roy Miller is in Florida. The community is changing. Growing. We're an hour and a half from the mainland, at least half an hour from the nearest sheriff's deputy. It would be good to count on backup in an emergency."

"What emergency? I'm not in any hurry to lose another waitress."

"Maggie deserves to get her life back. I'm doing the legwork on my own, and so far we have no ID on her photo."

"Not that I'm telling you how to do your job, but shouldn't you be looking for a man? The guy who hit her?"

"I would if I had a description. A reliable witness."

"Weren't you there?"

"I'm not a witness." In his mind's eye, he saw again a tall, wavering figure turn and leap into the fire. Not a *reliable* witness. "I never got a good look at the guy."

"Hm. He'll be from Away, I can tell you that much."

Caleb's attention sharpened. "How do you know? Has Maggie talked to you?"

Antonia shook her head. "But the men around here . . . I'm not saying there aren't some who would hurt a woman.

They have a bad day, a bad season, they take it out on any woman fool enough to live with them and put up with it. They don't go after strangers on the beach."

"Women are more likely to be attacked by someone they know than a stranger. Spouses, family members, neighbors. Coworkers, sometimes. I need to know who knows Maggie." He glanced toward the heavy metal door at the rear of the restaurant. "How's she doing?"

"Well, she's no cook. And you'd swear the girl never saw a cash register before in her life. She catches on quick, though, I'll give her that. And she's good with customers." Antonia's eyes gleamed. "Male customers, especially."

Caleb refused to rise to her bait. "I meant, how is she feeling?"

"Ask her yourself."

"I'll do that." He limped toward the entrance.

"Where are you going?"

He glanced over his shoulder. "Inside. To pick up Maggie."

"She's gone," Antonia said.

A bad feeling settled in the pit of Caleb's stomach. Tension gripped his neck. "Gone where?"

"How should I know? She left as soon as her shift was over." Antonia's gaze was almost pitying. "Must be fifteen, twenty minutes ago."

"I told her I was meeting the ferry."

Antonia shrugged. "Maybe she doesn't like to be kept waiting."

He knew that. Damn it.

When he found her, they were going to have a little talk about this habit she had of disappearing every time he was a few minutes late. He was a cop, damn it. He didn't punch a clock like—well, like everybody else. Maggie had to learn to accept that.

Sherilee never had. In the brief months they'd actually lived together before Caleb's deployment, his ex-wife complained he was never there for her. She objected to the late nights, the canceled dates, the interrupted phone calls. The fact that even when he wasn't working, he checked out on her sometimes in his head. In his heart.

No wonder the marriage hadn't stuck.

Caleb dragged in a quick, frustrated breath.

Neither had Maggie.

13

SHE HAD RECOGNIZED HIM.

The thought cracked like lightning, blinding, scorching.

Not the human body he inhabited, of course. But she had definitely reacted to his presence, his essence, within. She must die.

No, the man thought, horrified. What . . . ?

He dug his fingers into his temples as the mother of all migraines threatened to burst his skull. His stomach lurched. He fought for control, bile burning his nose. Saliva pooled in his mouth.

He must be hallucinating. He clung to that rational thought. He wasn't opposed to all killing. Hell, he'd argued in favor of capital punishment. But he never thought . . . He never would . . .

Sparks detonated in his head, danced in his vision.

Nononooo . . .

He fell to his knees, still clasping his head.

* * *

The gannet rode the currents of air as easily as a selkie in the water, white wings shining like sails in the sun, yellow head cocked to follow Margred's progress. At one with its element, it floated, graceful and free in the cool blue sky.

Landlocked and sweaty, Margred stopped to glare upward. Stupid bird.

The sun beat on her head and chest as she pushed through a tangle of beach roses and blackberry bushes. Trailing canes hooked her skirt and hair. Thin scarlet scratches sprang up on her arms. Midges swarmed, attracted by the scent of blood.

She wanted the sea, the rhythm of the surf, the rocking of the waves, the freedom of the water. She wanted to plunge and dance in the depths, to glide like the gannet. She longed to be herself again, not this clumsy two-footed creature stumbling over the coarse grass, bleeding and beset by insects.

Beyond the golden crest of the hill, the ocean glittered like a promise. But she could not see the beach. Where was the gannet leading her?

The thicket thinned to clumps of prickly juniper and spicy bayberry. A wind skipped over the hill, stirring her hair, refreshing her spirit. Margred lifted her face to the breeze.

The land fell away to wrinkled rock dotted with glasswort and goldenrod and then to stony beach.

Margred breathed deep, the smell of the earth infused with the salt of the sea, gazing down at a cove cupped like water between fingers of rock. The waves winked in the sun, teasing. Tantalizing.

There, at the water's edge, standing by a tide pool of swaying brown rockweed, Dylan waited alone.

Without Conn.

And almost without clothes, Margred noted with a ripple of new awareness. Human awareness. A pair of low, wet, ripped shorts hung from his narrow hips in an apparent concession to modesty. Hers? Or his? Dylan might be the prince's creature now, but he had been raised human for thirteen years.

His dark hair was sleeked back, touching his broad, bare shoulders. His bare feet balanced on the rocks.

So she had one advantage, at least. She had shoes.

She crunched in them over the pebbled beach.

At the sound, Dylan turned. He made a move toward her, quickly checked.

Selkies did not touch, even in greeting. Only to fight, or to mate, acts of possession as much as passion.

You do not own me, she had told Caleb. Any more than Antonia owned her cat.

Was he looking for her? Margred wondered suddenly. Worried about her?

She pushed the thought away. She had other things to worry about. Like his brother.

She stopped, raking her hair back from her hot face. "You could have chosen a more convenient meeting place."

Dylan shrugged. "This is convenient for me. There's a private island a few miles east of here—an easy swim, in either form, and undisturbed, if you don't count the birds and an occasional kayaker. I keep a few things there."

"Is that safe?"

"Safer than here, apparently." His gaze narrowed on her forehead. His mouth formed a flat line. "Is my brother beating you already?"

Self-consciously, Margred fingered the bump at her hairline. "Your brother saved me. Or didn't Conn tell you?"

"The prince keeps his own counsel always."

"Yet he sent you."

Dylan bowed. "As you see."

"Why, if not to help?"

"To find out what happened to you. The *muc mara's* account made no sense."

"So Conn sent you on a family visit." She watched him stiffen as that arrow struck home. "Why did you not tell me Caleb was your brother?"

"Why didn't you tell me you were shagging him?" Dylan shot back.

Beneath that cool facade, there were currents swirling she did not understand. Rivalry or injured pride or . . . He had wanted her once.

She shrugged. "I did not think the relationship had any relevance to you."

Dylan showed his teeth in a thin smile. "I could say the same."

"Who was your mother?" Margred asked.

Dylan looked out to sea. Perhaps, like his brother, he needed encouragement to talk.

"Did I know her?"

"You probably know of her. Our dam was Atargatis."

Margred hissed in surprise.

Atargatis was one of the ancient ones, almost as old as Llyr himself. Legends and prophecies clustered around her name like barnacles on a rock.

"I did not know she was still alive."

"She's not. She drowned shortly after returning with me to the sea. Trapped in a fisherman's net." Dylan's mouth twisted. "Ironic, since our father was a fisherman."

Margred shivered. "But she is immortal. She would have been reborn again."

"Maybe. I've never looked for her. What would be the point?"

"She is your mother."

"I don't need a mother anymore. Especially not one years younger than me with only vague memories of who I am."

She smothered a flicker of sympathy. "You would rather attach yourself to the prince?"

"I enjoy the prince's favor. Conn believes there is power in our lineage, although the prophecies speak only of the daughters of our house."

The daughters . . .

Margred's breath caught. "Your sister?"

But Dylan shook his head. "Lucy is not selkie. She has

never Changed. I know. Conn set me to . . . watch her, for many years."

"And your brother?"

"What of him?"

"Do you spy on him, too?"

"He left the island," Dylan said flatly. "Where he went and what he did after that is no concern of mine."

Margred tilted her head. "So you only care who he fucks?"

Dylan's lean face flushed.

"Did you know he had been wounded?" she asked.

"Caleb? When? How?"

"He was a soldier in the desert. He still has scars."

And nightmares. But she would not expose those to Dylan. She had perhaps said too much already.

"Is that why you stay with him? Because you feel sorry for him?"

"No!" Whatever she felt for Caleb was not pity. Nor was it any of his brother's business. "I stay because . . . because I cannot leave. My pelt was stolen from me. Destroyed. Conn did not tell you?"

"He said—the *muc mara* claimed you were attacked. By demons. Which is crap."

"Why?"

Dylan regarded her with patient disbelief, his expression so like Caleb's that Margred's stomach tightened. "Elementals do not prey on other elementals," he said.

"Wrong. The demons have been warring with the children of the air since the creation of mankind."

"A war that has nothing to do with us."

Margred arched her brows. "Even though you are half human?"

Dylan stiffened. "I am selkie. Anyway, the fire spawn have no reason or excuse to attack you."

"I was not aware they needed an excuse."

"Of course they do. Margred, think. The children of the sea have always been neutral in Hell's war on humankind. Why would a demon target you and risk the king's anger?"

His argument shook her. But she said, "Oh, as if Llyr would even notice."

"Conn, then," Dylan said. "He would not ignore an attack on one of his people."

She glared at him. "No, he would just send you, and you would declare it to be impossible."

"At least admit it is unlikely. Why would the fire folk upset the balance of power?"

"I don't know. I am not a politician." Frustration welled inside her like an underwater spring. She had told Caleb as much of the truth as she dared, and he had not believed her. Now Dylan did not believe her either. "I want my pelt back."

Sympathy softened the hard lines of his face. "Margred . . ." He reached for her.

She bared her teeth.

His arms dropped back at his sides. "Be reasonable. Why would a demon take your pelt?"

"To destroy me."

"To what end?"

"I tell you, I don't *know*." Despair made her shrill.

"Isn't it more likely you were attacked by a human? A fisherman," Dylan suggested. As if she could not tell the difference between a man who made his living from the sea and a demon who dwelled in the fire. "Or a poacher who wanted your pelt."

"And so he waited until I conveniently stepped out of my skin before throwing it onto the fire? How does that make sense?"

"More sense than this notion that another elemental wants to end your very existence."

"I smelled a demon," she insisted.

"And what did it smell like?"

"Like fire."

Dylan sneered. "Your pelt is burning, and you smelled fire. How extraordinary."

She hit him, hard, across the face. His head snapped back. Her palm burned.

She did not care. Her heart was on fire. "Mock me at your peril, Dylan. I die a little every day, trapped in this place. In this body. When I am gone, I am gone forever. Without my sealskin, I am not immortal anymore."

The red imprint of her hand stood out against Dylan's cheek. The rest of his face drained of all color. All emotion. "And if you had it, would you be content to let these accusations go?"

If she had her pelt . . .

Hope unfurled inside her. She would be free. Free to return to herself. To the sea. Free to—

Leave Caleb.

The thought lodged like a stone in her chest. She could not breathe.

This was what she wanted, she reminded herself. The sweet, deep, cloudy sea, brimming with form and color and life. Swaying forests of kelp, carpets of anemones, swathes of coral and sponges. Who would crawl over the crust of one quarter of the world for a span of years when they could have the world's oceans and centuries of freedom to explore?

Would you be content?

She opened her mouth, but the answer would not come. Her fingers tangled in the necklace at her throat.

Dylan's gaze shifted to a point beyond her shoulder. He went still with a kind of coiled energy, like a moray eel whose prey is in sight. "Hello, brother," he said silkily.

*   *   *

Brother, my ass.

Caleb leveled a checkpoint glare at the asshole crowding Maggie, itching for an excuse to cuff him and drag him to the station. He could take him. The guy was younger and taller—longer reach—but he didn't carry much weight. Untrained, probably. Unarmed. Unless he had a knife in his shorts pocket.

Caleb had watched them as he came over the hill, Maggie practically on tiptoe, getting in the guy's face, talking with him, arguing with him. The unconscious intimacy of their pose had stuck in Caleb's throat. Struck at his heart.

And then Maggie hauled off and slugged the guy, the sound echoing off the rocks like a rifle shot.

At least he hadn't tried to hit her back.

Yet.

"Who the fuck are you?" Caleb asked.

Those flat black eyes widened slightly. "Don't you recognize me?"

Something about that taunting tone, that twisted smile, got under Caleb's skin. A splinter of doubt worked its way toward his heart.

He used to dream his brother would come back. Show up at a ball game or ring the bell one Christmas morning or be there by Caleb's hospital bed when he opened his eyes.

Not appear half-naked on his island, threatening his woman.

Caleb shook his head. If Dylan lived, he would be— what now? Thirty-six? Thirty-seven? This guy couldn't possibly be his brother.

"Nope," Caleb said.

"I'm crushed."

Caleb didn't smile. "Can I see some identification, sir?"

"I don't have any." The guy jerked his head in Maggie's direction. "Ask her who I am."

"Maggie, do you know this man?"

"Yes." Her chin went up. Her big dark eyes hit him like a punch in the gut, harder than the realization that she must have been lying to him, playing him from the start. "And so do you."

"The Prodigal Son returns," Asshole said lightly. "Wasn't that the story Mrs. Pruitt liked so much? Aren't you supposed to kill a fatted calf or something?"

Caleb felt like killing something, all right.

Mrs. Pruitt . . . God, he hadn't thought of her in years. Growing up, every kid on the island had been forced to attend her week-long vacation Bible school at least once.

Every kid on the island, Caleb told himself.

Not just the Hunter brothers.

His gaze switched from Asshole to Maggie, standing between them, drinking in every word.

"I'll have to ask you to come down to the station, sir."

"No," the guy said.

"Why do you need him to go to the station?" Maggie asked.

He wasn't questioning the guy in front of her. "Why did you slap him?"

She shrugged. "He annoyed me."

"Good enough for me. Jeep's that way," Caleb said, gesturing up the hill.

Offshore, the waves churned, up and down, like a washing machine's agitation cycle. Caleb eyed the white water and thought, *Rip current.*

"You can't make me go anywhere," Skinny sneered.

Caleb's jaw set. What was this, fifth grade? He pushed away a memory of Dylan yelling, tearful, dancing out of their father's reach. *You can't make me.*

"You don't have the power," the man added scornfully.

"I have power."

Caleb tapped his chest. "I've got a badge." More than his anger, more than his gun, that gave him authority to act. "Let's go."

And then the sea reared up like a living thing and struck the beach in a ten-foot wave.

The surge smashed into Caleb, knocking him off his feet, carrying him in a rush up the beach. Water and sand roiled around him, roaring in his ears, blocking his nostrils, green and gray and gold speckled with grit and bubbles.

The wave hurled and rolled him, scraped and raked him. His boots dragged like weights over the rocks. He fought the surge, struggling for balance. For breath.

Panic squeezed his lungs. *Maggie.*

He clawed free of the undertow, staggering to his feet, and saw her standing a few yards away, her wet, white clothes clinging to every perfect curve, ankle deep in foaming water.

She pushed her sopping hair back from her face. "Now I am really annoyed."

Caleb almost grinned. He coughed to clear his lungs and spat, wiping salt from his mouth. "Where is he? Where's—"

The man who claimed to be Dylan.

Maggie shielded her eyes against the bright sunshine, gazing out at the impossibly calm sea. The quiet water withdrew, whispering, leaving her bare feet planted firmly on a patch of sand. "There." She pointed to a sleek, dark head bobbing through the waves offshore. "Say good-bye to your brother."

"Fuck," Caleb said wearily and reached for his phone. Would it still work?

"What are you doing?"

"Calling for rescue. He's caught in the tide."

"He's not caught. See?" She put her hand on his wet sleeve, compelling him to look. "He's swimming."

Caleb watched. Instead of being sucked out to sea at top speed by the current, the black, bullet-shaped head appeared to be moving easily, parallel to the shore. "He's still too far out. He can't swim that long. Nobody could."

"No man."

Caleb frowned. "That's what I said."

"No *man* can swim that long. Dylan can." Maggie smiled at him, her eyes sane and a little sad. "Your brother is not human, Caleb."

14

CALEB'S FACE CLOSED LIKE A CLAMSHELL, SMOOTH and hard.

Margred's heart sank. He did not look like her lover. He looked like . . . well, like a man who spent his days questioning the actions and motivations of other men. She almost wished her words back.

Too late.

She had owed him the truth since he rescued her on the beach. Since she learned of his mother's identity. Maybe from the moment he first came in her body and whispered his name in her hair.

"You've had a shock," he said. Polite. Detached. "Let me take you to see Donna Tomah."

He did not believe her.

She had not expected him to, and yet she was tempted to smack him the way she had slapped his brother.

"I do not need a doctor. I need you to listen."

"Oh, I'm listening. You ought to have your head examined."

Her lips drew back from her teeth. "You said you wanted the truth."

"That's right. Facts, not fairy tales."

"So you will not listen to any facts that do not fit your particular theories?"

That got him, she saw with satisfaction. His mouth flattened to a thin, grim line. "Right. All right. Go ahead."

But now that she had his attention, the enormity of her task overwhelmed her. She touched the necklace around her throat. For reassurance? "I am not sure where to start."

His expression did not soften, but his green eyes, meeting hers, were patient and steady. Caleb's eyes.

Cop's eyes.

"The beginning is usually a good place," he said.

Margred opened her mouth. Shut it. At the bottom of the tide pool, a crab rummaged through a pile of periwinkle shells, tapping, weighing, discarding.

"Perhaps we should sit down," she suggested.

His eyebrows rose, but he folded his long body and sat, stretching out his injured leg, his wet boots scraping on the white limestone forts of a barnacle colony. The sun teased golden glints from his damp hair, touching his face with color. His throat looked strong and faintly sunburnt, tempting her to test its temperature with her lips.

She sat a few feet away—she had to be able to think—and spread her skirt to dry.

Caleb waited, his silence pulling at her.

She picked at a loose white thread, searching for an end. For a beginning. Written texts were rare among her people. Their history was passed and preserved for each generation, each incarnation, in the eternal song of the whales. How would it sound to Caleb?

She took a deep breath. "Before—well, before anything was, the Spirit of the Creator moved upon the face of the waters."

Caleb's mouth twitched. "Maggie . . . when I said the beginning, I didn't mean all the way back to Genesis."

"What is Genesis?"

His expression closed again. "Never mind. Go on."

Margred bit her lip in vexation. In centuries past, when the mer revealed themselves to the sons and daughters of men, they were regarded with awe and worship, lust and fear. Margred did not expect Caleb's worship exactly; but neither was she prepared for his studying her like a scientist observing some new species of marine life.

It was easier, she found, not to look at him at all. "Out of the void, He formed the elements. And as each element took shape, its people also came into being—the children of earth and sea, of air and fire."

"People," Caleb repeated. "Are you talking Adam and Eve here?"

She shook her head. "Humankind came later. Much later, long after life crawled from the sea and walked on the land. But then the Creator breathed His immortal spirit into mortal clay. Many elementals resented this new creation— particularly the children of fire. The children of air defended the Creator's decision, appointing themselves heralds and protectors of humankind. While the children of earth and sea, forced to cohabit with you, chose to avoid you as much as possible." Margred shrugged. "Sometimes it is not possible. And then legends—or children—are born. Your own mother—"

"No," Caleb said.

"Your mother came to your father out of the sea." Now Margred dared to look at him. "As I came to you."

His eyes were splinters of green ice. "You're telling me my mother, Alice Hunter—"

"Atargatis."

"And you are . . . mermaids?" His voice cracked in disbelief.

Margred nodded. "Well, not mermaids, exactly. Selkies."

"What's the difference?"

"The mer may take different forms. Fish or mammal or—"

"Prove it."

"Excuse me?"

"Turn into a—what is it you turn into?"

She stiffened at his tone. "A seal."

"Right. Turn into a seal."

She struggled for patience. He wanted facts, he'd said. Proof. It was his nature, the nature of his job.

It was not her nature to justify or explain. But for his sake . . .

"I can't," she admitted reluctantly. "The last time I swam to the island, the night I was attacked, my pelt was stolen from me. I cannot Change form without my sealskin."

He raised his brows. "Convenient."

"Not for me," she snapped. "Nor, I imagine, for your mother."

"Leave my mother out of this."

"I would not even if I could." Moved beyond her people's customary boundaries by her need to convince him, Margred reached out to him, laying her fingers on his arm. His sleeve was stiff and sticky with salt, his muscles hard as iron. "The sea is your heritage, Caleb."

"Maybe," he said, his tone dry. "But I don't turn into a seal and bark when the moon is full."

Stung, she snatched back her hand. Stupid man. "The moon has nothing to do with it. Most human-selkie offspring are mortal. Human genes and the human soul are what you would call dominant traits."

"But you said that guy—"

"Your brother, Dylan."

"He's not my brother. My brother is gone. Besides, he's too young."

"Selkies do not age as mortals do. Only when we are in human form."

"He sure as hell looked human to me."

"It wasn't until he reached puberty that his true nature revealed itself. When Dylan was thirteen, he Changed for the first time." She gazed into Caleb's cold, closed face, the chill settling at her heart. "That's why your mother returned to the sea. To protect her son."

A muscle worked in Caleb's jaw. "She had another son. And a one-year-old daughter."

Margred heart ached for him. For them all. "She had no choice. And she paid dearly for it. She lost her children and her life. Dylan—"

"Look, I don't need some crazy story to justify what my mother did," Caleb interrupted. "And you don't need to lie to cover up whatever it is you've done."

Margred scrambled to her feet. "I am not lying."

"Maggie . . ." His expression was patient. Weary. "This guy—the one you claim is my brother—did he hit you? Hurt you? Threaten you in any way?"

She blinked. "No. I slapped him."

"Good for you. How about before?"

She continued to stare at him, baffled.

"On the beach," Caleb clarified. "The night you were attacked. Was it the same guy?"

"Oh, no."

"It was dark, you said. He came up behind you. Maybe you didn't get a good look at him."

"I did not see him at all." She had told him that much already. "But it was not Dylan."

"How can you be sure?"

"It was a demon."

Silence fell. Long moments passed, filled only by the whispering surf and the snickering wind.

Her throat clogged. *Dylan* had not believed her. Why did she expect Caleb would? Because he was her lover? When had that come to mean anything more than—

She trembled. When had that come to mean anything?

"All this talk about mermaids and demons . . . It's a problem," Caleb said, still in that measured, dispassionate voice.

Disappointment was sharp as salt in her mouth. "*Your* problem."

"Say *ours*." He stood. "I want you to come to Portland with me to see Dr. Crawford."

She lifted her chin. "I am not sick. Or stupid. I do not want to see another doctor."

"It's for your own good. Trust me."

"Why should I trust you? You don't believe me."

"I believe something bad happened to you," he said carefully, "and your mind is dealing with it the best way it knows how. So you've come up with a story to explain—"

She thrust out her foot. "Explain *this*."

He glanced down at her bare foot, up into her eyes. "What?"

"My toes are webbed." She wiggled them to prove it.

Caleb grabbed the back of his neck. "Maggie, they're still toes." His tone was patient. Pained. Caring. "Not fins or flippers. I need more from you than that."

She closed her eyes so she would not see the pity in his. "So do I."

She needed him to believe her.

And he couldn't. Wouldn't.

Damn Dylan, anyway, for leaving her alone to fight his brother's skepticism. Maybe he had not expected her to tell Caleb the truth.

Or maybe he had. Maybe Dylan, more experienced in the ways of humankind, had anticipated Caleb's reaction and chosen to spare himself his brother's disbelief. His rejection.

You are selkie, or you are not.

She was not wholly selkie. Not any longer.

But she would rather be half selkie, banished from the ocean, crippled by the loss of her pelt, than be dismissed as a damaged crazy woman by the human she was having sex with.

She could use her magic to prove herself to him. Summon a wave, as Dylan had. Summon a storm, and dump it on his unbelieving head. But she should not have to. He should trust her.

"Let's get you back to the house," Caleb said gently. "You can change out of those wet things, and—"

Margred opened her eyes. "Getting naked with you is not going to help."

He smiled a little. "I wasn't suggesting we solve our problems with sex. Although if you like the idea—"

"I want to go to your sister's."

Caleb looked wary, like a man approaching a shark on the beach. "Sure. We can stop at her place on our way home."

"I am not going home with you." Her hands trembled, but her voice was quite steady, firm with her decision. "Not until you can accept me for what I am."

Caleb raised his eyebrows. "It didn't matter to you before."

He didn't matter to her before.

But now it did. He did.

And she was not backing down.

15

~≋~

IT AMUSED TAN TO FEEL HIS HUMAN HOST WRITH-ing on the floor in ineffective protest, its thin, diluted spirit no match for his pure will.

The very creation of man was demeaning to the sacred. Mankind's continued existence was an affront. Yet the Creator doted on this short-lived, bastard hybrid, had given it dominion over the creatures of the sea and earth and air.

Incomprehensible. Insulting, really.

Of course, mankind had screwed up. Better that all creation were cleansed in fire than be polluted by the presence of this vermin.

Tan forced the human to drag itself across the floor on hands and knees toward the glowing fish tank on the other side of the room.

The balance of power between Heaven and Hell rested on a knife's edge. Sea's children had remained weakly neutral for too long. For centuries, Hell had watched human-kind despoiling the oceans, taking selkie pelts, eroding the sea folk's patience.

And still the mer did not act. Llyr withdrew deeper and deeper into the sea and self-indulgence. Conn clung to the status quo.

It was time to tip the scales in Hell's favor.

Manipulating nerve and sinew like puppet strings, Tan jerked the human upright beside the aquarium. Small fish glided in their bright, contained world, smug in their beauty, insensible to their danger. Smiling, he removed the lid of the tank. The human's hands trembled.

Tan was charged with the murder of the mer in ways and places that would put the blame squarely on humankind. If enough selkies died by human hands, if enough lost their immortality through human action, they would be forced to side with their fellow elementals in self-defense. And if Tan could eliminate Atargatis's line at the same time, he would ensure Hell's new allies never became a threat.

So complicated.

So clever.

Tan plunged a hand into the tank. Fish scattered. Not—quite—fast enough. Tan glanced at the small, striped creature shining between his fingers. An angel fish. How . . . appropriate.

He savored the frantic flutter against his palm, its frenzied struggle to breathe, to survive. He licked the smooth, scaled skin, inhaling the fish's delicate scent, its desperation a delicious seasoning to the human horror rising at the back of his throat, the denial beating at the back of his brain.

He opened his mouth wide.

Oh, the delight of it, the squirming, wriggling pleasure against his palate, over his tongue. A silent scream echoed in his head at the cool burst of living flesh, crunching, slurping. Tan forced his host to chew, to swallow, compelling his clenched throat muscles to relax, running his tongue along his teeth, savoring his shudder. The body he inhabited gagged. Retched. It was delicious, that taste of bile and self-loathing mingled with the juicy living sacrifice.

Very tasty. Almost . . . satisfying.

Tan deserved his bit of fun. Even though the necessity chafed him, he had been discreet, careful not to risk any action that would arouse the suspicion of the sea prince, Conn, or the attention of Heaven's general, Michael.

He had not murdered the selkie Margred in front of a witness—even a human witness.

But now that Margred had recognized him, well . . .

She must die.

Iridescent scales spangled his hand like jewels. Like tears. Hot moisture streamed helplessly from his host's eyes.

Smiling, Tan reached the human's hand into the tank again.

* * *

Caleb scowled through the windshield at the quiet streets of his town, his nerves twitching and his senses straining for . . . what? He wasn't in Mosul anymore, where every turn in the road could hide roadside bombs or enemy fighters. Kids with rocks. Potholes.

Okay, yeah, there were potholes in Maine. That didn't explain the itch at the back of his neck, that *uh-oh* feeling in his gut.

Maybe he was just stalling, delaying the moment he would return to his silent, empty house.

He'd lived alone before. After his desert trailer "can" and his experience in the hospital ward, he'd looked forward to living alone again.

He should go home. With Maggie gone, he could do whatever the hell he wanted. Strip to his underwear, ice his knee, channel surf the TV . . .

When his cell phone rang, it was almost a relief. He glanced at the display, his pulse kicking up as he recognized the number of Antonia's restaurant. Maggie's shift had ended hours ago, but maybe . . .

"Hunter."

"Cal, it's Regina." Her voice was brisk, but he could hear the worry under it.

He was already swinging the Jeep in the direction of the restaurant. "What's up?"

"Nothing, really. We're closing, and one of our patrons has had a little too much to drink."

Had to be something, Caleb reflected. Regina wasn't rattled easily, and Antonia scared most drunks. "Did you get his keys?"

"First thing," Regina assured him.

"So?" He was grateful for the distraction. But he wasn't a damn taxi service.

"He threw them at me," Regina said. "Broke a couple of bottles. If you could stop by—"

"On my way."

"The thing is . . ." Her hesitation vibrated over the line. "I don't want you to think I'm overreacting to some broken glass. But you should know the guy . . ."

Her caginess intensified his sense of something wrong. "What?"

"It's your father."

His father.

Caleb's gut cramped. Of course. Growing up the son of the town drunk should have prepared him.

How many times before Caleb got his driver's license had Chief Miller brought his father home at closing time? And those nights, humiliating as they were, were better than the mornings when Bart Hunter hadn't showed up at all, when Caleb stared out his classroom windows hoping Lucy had made it to school, wondering how he would take care of her if their dad never came back.

"On my way," he repeated.

*   *   *

Bart Hunter stood among the restaurant tables like a fir amid the rocks, bleached by the sun, stripped by the wind and rain, upright only through force of habit and the grace of God.

Caleb felt an old, familiar helplessness rise like bile and bit back a curse.

"You want to press charges?" he asked Regina, who was

sweeping up broken glass behind the counter. The rich, fruity aroma of the wine battled with the scent of pine cleaner from the bucket at her feet. The smell made Caleb sick.

She wiped her hands on her apron. "I want him out of here. I'll charge him for the wine."

"The wine, her labor, and a two-hundred-dollar fine," Caleb told his father.

Bart sneered. "For what? Bad parenting?"

"Disorderly conduct," Caleb said evenly. "Now get in the Jeep."

Bart swayed. "I need another drink."

"Coffee?" Regina suggested.

"No," said Caleb.

"I want coffee," Bart said.

Regina looked at Caleb, uncomfortable understanding in her eyes. "On the house. You look like you could use it."

He was fourteen when he figured out pouring coffee down a drunk only produced a wide-awake drunk. But he appreciated the gesture. "Fine. Thanks."

He watched her set the coffee on the counter, watched his father steady the mug with two hands.

Regina followed the direction of his gaze. "I didn't serve him, I swear," she said in a lowered voice.

"Who did?"

"He was at the Inn most of the night. They kicked him out, and I cut him off."

"Appreciate it."

She shrugged. "No biggie. Stop brooding and drink your coffee."

He raised his mug.

"How *are* you sleeping?" Regina asked.

He had nightmares.

He missed Maggie.

This morning he woke up edgy and lonely and raw, and seeing his father like this again wasn't helping his mood one bit.

He blew on the hot brew, regarding Regina cautiously over the rim. "All right."

"Alone?"

He lifted his eyebrows. "Are you asking? Or offering?"

Regina cocked her hip against the counter, crossed her arms over her chest. "You told me to keep an eye out for anybody giving Maggie a hard time. You're not making things easy for her."

"Is that what she said?"

Regina snorted. "Oh, yeah, she talks to me all the time. Because we're such close girlfriends."

"She needs friends," Caleb said quietly. "She's all alone right now."

"So, what's she doing staying with your sister?"

Good question.

He set his mug down with a snap. "Her choice."

"That's right, blame the woman. Bet you hear that all the time. 'Officer, she was asking for it.' "

He leveled a look at her, and she flushed.

"Sorry, that was unfair," she admitted. "But why don't you go after her? It's obvious you're both miserable."

So he wasn't the only one suffering. He was glad. Which made him a selfish bastard, because . . .

"She was right," Caleb said. "I'm too close to her case. I can't be involved with her and do my job."

"Maybe she needs you to do more than your job."

His job was all he had. All he knew how to do. Weigh the facts. Keep the peace. Protect the innocent.

Only with Maggie, the facts were all mixed up with his feelings. His gut wanted to trust her. His head told him to dismiss her as a nutcase. And his heart . . .

He drained the dregs of his coffee. "Come on, Pop. You've had your fun. Let's go."

"You can't talk to me like that. I'm your father."

"Which is the only reason you're not sleeping it off in a holding cell tonight."

They drove in silence as thick and cold as a coastal fog.

Not looking at each other. Not speaking. Just like any car ride twenty years ago.

Except now Caleb could ask—*had* to ask—the questions that lay unanswered between them.

"Why did Mom leave?"

"What the hell difference does it make? She left. Took the boy with her."

Caleb wasn't a kid anymore. He was used to dealing with uncooperative and hostile witnesses.

"Where? Where did they go?"

"Back where she came from." Bart turned his face to the darkness beyond the window. "Damn her."

"Where's that?"

"None of your damn business."

"She's my mother."

"She was my *wife*!" Bart roared. "Fourteen years I lived with that woman. Loved her. But that didn't stop her. Oh, no. First chance she got, she ran off."

"Where?"

His father slumped against the door. "I'm going to be sick."

"Not in the Jeep."

Caleb managed to pull over and open the passenger door before Bart lost it in a violent, stinking stream.

Caleb handed him a handkerchief and helped him back into the Jeep.

His father couldn't hit him anymore to shut him up. But being dog sick in a ditch and then passing out in the back-seat were just as effective.

Caleb steadied the old man out of the vehicle and up the porch steps. At least with the poisons out of his system, there was a chance Lucy wouldn't have to clean up after him tonight.

Propping the old man under the yellow porch light, he patted him down for his keys.

The door cracked open. Lucy stood in the illuminated rectangle, barefoot and with her hair in a braid. She looked about twelve years old.

"Is he all right?"

"He's drunk," Caleb said bluntly. "Go back to bed."

Her wry smile didn't quite reach her eyes. "News-flash, big brother. My bedtime's after nine o'clock now. And I have as much experience putting him to bed as you do."

Guilt twinged. "So take a night off."

Lucy stepped back as Caleb supported Bart over the threshold. Laughter and applause wafted from the television in the living room, and then Maggie was there, taking in the scene with her big, dark-as-chocolate eyes.

Caleb's heart pumped like a fist, knocking the air from his lungs.

Bart trembled. "Who's that? Who are you?"

"That's Maggie, Pop." Caleb nudged him toward the stairs. "She's staying here for a few days."

Bart lurched forward and gripped her arm, hard enough to bruise.

Wincing, Maggie tried to peel his fingers from her arm.

"Easy." Caleb grabbed his jacket. "Let her go."

His father barely noticed, thrusting his head forward to peer into Maggie's face. "Are you her? Have you come back?"

Maggie made a soft, protesting sound.

Caleb shook his father by the collar. "Let her go," he repeated through his teeth.

Bart dropped her arm and swung at Caleb.

He didn't have time to duck. The punch glanced clumsily off his jaw, stunning him. It had been years since his father hit him.

He wanted to hit back.

But he never had. Even when he was big enough. Strong enough.

He caught his father's fist on the next swing, pulling his arm up and behind him. "Enough," he growled.

Bart made a sound, a terrible sound like wet rope rattling through rusty hinges, and collapsed against him. It took Caleb several long moments to realize his father was weeping. He supported his father's tall, wasted body, rage and pity churning in his stomach.

"I am sorry." Maggie's beautiful face was grave, her tone gentle. "She is not coming back."

Caleb frowned. "Do you know each other?"

"Her eyes . . ." Beads of perspiration dotted Bart's pale face. His breath was rank.

"What about them?"

"She has your mother's eyes."

Baffled, Caleb met his sister's gaze, gray green as his own. "Lucy?"

"The other one," Bart mumbled. "Staring at me. Your mother's eyes . . ."

"He's sick," Lucy said. "Let me take him upstairs."

"I've got him," Caleb said grimly.

Whether he wanted him or not.

*   *   *

Margred watched Caleb help his father up the stairs. Despite the impatience in his voice, the frustration in his eyes, there was such strength inside him.

Such tenderness.

"He should have a care for his leg," she murmured.

"Caleb's better at taking care of other people than himself," Lucy said. "He raised me, you know."

Margred tilted her head. "Until he left to fight."

"Actually, he went away to school when I was nine. It was that, or haul lobsters with Dad, and by then they could barely stand to eat dinner at the same table, let alone be cooped up on the same boat twelve hours a day. Caleb put up with it as long as he could. He's a good brother." Her gaze, earnest and unguarded, met Margred's, and for a moment Margred felt a buzz, a click, a— The girl looked away. "He's a good man."

Selkies did not think in terms of good or bad. They simply were, and their existence was enough. But for humans, whose lives were short and messy, whose choices determined the eternal fate of their souls, good and evil had meaning.

Caleb *was* a good man, Margred realized, feeling an ache like a bruise at her heart. Whether he believed her or not, he was trying to protect her. To care for her.

And one day he would die.

How could he stand it?

How would she?

Her mate had died, and she had mourned him. But her life with him had not been very different from the centuries that had gone before or the decades since: sunlight, sea, and storm, the cycle of the seasons, the richness of the ocean, the freedom of the waves. Fifty years later, she could not recall his touch or the timbre of his voice.

Caleb limped down the stairs, his wonderful green eyes sober, his mouth tight with pain, and she felt a pang in her belly.

He had moved her. Changed her.

Even if she could go back to the sea, would she ever be the same?

"How's Dad?" Lucy asked.

Caleb's expression softened when he looked at his sister. "Asleep."

"Oh. Oh, well, that's good." Lucy shifted her weight from foot to foot. Shifted her gaze from Caleb to Maggie. "I think I'll watch the rest of my show up in my room. Good night."

" 'Night, Lu."

"Good night," Margred echoed.

Lucy's footfalls sounded going up the stairs.

"You want to tell me what's going on?" Caleb asked quietly.

She arched her eyebrows. "I have been watching television with your sister. It is very . . . educational."

Caleb's mouth quirked. "Honey, it's *American Idol*, not the History Channel." He pressed a button, and the set went dark. "What was that business with my father? He acted like he recognized you."

"He did. Or rather," she corrected herself, "he recognizes what I am."

"What the hell is that?"

The question buried itself like a knife in her chest. She had told him, and he had not believed her. "Did you ask him?"

"I can't get a straight answer out of the old man when he's sober. He makes even less sense when he's drunk."

She lifted her chin. "And as long as you can tell yourself he is drunk and I am crazy, you don't have to believe either of us."

He shook his head. "I didn't come here to fight with you. I've missed you, Maggie."

Her heart shook. She crossed her arms to hold it in her breast. "After one day."

He smiled wryly. "After five minutes. That's how long it took me to realize I could have handled things better yesterday. I was angry. Jealous, I guess. And I took it out on you." His gaze met hers, all nerves and need, and she felt the jolt in the pit of her stomach. "Come home with me, Maggie."

His admission moved her. But it was not enough. She drew a shaky breath. "You do not trust me."

"I want you."

"You do not *know* me." The words burst from her.

He raised his eyebrows. "That didn't stop us before."

"It did not matter before."

He had not mattered.

And now he did. Margred bit her lip.

It was as simple—and as painful—as that.

16

❦

THE SELKIE PROVED STRONGER THAN THE HU-
man. More resistant to Tan's will, and slow to die.

The first was an inconvenience, the demon thought,
looking down at her naked, bleeding body. Which made the
second rather handy. The longer she lived, the better chance
he had of teasing information from her.

When Tan first sensed the arrival of another elemental on
the beach, he'd been almost disappointed his victim had delivered herself so easily into his hands. More disappointed
when he struck her down and realized she was not the one
he sought.

But she served his purpose.

Or she would, if he could persuade her to give up her
sealskin. Unfortunately, she was proving resistant.

Tan frowned, tapping his teeth with the knife. He appreciated his adversary's strength almost as much as he enjoyed her weakness. He spread his other hand on the
selkie's breast and let it rest there, unmoving. Not to inflict
pain, not this time, but to prove she was as much in his

power as his human host. He could do anything he liked with her. With both of them.

And had, for the past hour.

Long enough for the babbling self-loathing, the screams of mental anguish, the incoherent protests of his human host to run together and fade into forgotten background noise, like a radio left playing for too long. Such a shame. Tan missed the thrill of awareness, his host's weak struggles for control. Forcing his will on the human as he forced his touch on the selkie was an exquisite added zest, a doubled delight.

But now, as Tan gazed down at his hand on the selkie's breast, her bound and naked body, her perfect skin—well, not so perfect anymore—he realized his host's male parts had swollen, pressing and twitching against the front of his pants. His body responded to the straining limbs, the quivering flesh, the slipperiness under his hands.

Tan pinched her nipple, drawing blood.

Ohgod, ohno, ohplease . . .

Delicious.

Idly, Tan took out the human's cock and fondled it, savoring this fresh sensation, relishing the new wariness in the selkie's eyes. He would not scare her with sex. She was selkie, after all. An opponent worthy of his effort.

But he had her attention now. Oh, yes.

"Nothing to say, dear sister?" he taunted.

He had brought her here to talk. To talk, and to get her away from the sea, where she might draw on the water's power. Unfortunately, he could not allow her to scream. Someone might notice, and he really did not want to be interrupted again. He had been forced to abandon his last job half-finished, destroying his victim's pelt but not her human body. She was beyond his reach at the moment, hedged about by humans. He could not reach her without drawing the unwelcome attention of both Heaven and the land beneath the wave.

But this one . . .

He had stuffed a sock in the selkie's mouth and bound

it—like her wrists and ankles—with thick tape. Tan had found the tape, the saw, and some pliers in the garage. Human technology might be polluting the earth, but he could not deny their tools were occasionally useful.

He ripped the tape from her jaw, taking some of her hair with it. She moaned.

"Patience," he chided.

He worked the gag, wet with blood and saliva, from between her torn lips and waited.

"Water," she croaked.

He needed her to be capable of speech. But she was mer. Water was her element. He must be careful not to revive her too much.

"Tell me where you left your pelt, and I will let you drink."

She worked her mouth. Glared at him with her remaining eye. "Go to hell, demon."

Tan appreciated her humor—if, indeed, she wasn't past the point of relishing her own joke.

"Certainly I will. After you tell me." He squatted beside her chair. The cock jutted, red and eager, from his gaping zipper. "Tell me," Tan coaxed. "Tell me, and we will end this, and you can return to the sea."

He lied. Even if he would set her free to accuse him, she could never go back. Not if he possessed her sealskin.

And she knew it, cunning female, which was why she had hidden it so well. Resisted him this long.

"I am selkie," she panted. "Whatever you do to this body, you cannot end me. I will not die."

Tan straightened and stood over her. *Nonononnonooo . . .*

"You will not die," he agreed. He stroked his host's cock, his hand slick with selkie blood, pleasuring himself with the human's horrified excitement, the elemental's impotent rage. "But I can make you wish you had."

*　　*　　*

Fog shrouded the beach and clung to the rocks like a thin film of tears. The trees rose against the dawn like the black masts of pirate ships, silent and threatening. The gray waves whispered and mourned.

Artist Lisa Stewart fingered the plastic bags in her hoodie pockets, dutifully grabbed when she left the cottage with Buster and Brownie. Most people slept in on their vacations. But morning was the best time for the dogs, the only time Lisa could risk letting them run free on the beach.

Buster raced up and down in joyous swoops and bursts of speed. Brownie sniffed along the water's edge at whatever the tide had left behind. Rock weed. Mussels. Limpets. Gull droppings.

A big white bird with a yellow head and a cruel, curved beak stood in the shallows, cocking a blue-ringed eye at the dogs. Lisa caught her breath. She'd never seen a gull that size.

Buster bounded out of the mist, pink tongue dripping. The bird screeched and lifted off, its black-tipped wings beating the air. Barking, Buster charged down the beach after it.

Lisa grinned. But as long minutes passed with no sign of the dog, her smile faded.

She whistled and lengthened her stride, Brownie trotting at her heel. Her sneakers crunched and slid on shingle and shale. Her breath rasped. The smell of the ocean, life, death, and decay, hung heavy in the damp air.

There. Relief washed over her.

Wasn't that—yes, there was Buster, inching toward the shallows on his belly, completely ignoring the big white bird perched only yards away. His big dark eyes fixed on a rounded lump that rose from the wet shore like a dark jewel on a belt of beaten silver, its reflection staining the gritty beach, bleeding into the retreating water.

"Buster!"

Brownie whined and pressed trembling against her leg. The bird squawked and launched heavily into the still air.

Buster's hips wriggled. His top knot quivered. A wave rushed in and faded away, stirring the rusty seaweed clumped along one side of the rock.

Lisa frowned. Not a rock. A dolphin beached by the tide? She tightened her grip on the leash and took a step closer. A seal? Or . . .

Her stomach plunged. She pressed her shaking fingers to her mouth.

A body.

*   *   *

In her dreams, the heavens wept blood and the oceans blazed. Margred struggled to breathe.

Pain sprang at her out of the dark—brutal, insulting, slamming her onto the rocks. Her palms burned. Fire exploded in her head. In her knees. She tried to cry out, but the fire stole her voice, eating the soft tissue of tongue and palette, searing her throat.

Margred tossed, her breathing harsh, her heart racing. She was burning, drying, drying up . . .

She moaned and opened her eyes.

Gray dawn licked at the edges of the window shade, the paneled walls, the row of books by Bradford and Conan Doyle. On the shelf below sat a picture of the child Caleb with Lucy on his lap.

Caleb. She was in Caleb's room.

And Lucy—all grown up now—hovered in the doorway, wearing an apologetic expression and a green T-shirt with the word CLIPPERS across her breasts. The shadow of Margred's dream clouded the younger girl's eyes.

Margred struggled from the shrouds of sleep. Something about the veiled depths of those eyes . . .

Lucy blinked. "Sorry to wake you." She held out her cell phone. Her eyes were bright and shallow again as sunlight on the sea. Warm, green eyes. Caleb's eyes. "It's Caleb. He wants to talk with you."

Margred sat up, sticky with sweat, and fumbled with the phone. "Hello?"

"Maggie."

Her heart gave a foolish skip. "Yes?"

"You're all right."

"Ye-es."

Why wouldn't she be?

But she was troubled by her dream, bothered by whatever she had seen or imagined in Lucy's eyes. She looked again at Lucy.

Lucy shrugged.

"What is going on?" Margred asked.

"I don't know yet." Caleb's deep voice was hard. Flat. "I'm on my way to find out. Stay put, okay?"

She appreciated his concern when he was so obviously preoccupied. But she resisted his assumption he could tell her what to do.

"I have work at ten," she said.

"Tell Antonia you can't make it. Somebody may be by later to talk to you."

"Then he can talk to me at Antonia's."

She heard his indrawn breath. "When they get there—"

They?

"Tell them the truth. As much as you can."

Maggie bit her lip in vexation. What *truth*? He didn't want her truth.

As much as you can? Or as much as Caleb and his mysterious "they" could accept?

"Caleb—"

"I've got to go," he said, still in that abrupt, official voice. "Maggie . . ."

She waited, her heart racing, her fingers curled around the phone, willing him to dispel the darkness cast by her dream with the light of his reason, his warm, strong, steady heart.

"Take care of yourself," he said, and disconnected.

*   *   *

The beach boiled with activity.

A temporary command post had been set up under the trees on the headland until the scene could be released and the whole police circus moved to the common room at the community center. Which would inconvenience a lot of islanders and piss off Antonia, but the mayor was the least of Caleb's worries now.

The medical examiner had come and gone, transporting the body to his office in Augusta. No bloated drowning victim this time. This woman had died recently. Violently.

Even Caleb, hardened by war and accustomed to death, had been shaken by the condition of her torn and naked body. The nature of her wounds.

The webbing between her toes.

But he couldn't dwell on the victim's feet. He couldn't think about Maggie. He'd reacted according to his training, calming the hysterical dog owner, notifying CID, securing the scene.

And then he stood by while they took over.

One of the state cops had accompanied the medical examiner to the mainland. By Caleb's count, that still left five detectives from CID, three techs from the Evidence Response Team, ten members of the Maine warden service performing a meticulous search of the surrounding woods and slopes, and a dive team searching for evidence offshore.

The mist had burned off. Caleb squinted against the glare, watching the sergeant in the shadows confer with his detectives.

God, he wanted a cigarette. His hands fisted uselessly in his pockets.

He needed something to *do*.

This was his island. His responsibility. But this wasn't his case. Outside of Portland, homicides in Maine belonged to the state. In the past, in the city, Caleb had worked Major Crimes. But here and now, all he could do was stand outside the crime scene tape with his thumb up his ass as the experts did their jobs.

He paced, getting sweatier and more frustrated as the sun crawled overhead, cutting the hill in light and shadow. The flat blue ocean mocked the bustle on shore, the turmoil inside him.

In his mind, he saw Maggie sticking out her pretty bare foot.

"Explain this."

"What?"

"My toes are webbed." She'd wiggled them to prove it.

"They're still toes," he'd told her. *"Not fins or flippers. I need more from you than that."*

His brain reeled. His gut twisted. How much more did he need?

Two violent attacks. Both on the beach.

Two women. Both with webbed feet.

My God, *Maggie* . . .

Sam Reynolds and one of the female detectives peeled away from the knot under the trees and strolled through ankle-deep weeds toward Caleb.

Caleb stood at attention and watched them come.

Reynolds massaged his mustache. "Got a minute?"

"As many as you need."

The state guy nodded toward his companion. "You've met Detective Hall."

Unlike the female cops on TV, Evelyn Hall was gray and plain, weathered as a barn and thirty pounds overweight. She had a fisherman's grip and a farmer's tan.

"Detective," he acknowledged.

"Evelyn." Her smile was more polite than friendly. Maybe it was a turf thing. Or maybe it was a gender thing. The state bureau was almost half and half, male and female. But Caleb bet any female state detective was used to the boys in local law enforcement giving her a hard time. "Our sergeant was wondering if we could sit down and discuss the case."

Caleb lifted his brows. "This case?"

Reynolds cleared his throat. "There's a good chance the same person committed both attacks. At least until we have the identity of the murder victim, the key to the crime is probably the first assault."

"So you're taking over my case."

Maggie's case.

"We're incorporating the two investigations. The sergeant understands you have experience with this place and the people."

"I have experience in homicide, too."

"We're not in Portland anymore, Toto," Hall said. "We have a dead naked woman at a tourist resort. The lieutenant's making this case a top priority."

"Too bad he didn't feel that way when I was asking for Maggie's lab results five days ago."

Or this murder might have been avoided. The unspoken implication echoed between them.

"Look, you'll still have a role in the investigation," Reynolds said.

Caleb narrowed his eyes. "A role."

Reynolds shrugged. "Take it or leave it."

"I can show you the report," Caleb said. "Back at my office."

His turf.

Reynolds nodded, conceding home field advantage. "We'll need copies," the detective said. "Notes, sketches, interviews—"

"There's a machine in the office," Caleb replied evenly. "You can copy whatever you want."

"We appreciate that," Hall said. "Right now, all we have to go on is the body."

Caleb's mind flashed back to purpling flesh and white-edged wounds and naked toes . . .

He controlled his face. His voice. "How soon can the ME conduct the autopsy?"

"Usually? Tomorrow morning," Reynolds said. "But the lieutenant is pushing for this afternoon. We need ID."

"Get me a photo," Caleb said.

"You want to put it out in the media?" Hall asked.

"If we have to. First I want to show it to Maggie—the first victim," Caleb said. "See if she recognizes her."

"We can do that," Reynolds said.

Caleb's jaw tightened. Not his case, he reminded himself. But—

"I can go with you," he said. "She knows me."

"We don't want to take up your time," Reynolds said.

"You have an objection to our talking to her alone?" Hall asked.

"No objection," Caleb said while frustration ate a hole in his gut.

It wasn't his job to object. And what the hell else could he say?

He could tell them Maggie thought she was a mermaid and completely destroy her credibility.

Or he could tell them he was beginning to believe her and completely destroy his.

"Does she remember anything yet?" Reynolds asked. "Did she see anything?"

"I did not see him at all," Maggie had said, her cheeks flushed, her eyes dark and earnest. *"But it was not Dylan."*

"How can you be sure?"

"It was a demon."

Fuck. That would go over about as well as her mermaid theory.

Caleb forced his jaw to unlock. "She doesn't remember. I think she doesn't want to remember. Sometimes she . . . imagines things."

"She lies."

The memory of Maggie's wide dark eyes and earnest voice rose like a ghost to accuse him.

"No," Caleb said firmly. "She believes what she's saying. She just—"

"I am not sick. Or stupid."

She had webbed toes.

"She's confused," he said.

Reynolds and Hall exchanged a look.

"Maybe seeing what this guy did to somebody else will help clear her mind," Reynolds said.

Maybe, Caleb thought. Or maybe it would convince her she shouldn't trust anybody.

Including him.

* * *

The two detectives flanked Margred, one on the ugly brown couch and one by the Hunters' living room fireplace.

Tell them the truth?

They would never believe her. Caleb had not believed her.

So Margred lied. Charmingly, easily, over cups of coffee.

Sitting between them, she told the same lies she had once told Caleb: She did not know. She did not remember. The male detective wrote everything down as if he believed her. The female had doubts—Margred could see the skepticism in her eyes—but she could not argue with Margred's pretty distress over her memory loss.

Margred felt no guilt. No betraying blushes, no awkward hesitations, no dropped glances gave her away.

She lied and smiled and sipped her coffee and wanted to wring Caleb's neck. Where was he? Why had he left her to deal with these people alone?

"Is Caleb coming soon?" she asked as she refilled the male detective's cup.

He smoothed his mustache, shooting a glance over his hand at the woman. With the careful instincts of the hunted, Margred noticed the look. Her pulse kicked up.

"We believe so," the woman said.

"Tell us about your relationship with Chief Hunter," the man—Reynolds was his name—said.

Relationship. Is that what they called it? Margred sat back down on the edge of her chair, folding her hands in her lap. "We are friends."

The man turned a page in his notebook. "Close friends."

She smiled at him. "Yes."

"How long have you known the chief?" the woman asked.

Margred tried to remember what Caleb told the doctor. "About a month."

She felt their sudden attention, like sharks scenting blood in the water.

"Since before the attack," Reynolds said.

Margred frowned. "Yes."

"You remember," the woman said.

Ah.

"I remember Caleb," Margred said. "Nothing else."

"So you really only have his word for it that you two were . . . close," Reynolds said.

Margred stopped herself from reaching for Caleb's necklace around her throat. "I do not understand."

"Were you two getting along? Before all this happened, I mean?"

Treacherous undercurrents swirled below the surface of the conversation. What did these people want? "Of course. I still don't understand—"

"We're trying to help you," the female detective said.

"Another woman was attacked on the beach last night," Reynolds explained. "If you know anything that could help us . . . anything at all . . ."

Understanding struck Margred. Caleb had once accused her of protecting someone. Did these two actually imagine she—

They could not possibly suspect he—

She straightened her spine. "Caleb is a *good* man."

Reynolds nodded. "I guess you feel you owe him a lot."

"Especially since your . . . accident," the woman put in.

Margred bared her teeth. "I do not owe him anything. I have money. A job."

Reynolds looked down at his notebook. "You work for a friend of his, don't you? Regina Barone?"

A bloodred haze rose in Margred's brain. For some reason, these humans were targeting Caleb. Threatening him. She bristled like a seal defending her pup. But she did not know how to protect him.

"He got me my job, yes."

"Was he with you last night?" Reynolds asked.

"He came by."

"What time was that?"

"I was watching television with his sister. You could ask her. Perhaps . . . nine o'clock? A little after."

"Tell me what happened then," Reynolds said.

Margred clasped her hands loosely in her lap, holding on to her temper. *Tell the truth,* Caleb had advised. Well, if it would help him, she would try. "Caleb gave his father a ride home from Antonia's. His father had had too much to drink. Caleb was very considerate, very calm. He helped his father to bed. Then he came downstairs and we talked for a while before he went home."

"How long?"

Margred shrugged. "Perhaps . . . an hour?"

Reynolds looked up. "So he didn't spend the night?"

If Margred could have lied, she would have. "No."

"Why was that?" the woman asked.

Margred's heart lurched. She could not possibly explain why they had quarreled.

"I was angry. Jealous, I guess. And I took it out on you." Caleb's gaze had met hers, all nerves and need, and she felt the jolt in the pit of her stomach. *"Come home with me, Maggie."*

She wished she had.

Too late.

"I was tired," she said. "A long shift at the restaurant."

"So you didn't have words?" the female detective asked. "A disagreement?"

"What are you suggesting? That Caleb was so upset by a lovers' quarrel that he went out and attacked some woman on the beach?" Sarcasm dripped from her voice. "You insult him. Caleb is one of the kindest, most honorable men I know."

"You haven't known him very long."

"Long enough to understand your suspicions are ridiculous."

"We don't suspect anybody yet. We're just trying to get a picture here."

The female detective leaned forward. "Chief Hunter

just got back from Iraq, didn't he? How's he handling that?"

Margred arched her eyebrows. "I imagine he is happy to be home."

"That doesn't mean he wasn't affected by the experience."

"Yes." Margred met her eyes coolly. "He limps."

The woman pressed her lips together. "Any signs of stress? Mood swings. Nightmares. Depression, maybe."

Nightmares, Margred thought, with a catch at her heart. He had nightmares.

"No." She rose. "Now, if that is all—"

"Not quite all." Detective Reynolds slid a manila envelope from his notebook. "We'd like you to take a look at last night's victim."

"Why?"

"You might have seen her before."

"If I did, it is unlikely I would remember. But of course I will look if you like," Margred added politely, and sat back down.

Reynolds slid a photograph from the envelope. Neither of the detectives looked at it, Margred noticed. They watched her instead.

She took a breath, steeling herself against betraying any reaction, and held out her hand.

Ah, no.

Her throat closed. She wanted to vomit. Her nails curled into her palms.

Hastily, the female detective loosened Margred's grip on the edge of the photograph before it crumpled.

Margred barely noticed. Her mind whirled. Her stomach churned.

"Can I get you anything?" Reynolds asked. "Water, maybe?"

Water...

Margred drew a ragged breath. Her heart pounded. "No, I will be fine."

"Do you recognize her?"

Margred shook her head in mute denial.

"Take your time," Reynolds said gently. "I know it's a shock."

"Yes."

Margred forced herself to look back at the face in the picture. An attempt had been made to clean it up, but nothing could be done to cover the livid bruising along the jaw or disguise the torn and bloody lips. The one eye swollen nearly shut. The other . . . puckered. Empty.

Margred hissed.

"You sure you haven't seen her before?"

"I am sorry," Margred said.

But she was not speaking to the detectives. She was talking to the woman in the picture.

The murdered selkie.

Gwyneth of Hiort.

17

THE DETECTIVES LEFT LUCY'S HOUSE, TAKING the photograph and their suspicions with them.

Margred shivered, wrapping her arms around her body. Gwyneth was dead, slaughtered and skinned like a baby harp seal. She could not dismiss the other selkie's fate. Or ignore her own any longer.

Whatever demon had attacked her out of the dark hunted still. He could, he probably would, return for her.

She hugged her elbows tighter. But it wasn't only her own danger that haunted her. If another elemental stalked her kind, if fire turned against water, more was at stake here than Gwyneth's death or Margred's survival. The very balance of nature would be affected. Which meant . . . destruction. For the earth and the sea and everything that inhabited creation.

Her kind. Caleb's kind. All.

Margred bit her lip until she tasted blood. This was the prince's responsibility, his fight. She was not prepared for this. Always going with the flow, immersed in the cycle of the seasons, in swimming and sunning and sex, she lacked the knowledge and training, the habit of thought or trick of temperament, to deal with a skirmish between immortals.

She was, as Regina would say, screwed.

Frightened of her own death and what lay beyond.

And for almost the first time in centuries, angry. Beneath her shock and fear, rage smoldered inside her like a lump of coal from a demon's fire.

Gwyneth had trespassed on Margred's territory, had coveted Margred's man. But poaching or not, Gwyneth had not deserved to die.

The front door opened. Margred jumped.

Caleb stood in the light of the hall, tall and grounded as an oak tree, with leaf shadow eyes and sun-tipped hair. Tiny lines of fatigue or frustration dug between his brows and bracketed his mouth.

He looked so good, so right, standing there, she forgot he did not believe her. Forgot she was annoyed with him. A great wave of worry and relief carried her from the couch and into his arms without thought or hesitation.

They closed around her. She clung to him, needing the solidness of his flesh to reassure herself he was here. He was whole. He was well.

His lips pressed her hair. "It's okay," he murmured.

Which only proved he had no idea what he was talking about. A demon hunted, and those two detectives had practically accused him of murder.

Margred closed her eyes. He smelled wonderful, like earth and sunshine, sweat and Caleb. His arms were strong around her, and his shoulder was as hard and rounded as an apple. His uniform buttons scratched her cheek. Even that friction was somehow reassuring, a reminder she was still alive.

She rested her forehead against his chest, absorbing the comfort and safety of his body.

Temporary comfort, she reminded herself. Illusory safety.

But all the harbor she had.

"You knew her," his voice rumbled. It was not a question.

She nodded against his chest. His heart beat under her palm, strong and sure.

His chest rose with his breath. "Who was she?"

"Her name was Gwyneth. She was selkie."

"I guessed."

Margred raised her head to gaze into his face. "How?"

A corner of his mouth indented, but his eyes remained sober on hers. "Webbed toes."

Ah. "Evidence," she said.

"Yes."

Margred stifled her disappointment. So he was not ready to take her story on faith. At least he was willing to listen.

" 'When you have eliminated the impossible, whatever remains, however improbable, must be the truth,' " she quoted. She felt his start of surprise and smiled. "Sherlock Holmes. I have been reading your books."

"Good for you." He rubbed the back of his neck. "This . . . woman, this selkie—what brought her here?"

Gwyneth's memory haunted Margred, the teasing note in her voice, the avid, speculative look in her eye . . . *"I hear you've had good hunting yourself. In . . . Maine, is it?"*

"The currents," Margred said.

"Bullshit."

Her pulse tripped. "It's true." Partly true, at least. Either Gwyneth had not been attuned enough to politics to be aware of Margred's predicament, or, driven by her appetites, the other selkie simply had not cared. "Your island is between the Arctic current and the Gulf Stream, like . . . like one of your hotels at an intersection. A convenient resting place for anyone making the ocean crossing."

Caleb's eyes narrowed. "And your friend just chose this moment to travel halfway around the world and get herself killed."

His belief was new and precious to her. She did not wish to jeopardize it with lies. But neither would she burden him with the responsibility of Gwyneth's lust.

"She was hunting."

"That's a long swim for something to eat."

Margred squirmed. Did he guess the real reason selkies came ashore at night? Did he remember their own first meeting on the beach and wonder?

"Gwyneth liked . . . variety in her diet."

"Hell of a price to pay for a snack," Caleb said. "It's my fault."

Her heart jarred. "No. You did nothing."

"Exactly. I should have believed you."

"I meant, there is nothing you could do," Margred said. "Not between a selkie and a demon. This is not your fight."

His jaw set. "It's my job to protect this island."

Fear and frustration made her sharp. "Those two people, the ones who came here, seem to think it is theirs now."

Caleb smiled grimly. "They can't catch the killer if they don't know what they're looking for. Evelyn Hall may look tough, but she's no Buffy. They have no idea what they're up against."

Who was Buffy? "Neither do you," Margred said.

"So tell me."

She was shaken by his belief in her. By her fear for him. "Demons are elementals. They take their form from the fire. You cannot shoot one with your gun or . . . or lock it in a cell."

"The thing has some kind of body. I saw it on the beach that night you were attacked. And I saw your friend. No fire, no spirit, did that to her. She wasn't burned. She was tortured."

Margred flinched. "The demon may have taken a human body. Temporarily."

"You mean, like you do."

She shook her head, rejecting the comparison. "No.

Earth and water—the sidhe and the mer—have mass, weight, shape of their own. The other elementals . . . Air at least has a little matter. But fire can only borrow substance."

Caleb's gaze sharpened. "So this thing, this demon—he borrowed a body?"

"A human host, yes."

"Good. If he's human, I'll find him."

Margred's stomach twisted. Caleb believed her. But he still did not understand.

And his ignorance could kill him.

"The human is not responsible," she said. "He is a vehicle. A victim."

"But if I catch him—"

"Then the demon will simply take possession of another host. It would take time for him to establish mastery over another's will, but—"

"How long?" Caleb interrupted.

"What?"

"How much time before this . . . thing moves on somebody else?"

"That depends on the strength and complicity of the host."

"You mean, if the human cooperates in torture. Murder."

"Yes."

A muscle worked at the corner of his mouth. "I am so nailing this fucker."

"Caleb." She touched his arm. "You cannot stop a demon."

"Maybe not." His eyes gleamed with a pure warrior's light. "But I can slow him down some."

His courage shamed her. Terrified her. "Why are you doing this?"

"Because I can. Because he hurt you." Caleb shrugged. He met her gaze, and all his soul was in his eyes, steady and unpretentious. "Because there's no one else."

His words lanced her heart.

So he would take responsibility on himself, she thought.

The same way he shouldered everything else, without pause or complaint—the raising of his sister and the care of his father, his duty to his country and his service to this island.

Her blood beat in her ears like the rush of the tide. She was not like him. She could barely comprehend him. He was a man bound and defined by his connections to others, while she flowed as the sea flowed, without tie or limits.

Margred hung a moment, suspended like the curl of the wave seconds before the crash. Contained. Perfect. Whole.

And then plunged, a long, glistening slide toward . . . what? She did not know.

There's no one else.

"There is me," she said.

* * *

Caleb looked at Maggie's dark, shadowed eyes and full, unsmiling mouth. The half-healed gash that ran under her hairline.

She was offering herself to him as an ally. A partner.

He fisted his hands lightly, resisting the urge to take, and shoved them in his pockets. "No way in hell," he said. "This thing's already beaten you once."

Her chin came up. "Bested me," she corrected. "I am still alive."

"Yeah, and I'd like to keep you that way."

He thought he saw her wince. But she didn't back down. He respected her courage. "You need my help," she said.

"I need you to be safe." His voice was firm. Flat. "You didn't see what he did to her."

"The detectives . . . they showed me a photo."

"Of her face. He did worse."

He would not describe the condition of her body. Bad enough that he would dream of it tonight, the multiple cuts and burns, the swelling around her wrists and ankles, the pale and purpling flesh of her fingers, breasts, and thighs.

He recognized the marks of torture, the signature of the

Iraqi death squads. In the past three years, he'd seen too many bodies dumped in canals and alleys, left like trash by the side of the road or the back of market stalls.

This was worse, because it had happened here, at home.

Because it could have been Maggie.

"Did he burn her pelt?" she asked.

Caleb scowled, pulled from his private nightmare. "What?"

"Her sealskin. Did you find it?"

He had spent a long, frustrating morning standing outside the yellow tape, observing the activity of the crime scene technicians, the wardens, the dive team. Nobody had entrusted him with the evidence log this time. But he would have noticed the excitement surrounding any major find. A car. Her clothes. A handbag.

Or even an unexpected, unexplained animal pelt.

He held her gaze. "No."

"Then he destroyed it," she whispered.

"There wasn't any evidence of a fire," Caleb said. And they had searched for one, seeking another connection between the two crimes. "Maybe he took it. Hid it."

"No." Maggie's eyes widened. "But Gwyneth might have. She was . . . adept at self-preservation. She would have safeguarded herself. Better than I did," she added with faint bitterness.

Uneasily, Caleb remembered Maggie's desperate struggle to reach the fire the night of her attack. *I need what he took from me.*

Could she be right about Gwyneth? Or was she projecting, hoping for . . . what, exactly?

"Before, you said a selkie without her sealskin can't change form."

"More than that. The sea is our life. Without it, we die."

"Everything dies," Caleb said harshly.

Maggie's eyes were shadowed and heavy with loss. "But not forever. Humans have souls. Selkies return to the sea."

He was a cop. He didn't know how to respond to her talk of souls. But he understood guilt. Motivation.

Evidence.

"Your selkie friend didn't hide anything. Not on that beach. The searchers combed the rocks and the surrounding woods. If her pelt was there, they'd have found it."

"The island," Maggie said.

"What island?"

"Dylan mentioned an island where he keeps a few things. If Gwyneth followed him here, she might have done the same."

Caleb couldn't think about his brother. Not yet.

"There are thousands of islands in Maine. We can't search every uninhabited rock in the ocean hoping to get lucky."

"This was a private island three miles east of here. You could find it." Maggie looked at him confidently, resolve shining in her eyes. "I could find it."

"I'm not letting you dangle yourself out there like bait."

Her lips curved. "Then it seems we are in this together."

He could not resist her. Not when she was right.

"Fine," Caleb said wearily. "Tomorrow I'll get us a boat."

"Why not tonight?"

"It'll be too dark to cast off in a couple hours, and way too dark to search. Besides . . ." He forced himself to meet her gaze. "I can't leave the island without Reynolds's okay."

"But . . . you are the chief of police."

"I'm also a person of interest in an ongoing investigation," he said evenly. In light of what had happened, he couldn't afford sentiment. Or outrage. Or even pride. "I volunteered to take a polygraph. I've offered them my financial records, my postdeployment health assessment, and my ex-wife's phone number. But it will take a while to clear the record."

Longer to clear his name.

"Then we must use the time we have," Maggie said.

He nodded. "I'll be done with the polygraph before lunch. What time do you get off?"

"Two o'clock. But I was not talking about our work schedules." She cradled his hand; placed it on her breast. Surprise held him immobile. "Take me home with you tonight."

His mouth dried. His mind blanked as the blood in his head rushed to his groin.

He worked hard to sound relaxed. In control. "That's the best offer I've had all day. But I can't."

So move your hand, dickhead.

But apparently he couldn't do that either. Her breast was so soft, the nipple stiff against his palm, and the sight of his hand spanning all that fullness, all that roundness, gave him another rush.

"Why not?" she asked.

He jerked his mind back but left his hand where it was. Why not? Er . . . "It's the middle of the season," he explained. "Every room on the island is booked. So we've got half a dozen detectives sleeping in shifts on jail cots and a sergeant catching naps on my couch. I'm not tiptoeing you past him to get to the bedroom."

Margred's lips curved. "Then we will tiptoe past your sister."

She was serious. She wanted him. Tonight. Now.

He struggled to laugh. To breathe. "You gonna smuggle me to your room?"

Her warm mouth skated over his jaw. "It is your room."

"Was my room." He cleared his throat. "We're not in high school anymore."

"I was never in high school." She nipped his earlobe. His bottom lip. "Teach me."

His eyes damn near crossed. He was already hard. Her voice, her hands, her breath slid over him, sluiced over him, warm and irresistible. She was a goddess risen from the sea, Aphrodite, bewitching him, seducing him, with the same hungry, skillful intent of their first time.

"I can't teach you anything," he said, his voice rusty.

"Ah." She cupped his face between her soft, warm hands and touched her lips to his. Drew back to smile into his eyes. "But you have."

His heart turned over painfully in his chest. This . . . this was different, he thought. The laughter and self-awareness in her gaze. The tenderness in her touch.

"Maggie . . ."

I love you.

Did he say it out loud?

"Shh. Upstairs."

She led him up the steps and down the hall to his room, both of them breathless, bumping, struggling with buttons, trying hard to be quiet. Her hands were all over him. His tongue was in her mouth. He backed her into the wall and—

Bang. The door to his parents' room—almost twenty-five years since his mother walked out on them and he still thought of it as his parents' room, how pathetic was that? Anyway, the door flew open, and his father swayed, framed in the doorway.

Caleb twisted, putting Maggie behind him, shielding her with his body.

Unnecessary. Bart never glanced at her, her untucked blouse, her kiss-swollen mouth.

Fixing his gaze on Caleb, he growled, "She won't stay. She'll leave you like your bitch of a mother left me."

He staggered past them to the bathroom. The lock clicked. The toilet seat banged. And then the unmistakable sound of peeing hissed through the closed door.

Caleb's jaw tightened. "Just like high school," he said bitterly.

Maggie stroked the knotted muscles of his back. She pressed her lips between his shoulder blades. "Come to bed."

He wanted to. He wanted to close his eyes and lose himself in her for a while. Like maybe forever. "I have things to do."

"Yes." She tugged him. Turned him. "Me."

That surprised a laugh from him. How could she want him after seeing that? After knowing who and what he'd come from?

But she did.

She rose on tiptoe and kissed him, the corner of his eye, the underside of his jaw, the hollow of his throat. All the neglected, unexpected, tender places.

His heart swelled. "Maggie . . ."

"Shh."

She pulled him into the stark brown room where he'd spent his childhood. Vaguely, he noticed changes: a bright skirt tumbling off a chair, extra pillows softening the narrow bed. The room even smelled like her, like woman, like Maggie, shampoo and lotion and, under that, the deeper, wilder notes of the sea. He breathed them in like a patient released from a hospital, like a man returning from the desert.

Her touch flowed over him like rain, warm and healing. He was parched for her, his mind restless as blowing sand, his spirit dry and discouraged. She poured herself over him, her mouth lush and giving. Her hands stole over him, under his shirt, over his chest, rousing him to life.

He grabbed at her. Smiling, she slipped through his grasp to his bed, sliding backward until she lay against the pillows. He drank in the vision of her long hair waving against the white sheets, her skin shining like pearl through her open blouse, the white globes of her breasts. He forgot . . . everything else. There was only now. Only her, her smooth thighs and her warm smile and her great, dark, unfathomable eyes. He yanked at his belt, tore at his shirt. She was rain, water, life, and he was dying for her, his hands shaking, his touch feverish as he sank beside her on the bed, reaching, touching, wanting—

She was so warm. So soft and pink and slick. He spread her with his thumbs, loving the feel of her, ripe and wet, the sight of his tanned hand working in and out against her silky thighs, her soft, dark bush. He bent to kiss her, to drink from her, dizzy with her scent. Her sweetness. She gasped and moved with him, under him, rising and falling like the sea, and his blood pounded in his head. He was drowning, drenched in her. He felt her crest around his fingers, against his mouth, as he suckled her.

She tugged his hair. He indulged them both with one long, last, lingering lick before he dragged his body over hers—wet, quivering, *his*—and shoved his scarred knee between her thighs.

Her hands pushed at his shoulders. "Your leg—"

He didn't care about his leg. He didn't care about anything except being inside her as close, as deep, as far as he could go. He straightened his arms, shifting his weight. She rose to meet him; strained to take him.

Theirs eyes linked. Locked. With one swift, deep thrust, he entered her.

She gasped and shuddered.

So did he.

They plunged together, fused by sweat and passion. Complete. Connected. Whole. He was part of her as he had never been part of another being in his life. Her legs wrapped his. Her hair tangled his fingers, a net of texture and fragrance. She tightened around him, a silken fist, and he turned his face into her neck and spilled himself into her, gave himself up to her, body and soul. She shuddered again, vibrating under him, her nails digging into his shoulders.

The last shimmering wave retreated, leaving him beached and breathless on top. Wrecked. At peace.

When he could breathe again, when he could speak, he raised his head and said it.

"I love you."

* * *

Margred lay stunned under him, trying to regulate her breathing and her thoughts.

Caleb's words curled warm against her heart. *I love you.* Selkies did not do love any more than they did miracles. He loved her?

What was she supposed to do about that?

What was she supposed to say?

"Thank you."

Wrong answer. She saw his eyes cool, felt him distance himself even as his body still filled hers.

She moistened her lips and tried again. "You honor me."

"No, I make you nervous," Caleb said. "What are you afraid of?"

It was hard to be honest with him lying on top of her, lodged inside her, studying her face with assessing green eyes. Hard to think with her body still thrumming and moist from sex.

She wanted him again. Possibly she would want him forever. Maybe that was why she was afraid.

"We are very different," she said.

"That's why we work. You told me once I lived in my head. With you . . . I feel like I've found my heart."

Whatever breath she had left escaped in a soft rush. "I cannot think when you say such things to me."

His eyes narrowed. "Maybe I don't want you to think. Tell me how you feel."

"I . . . care for you," she admitted. "More than I have ever cared for anyone in seven hundred years of existence."

His body went very still. "Seven hundred—"

"Years. I am immortal."

"My mother wasn't. You said she died."

He told her he did not want her to think. But she could almost hear his brain ticking like the clock in the hall. "Her life—her present life—ended. But because she returned to the water, she will be born again on the tide and the foam."

"And that was more important to her than her husband. Her children."

Margred thought of pointing out that Atargatis had taken Dylan with her, but his mother's choice would hardly soothe Caleb's feelings. "She was selkie." Margred defended her. "We belong to the sea more than we can ever belong to another."

"She stayed with my father for fourteen years. I thought they were happy."

Ah. Margred bit her lip, the tiny pain an echo of the one at her heart. The boy Caleb had believed he was the child of love, of a true union between husband and wife. Atargatis's desertion not only had deprived him of his mother, but had tarnished his earliest memories and perceptions of family.

He deserved better of her. He deserved love.

Or at least the truth.

"They were too different." As she and Caleb were different, Margred reflected with a pang. "Your father possessed a selkie. He never had her love."

A muscled worked in Caleb's jaw. "You think I'm trying to possess you?"

He already had more of her than she had ever given another, even her long-dead mate. Her feelings for him filled her like a pregnancy, crowding and pushing inside her. She felt swollen, stretched into someone—something—she almost did not recognize.

Doubt wrapped tentacles around her heart. Could she ever be what he needed? Could she give him more than his mother had given his father?

What would it do to her to try?

The fear in her chest tightened, squeezing the air from her lungs. And what would it do to both of them if she failed?

"I think," Margred said carefully, "that you belong here, in this place. With these people."

"And you don't."

"I am selkie," she repeated. Her words sounded thin, even to herself. "The ocean is our element. Its magic is in our blood. We must return to it or die."

"You can't return. What if you're going to die anyway?"

His question quivered like an arrow in her heart. And yet it was the wrong question.

She saw the instant he realized it, watched his eyes chill, felt his body brace like a warrior's for a blow.

"If you had your sealskin," Caleb said quietly, "if you could return to the sea, would you stay here with me?"

Would she give up all the seas and eternity to live on land with this one man until they both were dead?

Her mouth dried. She did not, could not, answer him.

But that was all the reply he needed.

18

~❈~

"WELL, THAT WENT WELL," CALEB SAID AS HE
left the polygraph examiner in possession of his office—the
only space on the island that hadn't already been taken over
by the state's task force.

He lied.

Not for the first time that morning. But even with
Caleb's right arm in a blood pressure cuff and finger plates
wired to his left hand, even with rubber tubes around his
chest and a digital readout confirming the truth of every
word, there was no way the examiner was going to believe a
story about a seven-hundred-year-old mermaid being
stalked by a demon.

Sam Reynolds stood in the doorway of the small break
room that housed the coffeepot and the copy machine.
"Don't worry about it," he said. "Three hours on the box
would have my mother sweating like a pig. You already
passed my test."

Caleb raised his eyebrows. "DNA results back already?"

The state dick snorted. "Who do you think we are, the
FBI?"

"So why the sudden change of heart? Unless you're grateful that I let you sleep in my jail cell instead of on the beach."

Reynolds shrugged. "You gave us the DNA sample. You volunteered for a polygraph. If you were guilty, you would have told us to pound sand. So either you're thick-as-a-brick dumb or you're innocent."

Caleb was not in the mood to be mollified. The woman he loved wanted to leave him, he'd been shut out of the task force meeting that morning, and the sergeant in charge didn't trust him to direct traffic.

He rubbed the back of his neck with one hand, his gaze traveling from the flashing copy machine to the stacks of paper lined along the counter. "What are you doing?"

Reynolds fed another sheet into the machine. "Copying your case notes."

Caleb cocked an eyebrow at Edith Paine. The reflection from her computer screen—bright white cards against a brilliant green background—gleamed in her glasses. "I don't make copies," she announced. "I don't get coffee either."

"Good to see you keeping busy," Caleb drawled.

Edith clicked on another card. "Don't start with me. That phone's been ringing off the hook all morning. Every busybody on the island has been through that door. The summer people want armed escorts to go swimming, and the homeowners want you to arrest the rubberneckers for trespassing."

The vise gripping the back of Caleb's neck tightened. "Whittaker?"

"Haven't heard from him."

Caleb frowned. That was odd. "Did he go to the mainland?"

"And miss the excitement?" Edith sniffed. "Not likely."

"He could be sick. I'll check on him when I do patrol."

The island was hard on those who lived alone. Visiting shut-ins and the elderly was good community relations.

And in this case, visiting Whittaker gave Caleb an excuse to recanvass the area.

If he's human, I'll find him.

"Who are you talking about?" Reynolds asked.

His questions jarred Caleb from his thoughts. "Local lawyer," he said briefly.

"Local blowhard," Edith muttered.

"Well, if you're going out, watch out for reporters," Reynolds said. "A Channel Six news crew came over on the ferry this morning."

Edith kept her eyes on her game. "They're at Antonia's. Regina called."

Caleb's tension spiked. He'd just spent three hours lying on a polygraph exam, and Maggie could blow it all in a five-minute interview with a couple of tabloid headlines. MERMAID BEDEVILS LOCAL COP. DEMON HUNTS OFF COAST OF MAINE.

Screw patrol. Maggie needed him, whether she admitted it or not.

* * *

News of a nude blond corpse on the beach attracted more folks than a Rotary Club clambake.

Like a winter storm, the threat to their island brought the locals out in search of food, company, community. When Caleb pushed open the door to Antonia's, a wave of noise rushed to greet him: babbling voices, clattering dishes, the hiss of the grill. The smell of fish and onions, fries and coffee, floated on the air.

Caleb scanned the packed booths, the line snaking between the tables, the weathered faces around the room. New England faces, most of them, with Viking eyes and Puritan mouths.

Where was Maggie?

Regina slapped two plates from the pass-through on top of the counter. "One chowder, tuna on wheat, lobster roll with fries. Come get your order or I'm giving it away to the next person in line."

No waitress, then. No Maggie. Caleb's gut cramped. Couldn't she stay put just once?

Eight-year-old Nick scuttled among the pushed-back chairs and denim-clad legs, clearing tables.

Where the hell was she?

Regina caught his eye and jerked her head toward the kitchen. The knot in Caleb's stomach eased.

He took one stride, quickly checked as some asshole slid out of a booth and into his path. White male, mid-thirties, blow-dried hair, bleached smile. Not an islander, despite the vaguely familiar face. Caleb made him for the Channel Six reporter before he opened his mouth.

"Chief Hunter?"

Caleb nodded warily.

That raised a stir and a flurry of questions. Somebody thrust a long black microphone under his chin like the muzzle of a gun. Caleb's jaw set, but he didn't reach for his weapon. *Veteran makes progress in adapting to civilian life.*

"Do you think World's End is still safe for tourists?" the reporter asked.

Loaded question. Caleb would have preferred the gun. Conversations stopped all over the restaurant as locals and summer people waited for his reply. *Counted* on his reply for their safety and their livelihoods. Caleb ground his teeth together. He wasn't sacrificing either one to some asshole reporter.

"People need to be aware of their surroundings and take precautions wherever they are," he said carefully. "Excuse me."

The microphone bobbed in his face. "What about the vicious attacks on two women on your beaches?"

"CID is investigating both crimes," Caleb said. "Lieutenant Jenkins can give you a statement."

Sidestepping the reporter, he shouldered past the guy with the mike.

"What do you know about the deceased?" the reporter called after him.

Her name was Gwyneth. She had webbed toes. She was

an immortal sea creature who had been murdered by a demon.

Now *that* would make headlines.

"No comment," Caleb said, and pushed through the door to the kitchen.

Maggie stood at the big double sink, up to her elbows in greasy pots and foam. She looked messy, hot, and human, her ivory cheeks flushed, her hair curling in the steam.

The sight of her lodged in his chest like shrapnel. He bled internally.

Antonia slapped a row of frozen patties down on the grill. "Go away. She can't leave."

"I know," Caleb said quietly.

If you had your sealskin, if you could return to the sea, would you stay here with me?

His hands clenched at his sides.

Maggie raised one damp wrist to push her hair back from her forehead. Her gaze sought his. "My shift ends at two," she offered.

Her tentative overture made his heart beat faster. His nerve endings flared to life.

Pathetic.

Caleb hooked his thumbs in his belt loops, awkward as a boy hanging around the locker of his high school crush. "I'll be back then. I just stopped by to see how you were doing."

She shrugged, the gesture somehow encompassing every damn thing that was wrong with this day. "As you see." Her crooked smile cracked his heart. "And you?"

If she could lie, so could he. "Fine."

"Those detectives . . ." Her eyes searched his. "Are you still a—what did you call it?—a person of interest to them?"

Her concern was almost enough to make him hope she might stay. But he wasn't focusing on his problems while her life was at stake. "I'm fine," he repeated. "I'm here."

Maggie crossed her arms over her apron. "I can see for myself they did not lock you up. What did they say to you?"

She was made of tougher stuff than Sherilee. His ex-wife had never demanded he talk about his job. Had never wanted him to. Her lack of interest in something as basic as his work had driven them apart.

Or was it his inability to share himself with her that had driven her away?

"They're not telling me much of anything," he admitted. "I'm closed out of the investigation."

"They are stupid."

Her fierceness made him smile. "Reynolds is all right. Anyway, they have no idea what they're up against. What they're looking for."

"So what will you do now?"

"My job. CID can't stop me from talking to people. They're concentrating their attention on the cove, where the body was found. But that night on the point . . . I saw something. All I can do is hope this latest incident will encourage another witness to come forward."

"Ticket up!" Antonia bawled through the pass-through. She turned to Maggie, planting her hands on her hips. "And you can take the garbage out. I'm not paying you to stand around making moony eyes at the chief."

Maggie stiffened. "I do not make moony eyes."

"I call it like I see it," Antonia said.

"I've got it," Caleb said, to keep the peace. "You're not paying me to stand around either."

He hefted the bag from the can by the door.

"Take care," Maggie said.

"He's not going to drop it," Antonia said. "Or are you worried the door's gonna hit that fine ass of his on the way out?"

Caleb glanced at Maggie, pink-cheeked with steam or—was she actually blushing? "Easy, Mayor. That's sexual harassment talk."

"Ha. Don't get your hopes up."

Good advice. But . . . *moony eyes?*

"I call it like I see it."

He was smiling as he hauled the trash out the back door.

Gulls yammered and circled over the alley as if the Dumpster were a fishing boat at cleaning time. Caleb slung the trash bag up and in, startling a chorus of protest from the gulls and a sudden, furtive movement at the edge of his vision.

Sniper.

His hand dropped to his gun.

Son of a bitch.

He caught himself, his brain wresting control from his instincts. Not a sniper. Only a rat or a raccoon after garbage. Or the cat, what was his name, Hercules.

Caleb shook his head in disgust. Yeah, all he needed to boost his credibility was to get caught discharging his weapon at the restaurant cat.

Still, something wasn't right. He felt it, like the beat of his blood or the rasp of his breath, an instinct honed in other doorways, other alleys half a world away. He heard a scrape, caught a flicker of shadow just around the corner.

Not a rat, not a rat, not a rat, his pulse drummed.

He hugged the side of the building, using it for cover, his gun ready at his thigh. He angled his head for a quick sneak peek.

And came face to face with the bleary-eyed, haggard visage of his father.

Confusion robbed Caleb of breath. Of thought. "Dad?"

Bart Hunter blinked, thrusting his head forward like an old sea turtle.

Shit. Caleb's fear blurred into anger. "What the hell are you doing? I almost shot you."

"Took the day off," his father said. "I'm entitled, aren't I? A man's entitled to a day off after forty fucking years on a boat."

"Entitled, fine." Caleb bit out the words. "What are you doing here?"

Bart dropped his gaze. "Came to see that girl of yours. Maggie."

Maggie.

Caleb's blood ran cold. "Why?"

Bart drew himself up. At sixty-three, he was still tall, lean, and weathered as a spar. Tough enough to go out day after day, year after year, despite hangovers and fog. Vigorous enough to set his traps and haul his catch.

Strong enough to overpower a selkie? Caleb's hands clenched into fists.

"Since when do I have to give you reasons?" Bart blustered.

But Caleb was done with his years of lies and evasions. "What did you do with the sealskin?"

Bart's mouth opened. Shut. Opened again. "How did you find out about that?"

Rage surged inside Caleb. "Where is it?"

His father must have seen the violence in his face, because he stammered, "I don't know. She found it. Your mother. She took it. I never saw her again."

Caleb's fists loosened at his sides. "My mother found it."

"Yes. That's why she left us."

"And you don't know about another sealskin."

"No."

"Then what the *fuck* are you doing here?" Caleb roared.

The gulls in the alley flapped their wings, disturbed from their perch atop the Dumpster. The smell of garbage—grease and beer and cigarettes, spoiled meat and rotting vegetables—trickled down the alley, covering the fresh scent of the sea like an oil slick.

"Came to see if Maggie was all right," Bart muttered.

Caleb shook his head in disbelief. "So you decided to skulk outside until you caught her taking out the trash."

"Saw *him*," Bart explained. "Stopped."

"Saw who?" Caleb asked sharply. "Where?"

His father jerked his head in reply. *There.*

In the narrow space between the store fronts, sheltered from the wind and shielded from the gulls, a man huddled among the clumps of weeds and sodden paper cups like one of Portland's homeless.

Caleb inhaled sharply. Dead or alive?

Something about that long, angular figure . . . "Whittaker?"

Behind him, the birds circled and cawed. Cries of warning? Or calls of distress?

The figure raised its head from its chest. Even in the shadows, his face was very pale. His eyes burned feverishly in their sockets. Caleb fought a shiver.

"Man's hurt," Bart said. "Needs help."

Maybe.

He didn't appear injured. There was no sign of blood—his blood or another's—on his khaki pants and button-down shirt.

"Mr. Whittaker, can you hear me?"

The lawyer's face twisted. "Of course I hear you," he said in his usual pissy tones. "I'm sick, not deaf."

Caleb released his breath. He had to get a grip. Not everybody he encountered was auditioning for a starring role in *The Exorcist.* "Can you stand?"

"I'm not drunk either," Whittaker said. He got awkwardly to his feet, using the stone wall behind him for support. Just for one second, he staggered. His gaze sought Caleb's. "Help me," he whispered.

The hair rose along Caleb's arms and on the back of his neck. "What do you want?"

How much had he heard?

Whittaker blinked rapidly. "Well, for starters, you can help me to your car. I need a ride home."

Caleb assessed the situation. This was his chance to get another look inside Whittaker's house. All he had to do was give a lift to a man who might be possessed by a soul-sucking, flesh-shredding demon.

Not a problem. He had ridden with murderers in the back of his squad car before. He'd dealt with other evil that wore a human face. He had even lived through the desert hell of Iraq.

Keeping Whittaker in his peripheral vision, he walked around him to the curb and unlocked the Jeep.

Whittaker balked at getting into the backseat. "I'm not a criminal."

"Passengers ride in back," Caleb said. "Department policy."

"You could make an exception."

"He didn't for me," Bart contributed unexpectedly.

Caleb hooked his thumbs in his pockets. "You want a ride or not?"

Whittaker grumbled and got in.

Caleb shut the passenger door with relief. Demon or not, he didn't think the lawyer was going to claw his way through the metal grid between the seats.

Anyway, Caleb was armed. Whittaker wasn't.

He was trained in combat. Whittaker wasn't.

He was prepared—hell, he was *spoiling* for a fight. And Whittaker, poor SOB, probably had no idea and no defenses against the thing that had taken him over.

If the lawyer *had* been taken over.

Caleb got behind the wheel, keeping an eye on the rearview mirror. Whittaker slumped in the back seat, too weak even to sit up. His father loomed on the curb like a chain saw–carved totem of a man. They looked sick, stiff, unnatural.

But still human.

Caleb glanced down as he turned his key in the ignition. Maybe he was wrong about Whittaker.

And maybe, he thought grimly, he was making the biggest mistake of his life.

*   *   *

Tan's gaze drilled a hole through the human's thick skull. How he would love to take this one over. Tan wouldn't ride in the back then. Oh, no. He could do . . . He smiled slowly. Whatever he wanted.

Opening his mouth, he breathed in the human's mingled scent of sweat and spirit. Tasting. Testing.

The man's will burned like copper on Tan's tongue, flat and bright as an angel's blade.

Tan pinched his lips together.

Perhaps he would not exchange bodies just yet. His current host was still useful. Compliant. Tan did not want to expend energy establishing mastery over a rebellious host with his mission still only half accomplished.

Both selkies should be dead, their pelts destroyed.

Tan needed to act quickly before the mer discovered his involvement.

He shuddered. Or Hell lost patience.

As much as it galled the demon to admit, there might be other, better ways to use the man Caleb than by taking him over. He was not completely unintelligent. He was clearly determined. He was close to the selkie Margred. And judging from his questions in the alley, he, too, sought the pelt.

What if Tan allowed him to find it?

19

＊

THE AIR WAS HEAVY AND HOT, THICK WITH grease and garlic, unrelieved by the whirring kitchen fans.

Margred wiggled her swollen toes inside her sneakers, pretending to observe Antonia demonstrate how to cook clam strips in the deep fryer. Really she was watching the door.

And the clock.

One hour, twenty-seven minutes since Caleb had carried out the trash, promising to return. Eleven—no, *twelve*—minutes now since her shift had ended. She stank of smoke and sweat and crusted pots, and she wanted to go—

Home.

Her breath caught. Because in that instant she had not pictured the cold stone grandeur of Caer Subai or the sweet, cool freedom of the ocean.

She saw a house, tucked like a secret beneath the tall pines, and a wide bed with a view of the sea shining beyond the wood-paned windows. Caleb's house. Caleb's bed.

The vision rushed on her like a wave, stirring her to the

depths, flowing and filling the empty chambers of her heart. She pressed the heel of her palm to her chest, almost dizzy with dismay and a lack of oxygen.

She was selkie. She flowed as the sea flowed, following her whims and the currents. Ever changing. Eternal.

Caleb was hewed of New England rock, upstanding as the old stone church at the head of the harbor, rooted as an oak. For all his selkie heritage, he belonged to the earth. To the island.

Where did she belong?

She did not know. Only that in him, her restless heart had found harbor at last.

"Are you paying attention, girl?" Antonia demanded.

"No," Margred admitted.

"Moony eyes," Antonia repeated in disgust.

This time Margred did not bother to deny it.

One hour, thirty-two minutes. Every sixty-second tick lay heavy on her heart.

What if Caleb had found the demon? Or the demon had found him?

Her throat felt tight. She moved her hand to her necklace, closing her fingers around the shell. Caleb was more vulnerable than he believed. And his danger made her vulnerable in ways she had never imagined.

The door to the dining room banged open.

Caleb, Margred thought with relief. *Finally.*

But it was Regina who blew into the kitchen, her eyes stormy and red warning flags flying in her cheeks. Margred bit back her disappointment.

Antonia raised the wire basket from the hot oil. "What bug is up your ass?"

"That—reporter," Regina spat the word, "just asked me if the lobster was fresh. Yes, I said. Local, he says. We're on a freaking island off the coast of Maine. What does he think, we ship it from Florida?"

"Did you take his order?" Antonia asked.

"I took his head off," Regina said. "Asshole. I'll give him local lobster."

"You'll give him what he asks for," Antonia said. "Then he gives you money. That's how real restaurants work."

"I don't need you to tell me about restaurants."

Antonia crossed her arms. "Then why did you come back here?"

Regina ran a hand through her short hair. "Because if I stay out there another minute, I'm gonna kill one of your precious paying customers. Which is no big loss, but I don't want to set a bad example for Nicky."

"Fine." Antonia whipped off her apron and thrust it at Regina. "You're on the grill. Don't try anything fancy."

"Yeah, God forbid I do something crazy, like use real herbs or make my own mayonnaise," Regina muttered. She wrapped the apron strings around her narrow waist and shook salt over the clam strips, bumping Margred out of the way. "What are you still doing here?"

Margred bristled defensively. "Waiting for Caleb."

"Aww, that's so sweet."

She bared her teeth in a smile. "If you mock me, I will bite you."

Sympathetic laughter lightened Regina's angular face. "Yeah, yeah, sorry. Sucks, doesn't it?"

"What?"

"This. Men. Sex." Regina arranged clams and fries in a basket, somehow making a lettuce leaf and a few citrus wedges look like an elegant presentation. "Ticket up," she yelled through the window.

"I like sex," Margred said.

"Me, too. If I can remember back that far." Regina scowled at the next ticket and dumped a load of precut frozen fries into the wire basket. "But it makes you stupid. I always swore I wouldn't be one of those needy females who wasted her life waiting for some guy to acknowledge her existence. Then I met Nick's father and—*bam!*—I'm trembling in the prep line, all breathless if he so much as smiles at me."

Margred felt a shoot of curiosity, a tendril of concern,

cautiously unfurling within her. As if Regina was a friend. Her first human female friend. As if she, too, were developing roots in this place. "What happened with Nick's father?"

Regina shrugged. "Turns out he had even more trouble acknowledging Nick's existence. I got tired of waiting for him to, and I came home."

Margred felt she should offer something, some admission, in return. "I have never waited for a man before."

"Then you haven't dated in Boston. Those city guys all carry cell phones just so they can call you with excuses about how they're going to be late."

Margred could hardly explain they would not be late for a date with her. No mortal man had ever resisted her allure.

So where was Caleb?

One hour, thirty-six minutes.

She pressed her lips together.

Regina sighed, apparently misunderstanding the reason for her silence. "Listen, you could do worse than Caleb. He's one of the good guys. In fact, when I saw him again, I kind of hoped—"

The door swung open. Caleb loomed on the threshold, his big body radiating heat and frustration, his gaze raking the kitchen.

"You can see him now," Margred interrupted.

Regina flushed. "Oh. Well. Scratch that. Anyway, I—"

But Margred was no longer listening. The relief she felt at Caleb's return overwhelmed her. Annoyed her. She was not accustomed to caring for anyone. How would she bear it?

How did he?

"You're late," she said.

"Yeah." He didn't apologize. His face was hard and tired. "You're here."

She raised her chin. "Obviously."

His eyes, deep and turbulent as the sea, met hers, and she felt that funny little flutter again in her chest. *Home.*

"Thank you," he said quietly.

She shrugged, disguising the pleasure that look gave her. Her need was too new, too deep, too raw to expose.

"Let's go," he said.

Margred untied her apron.

Regina raised her eyebrows. "And hello to you, too."

But they were gone.

*   *   *

Maggie leaned back against the padded seat in the cockpit of the rental boat. Framed against the silver reflection of the water and the deep blue sky, she was so beautiful Caleb's throat tightened. His chest ached like an old scar.

She had waited for him. This once, at least, she had waited. He allowed himself a small satisfaction, a quiet hope, at that.

She caught him staring and lifted her eyebrows. "Do you know where we are going?"

He busied himself casting off the two stern lines so she wouldn't see the hunger in his eyes. "You said an island three miles east of Seal Cove. I figure we'll know it when we see it."

"If you see it," Maggie said. "Your brother may have cast a glamour."

Caleb settled into the seat beside her, making the small craft rock. Water, dark with shadows and sludge, slapped against the barnacle-crusted pilings. A compound of fuel, fish, salt, and decay wafted from under the dock. "What's that?"

"A glamour." She raised her voice over the low rumble of the engine. "A spell, you would say, to make you look. Or make you look away."

He still had trouble reconciling the brother he remembered with talk of mermaids and magic. "He can do that?"

She nodded. "To discourage visitors."

The dock slid away to starboard as Caleb eased into the waters of the harbor, giving wide berth to a school of sailboats wobbling in the shallows. "You said the island was some kind of way station, right? What good is a rest stop if nobody can find it?"

"Selkies can find it. I can find it."

"Fine. Then you can navigate," Caleb said.

Maggie shook out her hair, lifting her face to the wind. "As long as you do not expect me to drive."

"Not a chance."

She narrowed her eyes.

Caleb smiled blandly, rewarded an instant later when she chuckled and relaxed against her cushioned seat.

"Perhaps you are right," she conceded. "I would rather learn to sail anyway."

"I could teach you," he offered steadily. "If you stay." Their gazes met and held, the unspoken plea trembling between them. *Stay.*

She looked away, a flush climbing her cheeks. In the distance, a single kayaker struck out for open water, paddles glistening in the sunlight. "Who taught you?"

Caleb recognized and accepted the change of subject. "To pilot a boat? My father. I started going out with him— working stern—the summer I turned ten."

The year his mother left them.

He steered to avoid the strings of buoys, orange and white, red and yellow, that bobbed above a likely ledge. Fifteen years since Caleb worked the lines, and he still recognized the individual markings of each lobsterman's traps, still heard his father's voice name them, *Tibbetts, Dalton, Spratt . . .*

He didn't want to think about Bart. Not now. He didn't want to remember his father taking Lucy to the sitter's so they could go out on the boat together, just the two of them, and watch the sun rise over the sea and feel, in the quiet before dawn, that maybe the day held promise after all.

Caleb's hands tightened on the wheel. He didn't like the doubts that stirred inside him like something ugly crawling on the ocean bottom.

And he hated the question he had to ask, the question that had burned a hole in his gut since he'd stumbled on his father lurking in the restaurant alley.

He asked anyway.

It was his job.

"My father—he resented my mother for leaving. Is it possible the demon knew that? Used it. Used my father?"

"Possessed him, you mean?"

Caleb didn't flinch. "Yes."

"No," Maggie said certainly.

Caleb held himself very still, not daring yet to believe. "How can you be sure?"

"Because I would know. Living in the same house, breathing the same air ... I would smell it. Sense it. Caleb ..." She put her hand on his arm until he met those great, brown, perceptive eyes. "I would know," she repeated quietly.

Some of the tension leached from his muscles. His hands eased their death grip on the wheel. "Right. All right. Thanks."

They rounded the rocky point, plowing the deep blue water, leaving white-capped furrows in their wake. The Atlantic sparkled as far as the horizon. The breeze snatched at the dark streamers of Maggie's hair and molded her clothes to her body. She looked like some exotic figurehead sprung to life, full-breasted, bold, and gorgeous. The embodiment of every sailor's fantasy, every dream of home.

Caleb's chest constricted. Would she stay? Or would she go, taking his dreams and his heart with her?

He cleared his throat. "That's Whittaker's place."

She turned her head, studying the expanse of glass and shingle squatting on the headland. Turned back to smile at him, memory glinting in her eyes. "I recognize the cliff."

Oh, yeah. That cliff.

Where Caleb had found her swimming with the dolphins.

Where he'd backed her against the rocks and put his tongue in her mouth, his hands up her skirt.

He licked salt from his lips. "I went there today. To his house."

He watched, both glad and sorry, as the awareness in her eyes shifted. Sharpened. "Why?"

"His place overlooks the beach where you were attacked," Caleb said evenly. "He wasn't at the school assembly that night. He doesn't have an alibi for last night either."

She scowled at him. "And you went to his house? Alone?"

"I never got past the front door. He claimed he didn't feel well enough for company. Or questions either."

Her frown turned thoughtful. "If a demon has him . . . he may not be eating much. Or sleeping. The children of the fire are rarely considerate of their hosts."

"That would explain why he looks like shit," Caleb said grimly. "Unfortunately, it's not enough to convince a judge that Whittaker could be a murderer."

"But it convinced you."

Caleb hesitated. "Not . . . entirely. Not by itself. Look, in this job you've got to learn to trust your instincts. I went to his house, no bloodstains on the rug, not a damn thing out of place. Hell, I can smell pine cleaner from the fucking porch." Caleb shook his head, remembering. "This guy is smiling at me, closing the door in my face, and I see his fish tank. He's got one of those big ones. Expensive, like you'd see in a dentist's office, with the lights and the bubbles and the fancy plants. Well." Caleb swallowed. "It was empty."

"So, there was no water."

"Plenty of water," Caleb said grimly. "Filter running. Lights on. But the fish . . ." He stopped. Hard to explain, out here on the gentle chop of the sunlit sea, what made this one detail so chilling, so compelling. "All the fish were gone. I could see losing one or two. Hell, I can't keep a goldfish alive. But to lose them all, all at once like that, is . . ."

Disturbing.

Psychotic.

"Out of character," Caleb concluded.

"Not for a demon," Maggie said.

A long look passed between them. He felt the cold in the marrow of his bones.

"Right." He drew a long breath into tight lungs. "I don't have to worry about a warrant, then."

Her big eyes darkened with confusion. "I don't understand."

He had fought before, when the mission was unclear and the stakes weren't personal. This was a no-brainer.

"If Whittaker is what you say he is, this case is never going to trial," he said quietly. "It can't. Even if Whittaker could be convicted, I can't risk turning a demon loose on the prison population."

"What will you do?"

"Eliminate him. If I can."

He throttled down. Three miles out, the winking, wrinkled sea spread to the horizon, every swell blending into the next. The boat rocked, lulling his senses. But something about this stretch of water anchored his attention. A whisper of surf, a whiff of pine . . .

He watched a gull plummet out of the sky and disappear into . . . nothing, and knew. He felt the rock pushing up from the ocean bottom, poking through the surface like broken bones, and looked to Maggie for confirmation.

She nodded. "Here."

As if her word had raised a curtain, land began to form out of the flat and featureless sea: a jumble of rock, a curve of shore, a line of dark firs marching down to the water like a series of descending notes.

Caleb released his breath on a short, wondering laugh. "Shit. It's Brigadoon."

A short dock emerged from the haze, jutting from the stony beach, and a tethered boat with furled sails.

His heart quickened. "Dylan's?"

Maggie shrugged.

Okay, Caleb would worry about that when he had to.

He secured the boat. Checked the clip in his gun.

"You cannot shoot a demon." Impatience frayed her voice. Or was it worry?

"Yeah, you said." He holstered his weapon, steadied by the familiar weight at his hip. "So, how do I kill it?"

She frowned at him. "Demons are immortal."

"So are selkies. That didn't stop Whittaker from taking out your friend."

"Because water is matter. Fire is not matter. It has no substance of its own. It cannot be destroyed. It can only be contained."

"Or extinguished."

Her mouth opened. Shut. "Yes."

"So, what do I have to do?"

"You should not do anything. I should—I must—bind him."

"Bind him how? You're not selkie now."

Her lips drew back. "The demon stripped me of my pelt. Not my power. I will find a way."

"Meaning you don't have a clue," he guessed.

"At least I have a chance," Maggie snapped.

"Sure, we have a chance." A soldier had to believe that, just as he had to believe some things were worth fighting for. "It would up our odds if we could get our hands on that pelt."

"Why?"

"Exit strategy. Things go south, at least you can get away."

She frowned. "Using Gwyneth's pelt?"

"She doesn't need it anymore. Unless you people have rules against that sort of thing."

"I suppose . . ." Margred shook her head. "Selkies do not think that way. If the pelt came to me, it would be my gift to accept, the way I accept the rain or the sunrise or the bounty of the tide."

"There you go, then," Caleb said with satisfaction.

"My running away does not defeat the demon."

"Right. That's why I'm going back to kill the son of a bitch."

*   *   *

He had not heard her at all, Margred thought in despair.

Despite the swaying deck, his feet were firmly planted. The sun lay heavy and golden as a knight's armor on his shoulders. This strong, honorable man was prepared to kill for her.

Or die.

She shivered.

She had never acknowledged the claims of other partners to her loyalty or affection. Caleb had both.

She had never understood commitment or admired courage until she saw them in him. His example had challenged her. Changed her.

Margred narrowed her eyes. And now, she thought, he would just have to accept the consequences.

He was woefully mismatched in this fight. Somehow, she must convince him this was her battle.

"You cannot do this," she said.

His jaw set. "Yeah, I can. Fire needs an air supply, right? Or it goes out."

She blinked. "I—yes, I suppose."

"So, I crush his airway. Slit his throat. Cut off his head. He can't breathe . . ." Caleb shrugged. "He dies."

Margred stared. Easy for humans to contemplate death when their own lives were so short.

Or did the very brevity of their existence make life even more precious?

"If the demon dies, his host dies, too," she pointed out. "The human, Whittaker."

Caleb hesitated the barest instant. Long enough for her to read the cost of his decision in his eyes. "Collateral damage. Sometimes the importance of the target outweighs the effect of a strike. Whittaker's hardly an innocent casualty."

"I am not concerned about him. I am concerned for you."

"Honey, I can handle one middle-aged lawyer."

She raised her chin. "And how will you handle being arrested for his murder? What is *your* exit strategy?"

"I'll be fine," Caleb said steadily. "I can argue self defense or something."

She stared at him, baffled and frustrated. How could he dismiss so easily the life he had built with such deliberation, the job that meant so much to him? Didn't he understand the risks he ran?

And that was when she knew.

He understood too well.

He was not worried about his future because he did not expect to survive.

20

THE KEY WAS UNDER A LOBSTER BUOY ON THE front porch.

Just like home. Caleb closed his fingers around the tarnished metal key, wondering what other habits his brother still clung to after twenty-five years.

He raised his other hand to knock. "Anybody home?"

No answer.

"The door is unlocked," Maggie said.

Caleb tried the knob. Sure enough, it turned easily in his hand. "Selkies don't steal?"

She shrugged. "We flow as the sea flows. What one tide brings, another may take away."

Caleb grunted. "I'd like to hear you try to explain that one to a judge."

"Simple." Maggie smiled. "Pelts do not have pockets."

He narrowed his eyes.

"It is a joke," she explained earnestly.

A reluctant smile tugged his lips. "Yeah, I got it."

He'd just never heard her attempt an actual joke before.

Like a four-year-old's knock-knock joke, the effort was clumsy, endearing, and . . . human.

His heart stumbled. He pushed open the door.

Inside, the cabin looked like every other rundown vacation cottage in the state of Maine: the same knotty pine and peeling linoleum, the same rusted hinges and outdated appliances. Mildew grew around the refrigerator door. The shelves held a bottle of ketchup, a moldy half loaf of bread, and most of a case of beer. Caleb wondered where Dylan bought his groceries. Not on World's End.

Maggie wrinkled her nose at the smell. "I do not think Gwyneth hid her sealskin in the refrigerator."

"Right." Caleb closed the door. His brother didn't matter. Maggie mattered.

"I think I should look outside while you search inside," she said.

Caleb regarded the four square walls and narrow hall that led to the—bedroom? Bath? "Not much to search."

Maggie's lips curved. "You will be quick, then."

He didn't like splitting up. But on an island where his brother hadn't bothered to lock the door . . .

"Stay close to the house," he warned. "Where I can see you."

She gave him a limpid look through her eyelashes. "Of course."

That big-eyed routine set off alarm bells in his head.

But she had waited for him at the restaurant. *"Then it seems we are in this together,"* she'd said.

He wanted to trust her.

He had to trust her.

He strode down the hall.

*   *   *

Watching Caleb's tall, strong figure disappear through a doorway, Margred longed to call him back for a word, a look, a kiss . . .

Foolish, feminine, *human* need.

Impatiently, she let herself out the front door and crossed through the sunlit patch of yard, bright with daisies and sow thistle. When she reached the shadow of tall spruce, she cast one last look over her shoulder at the house.

And ran.

*   *   *

Caleb surveyed the room like a crime scene, hands in his pockets, gaze assessing, emotions firmly in check.

If this was Dylan's room, his brother's tastes hadn't evolved in twenty-five years. The navy spread was the same tough, ribbed material that covered the beds at home. The furniture was Vintage Motel. Only the king-sized mattress and an elaborately carved sea chest at the foot of the bed suggested Dylan had grown.

Changed.

A small frame on the battered dresser caught Caleb's eye. He stepped closer, bending to take a look.

Surprise tightened his throat. He recognized that picture. Hell, he was in it, ten years old, with Lucy on his lap. And beside them, scowling at the camera, was thirteen-year-old Dylan.

A memory pressed on Caleb's heart like an old bruise: their mother, laughing and excited as she framed the shot, ordering Dylan to smile. Had she known then that she was leaving? Had she kept the photograph to remind her of the children she'd left behind? Did his brother keep it for the same reasons?

Or was the picture simply like the bedspread and the mold in the kitchen, something Dylan had lived with so long he didn't see it anymore?

Not that Caleb gave a good goddamn about his brother's motivations.

He pushed back the curtain on the closet, revealing a surprisingly up-to-date men's wardrobe, and rifled efficiently through the bureau drawers before turning his attention to the sea chest at the foot of the bed.

His gaze kept skipping over it. Sliding away. Caleb

frowned. This wasn't like the glamour spell placed on the island. He could see the damn thing clearly. But he was oddly reluctant to approach it. Touch it.

Ignoring the recalcitrance in his mind, the tingling of his fingertips, he sank heavily to his knees and raised the lid.

His breath escaped in a silent whistle. *Jackpot.*

Like finding pirate treasure on the beach, a crusader's ransom, the pot of gold at the end of the rainbow. He stared at the pile of gleaming coins stamped with the images of goddesses and kings, Indians and eagles. Pieces of gold shining through rich, mottled strands of . . .

Fur.

A sealskin.

His heart hammered. Gwyneth's pelt? Or Dylan's?

Maggie would know.

He had to tell her.

He'd seen what the demon had done to her dead friend. Maggie complained Caleb didn't know what they were up against, but he understood evil. He was a cop. A soldier. He'd dealt with dead babies and abused wives, executed shopkeepers, blown-up school children. He knew what men could do to one another out of hate or greed, for high-minded, hollow political phrases or in the name of religion.

He had fought with insufficient weapons against enemies who could not be defeated, against poverty and crime and hopelessness, against zealots and insurgents.

He'd fight now because he had to. Because there was no one else, and Maggie could not face this thing alone.

But if they lost, if the situation went literally to hell, he wanted her to be safe. At least the skin would give her a chance to escape, to return to the sea she loved.

And if they won . . .

Caleb lowered the lid of the chest, annoyed to note his hands were trembling. He wouldn't let himself think about what Maggie would do if they won.

*   *   *

Maggie crashed through the wood on the slippery, over-grown path as if the hounds of Hell hunted at her heels.

Or a demon.

Hurry, hurry. Her feet pounded and slid on the carpet of pine needles. Her breathing rasped. In. Out. Her heart hammered in her ears.

She burst from shadow into sunlight. Blinded, she stumbled forward and thumped into something—someone—warm. Solid. Male.

She almost shrieked.

Hard hands gripped her shoulders. "Margred?"

She blinked at Dylan, fresh from the water, his skin like honey in the golden afternoon light, his pelt hitched like a towel around his lean waist. "What are you doing here?" he demanded.

She struggled for air. For explanations. *Hurry.* "I— Leaving."

"What?"

Margred inhaled. "The demon killed . . . Gwyneth of Hiort. Your brother—your brother found out."

"My brother doesn't believe in demons."

She didn't have the breath or time to waste in argument. "Does now. Trying to . . . stop it."

Dylan scowled. "That's absurd. A human can't defeat a demon."

Finally, someone agreed with her. But his words brought no relief. "So I told your brother. He will not hear me. But if I leave, I can draw the demon after me. He is not hunting humans. Caleb will be safe."

Bitter, angry, hurt, betrayed . . . but alive.

Dylan's face was stiff and pale. "You would set yourself as demon bait to save my brother?"

She refused to let him see her wince. "I have a higher opinion of myself than that. I thought to fight."

"You don't have the training. Or the power."

"I don't have a choice."

His black eyes flickered. "You could have come to me.

Or the prince. The birds carried the report of Gwyneth's death. Let Conn send a warden. They have the experience to—"

"Bugger Conn. And his wardens. By the time they show up, the demon may have switched hosts. Your brother could be dead."

The lines bracketing Dylan's mouth deepened. "Where is he?"

"Caleb? At the cottage." She thought of his probable re-action when he found her gone, and a fresh rush of pain and panic swept through her. *Hurry, hurry, hurry.* "I have to go."

Dylan let her pass, but she felt him hard on her heels as she jumped and slid over the rocks. "How did you plan on getting off the island?"

"I can still swim. It is only three miles to World's End."

"Faster by sail," Dylan said. "I'll take you."

"Yes." She did not question his motive in offering. Her mind was fixed on Caleb. She jumped on the dock. "Hurry. I need to disable the other boat."

Dylan stopped. "The powerboat? Why?"

Margred eyed him impatiently. He might comprehend the demon's power, but he had no concept of the warrior spirit that drove his brother.

"Because unless I strand him here, Caleb will go after the demon alone."

*   *   *

Caleb emerged from the cover of trees sweating and seri-ously pissed off. He had wasted precious minutes back at the house searching for Maggie, calling for Maggie, unable to accept she'd simply left him.

Again.

Maybe it made sense for her to comb the beach, but she should have told him her plans, damn it.

He scanned the flat seascape of black rock and bright water. Nothing moved on the beach but the wind and the blowing yellow tops of goldenrod.

But on the dock, he spotted a flutter of movement. A flash of skirt. *Maggie.* His lungs inflated with relief and sweet sea air. For a moment everything was okay.

Only for a moment.

She was stepping onto the deck of a boat. A sailboat. Dylan's boat. And Dylan was with her, working the lines.

Caleb's whole body went rigid. He didn't cry out. Didn't protest. This was, after all, what he had expected, what he'd known and feared all along.

He didn't ask what she thought she was doing either. Her plans were suddenly, painfully clear.

The sail rattled up the main mast. The boat jerked and quivered like a pony at the end of its tether. Maggie shook her long hair free in the wind, glancing back at the beach. Caleb knew the second she saw him. Her deep brown eyes widened. Her lips parted in distress.

He stomped toward the dock, cursing his limp and the wary look in those eyes, and spoke to her, only to her, not even acknowledging the one at her side. "Get off the boat."

She bit her lip. "I am sorry."

First a joke, and now an apology. She was making all kinds of progress. *Fuck.*

He gauged the twelve feet of water separating the boat from the dock. Even with a whole leg and a running start, he couldn't jump that far.

Urgency tightened his throat. He clenched his hands into fists. "Don't do this."

The sail fluttered and snapped, preparing to take her away from him.

"I must."

He held her gaze, desperate to make her understand. "You said we were in this together. Damn it, Maggie—"

"She's leaving," Dylan interrupted. "Get over it. It's not the first time."

"You shut the fuck up," Caleb snarled.

Maggie gripped the side of the boat, her knuckles white. "I love you," she said across the yards of open water.

The words should have made him feel better. They made

everything worse. A storm of need and rage and terrible fear howled in his empty chest.

"You picked a hell of a way to show it," he said.

Did he imagine it, or did her eyes fill with tears?

"You will be safe here," she assured him, while the boat strained and shuddered against Dylan's hold. The sail flapped frantically behind her like a trapped bird. "The glamour will shield you until I come back."

"When?" The single word cracked like a gunshot.

She flinched. "After. As soon as I can."

After she confronted the demon, she meant.

Assuming she survived.

"Maggie, for God's sake . . ." He was terrified for her. Furious. "If you love me, you've got to trust me. Trust us. Don't do this alone."

Dylan stood beside her, a possessive hand on her shoulder. "She's not alone. She's with her own kind now."

"You son of a *bitch*." Caleb lurched for the end of the dock.

And the boat leapt into the wind and away.

* * *

Caleb leaned over the exposed power head of the outboard motor, scowling at the tangle of loose wire where the spark plugs should be.

He wanted to rip something—the engine, his brother—apart with his bare hands.

Maggie was gone.

And he was trapped on fricking Brigadoon, unable to protect her, too far away to help her, deprived of the resources and procedures that would let him maintain even the reassurance of action, the illusion of control.

His hand tightened on the wrench. He'd scraped his knuckles on the swivel bracket. Blood and marine grease smeared his hands.

He should have told her about the pelt.

She hadn't stayed for him, but she might have for the pelt. He could have used it as a bargaining chip to force her to take him with her. If that didn't work, he would have given her the damn thing to protect her.

He would have given anything, done anything, to protect her.

But she was gone.

He rubbed at his face, at his eyes, which burned from the glare off the water and stung with unshed tears.

"Get over it. It's not the first time . . . She's with her own kind now."

Why the hell hadn't Dylan given her the pelt?

Caleb squinted out to sea, the gears of his cop's mind turning and engaging. What had his brother worn on the boat? Not a lot. Some kind of caveman fur at his waist.

So the pelt wasn't his.

Did he even know it was hidden in his bedroom? Or had Gwyneth placed the sealskin in the chest herself?

A blaze on the water riveted Caleb's gaze—the sun, striking a fiberglass hull or a lifted sail. His chest expanded with sudden, stupid hope.

Not a sail, he saw as the boat approached over the waves. The profile—red and fast—was too low. He could hear the buzz of a motor.

Caleb straightened slowly, prepared to watch the vessel pass him by.

But as the boat streaked closer without shifting course, his hoped morphed and grew. This could be his ticket off the island.

Caleb raised an arm to wave, but the boatman, a stick figure in the cockpit, didn't respond to his hail.

Of course not. *"The glamour will shield you until I come back."*

He reached for the open emergency kit on the deck behind him. Caulking gun, screwdriver, flashlight, matches . . .

Flares.

His hand closed on a long gold cylinder.

Glamour this, he thought with grim satisfaction.

The red signal arced and smoked into the sky.

Caleb watched the oncoming boat, his heart in his throat

and the sun in his eyes, and all he could think was, *Please*—a prayer to the God he hadn't had time for since Mrs. Pruitt's long-ago Sunday school class.

Please, God, let him see me.

Please let me get back in time to save her.

The boat slowed and swerved to approach the dock.

Caleb expelled his breath in a rush of relief and gratitude. *Thank you, thank you, thank*—

He froze.

God hadn't answered his prayers after all.

Because the man piloting the boat, with jerky movements and a fixed, bright smile, was Bruce Whittaker.

21

❧

MARGRED GAZED AT THE WATER RUSHING OFF
the bow, her stomach churning and her emotions in turmoil.

Dylan's hand rested on her shoulder. She shook it off.

"Your pardon," he said stiffly. "I thought to comfort
you."

She had not forgiven him for his taunt to his brother. Or
perhaps she had not forgiven herself.

"I do not need your comfort," she said coldly. "All I require of you is transportation."

"I should transport you to Caer Subai," Dylan muttered.

"Try it, and I am over the side before you trim your
sails," she warned.

His mouth tightened. "You would be safe there."

"I would be trapped. I have no pelt. I could never return
to the sea."

"All the more reason to consider Sanctuary. Without
your pelt, you will age and die. At least at the prince's court
you would not grow old."

Margred watched the horizon. Day after day after day after day, all the same, blending together. Never to grow old, never to die. *Never to see Caleb again?*

The prospect of eternity without him stretched before her like the cool, damp tunnels and corridors of Caer Subai. Echoing. Empty.

Like her life before she met him.

She shuddered. "I would rather die than live without pleasure or purpose."

Or love.

"You could have children," Dylan said.

Ah. Margred closed her eyes, struck to the heart by a vision of a son with Caleb's sea green eyes, a daughter with his sunlit smile.

She shook her head. "I told you once I have no ambition to be part of the prince's breeding program."

Dylan watched her intently, his expression cloaked. "There are other candidates for stud."

"None that tempt me." Her gaze traveled the foamy trail that led to the island and Caleb, his image drawing her as surely as the moon drew the tides. "Except for your brother."

"He's not my brother. He can be nothing to you. You can't look back."

Far to starboard, a red powerboat buzzed over the water like a hornet.

"Did your mother ever regret leaving your father?" Margred asked. "Did you never miss your home and your family?"

"We are selkie," Dylan pronounced. "We do not regret."

We flow as the sea flows. So it had been for seven hundred years of her existence. Why, then, did she feel trapped by the current, carried in completely the wrong direction?

Her mind returned to Caleb standing rigid on the dock, his fists clenched and his eyes bleak. She felt him like a weight at her heart, like the pull of the moon on the tides, and regret welled and spilled from her heart like blood.

"Perhaps then I am no longer selkie," she said softly.

Dylan scowled. "If so, my brother has succeeded where the demon failed. He has destroyed you."

Margred looked at him, surprised. She understood him. Once she would even have agreed with him. Selkies were among God's First Creation, superior in every way to the humans who strived and prayed and died.

And yet . . .

And yet.

Her beliefs had changed. She had changed, in her sinews and tissues, in the workings of her mind, in the depths of her heart. Caleb had changed her through some strange alchemy of soul. He had inspired her to courage and taught her to love.

For she did love him, with everything that was in her. But she had not trusted him. She had not believed in him the way he believed in her, the way he accepted her, the way he loved her. He had tried to tell her. *"If you love me, you've got to trust me. Trust us. Don't do this alone."* But she had not listened.

"Caleb did not destroy me," she said. "He made me."

"Made you human," Dylan spat.

Margred smiled, her heart suddenly sure. "Yes. Turn the boat around."

* * *

The thing that wore Bruce Whittaker's face smiled at Caleb, eyes flickering over the boat, the dock, the beach. Searching, Caleb thought. Looking for Maggie.

His hand went automatically to his gun.

"Chief," said the thing with Whittaker's mouth.

"Who are you?" Caleb asked.

The eyes widened. Whittaker's pale gray eyes, dancing with dreadful enjoyment. "Don't you know?"

"I recognize the face," Caleb said, angling his body, easing his weapon from its holster. "I didn't catch the name."

"Oh, very good," the thing approved. "You may call me Tan."

"Tan. Right," Caleb said, and shot him.

Or tried to.

The slide clicked uselessly in his hand.

"It won't work," Tan informed him. He lifted a revolver—.357 Magnum, plenty of stopping power there, the homeowner's defensive weapon of choice—from the powerboat's console and leveled it at Caleb's chest. "This, however, will. Throw your gun in the water."

Caleb's grip tightened. *Never surrender your weapon. Keep talking.* "Nice trick."

"Thank you. I suppressed the ignition of the primer in the cartridge. I could as easily explode it in your hands. But I might have use of them later."

Them. His hands? Caleb fought a chill at the thought of the demon using him. Using his hands.

"How's that?" he asked.

"You have something I want," Tan said from the deck of the boat.

He couldn't touch him. Reach him. Not yet. But like a criminal impressed with his own cleverness, the thing enjoyed the sound of its own voice. Caleb could use that. "Maybe we could bargain."

Tan smiled, a twist of facial muscles that revealed all of Whittaker's teeth. "I'd rather hear you beg."

Caleb's palms were sweating on the butt of the gun. Blood crusted his knuckles. "That didn't work too well for you with your last victim. Or you wouldn't be coming after me."

The demon hissed.

"Come on," Caleb goaded. "Make me an offer."

"Your life for the pelt."

The pelt. *Gold coins shining through the rich, mottled strands of fur.* Maggie's hope for escape.

Caleb gave a quick shake of his head. *No.* As if he held the power here instead of a worthless gun. As if he wasn't staring into the blind, black eye of a .357 Magnum in the hands of a creature that couldn't be killed. "We both know you won't let me live."

Tan shrugged, not bothering to deny it. "Then . . . a quick death."

Keep talking. Keep thinking. There had to be a way out of this. The fight never went the way you wanted it. You had to stay flexible.

"And in return, you want . . ."

"The selkie Gwyneth's sealskin. Yes."

"Why? She's dead."

"Let's say I want it to . . . remember her by."

Caleb fought another shudder of revulsion. Something didn't add up. The demon had burned Maggie's sealskin. It didn't make sense he would preserve Gwyneth's.

Like anything about this situation made sense. *Think. Talk.*

"You don't strike me as the sentimental type."

"My actions and my nature are none of your concern."

"I think you fucked up," Caleb said, deliberately provoking. *Keep him talking. Distract him. Find an out, an opening.* "I think she died before you got your hands on her pelt, and now you're screwed."

"She was weak." Tan spat the words. The muzzle of his gun wavered. "Her death was . . ."

"A mistake?" Caleb prodded.

The demon stiffened. "An inconvenience."

"So you didn't want her dead?"

"I wanted her *ended*." He waved the gun for emphasis. "The death of her body is a bare ripple in her existence. Her people will not care as long as the bitch can be sea born."

Caleb eyed the waving muzzle. A gun was only as effective as the person holding it. "You *want* her people pissed off at you?" he asked, taking a half step forward.

"Not at me. At you. The children of the sea are too tolerant of humankind. You overrun the earth, you pollute the water, you violate the very air, and still the elements suffer your existence. 'Because the Creator wills it so.' " Tan's mimicry was savage. "The sea king has wasted centuries in dreams and denial. His heir is too cautious to act. But they cannot ignore the deliberate destruction of their kind. Not when their numbers are declining."

The demon sounded like a fucking terrorist. As if wrapping an act of violence in self-justification and a noble cause somehow vindicated the death of the innocent.

Caleb controlled his anger. "So you disguise yourself as human, kill a selkie, and hope the humans get blamed."

"You will be blamed. Your own kind suspect you already. And when more die, even that selkie fool King Llyr will be convinced of your guilt."

Tension clamped on Caleb's neck. Pounded in his temples. *When more die . . .*

Maggie.

He had to stop this thing before it reached Maggie. Before she realized Whittaker wasn't on World's End and came looking for him.

He slid another foot forward, gauging the distance (*too great*) and his chances (*not good*).

Keep talking.

"Why would they care? I'll be dead. You kill me, that evens the score."

Whittaker's mouth flapped open. For a second, Caleb dared hope he'd gotten through to him or to the demon possessing him.

"Their deaths will not end with your death," Tan said, rallying. "And by taking your life, I will convince the selkie prince that our interests lie together."

One step closer. All he needed was a distraction. A bird, a boat, another fucking flare . . .

"Caleb!" Maggie's cry rang over the water.

Whittaker's head jerked. Good enough.

Caleb dove low and hard for the lawyer's stomach and crashed with him onto the deck.

*   *   *

The blast of the shot echoed over the water.

Margred sobbed. "Hurry!"

The boat sprang forward as Dylan summoned his power, calling the wind to fill the sails. Margred clutched the side with both hands, fear congealing in her stomach. Fear and guilt. She knew what Caleb faced. She should never have left him.

Caleb and the thin man—Whittaker?—rolled around the cockpit, thrashing and thumping into the seats and sides.

At least he was alive. Bleeding? Shot?

Her throat constricted. She could not *see*.

She lurched to her feet to get a better look, nearly pitching overboard as the sailboat came about.

"Damn it, sit," Dylan barked.

She dropped to a seat, her heart forcing its way to her throat. "Hurry."

Over the rush of wind and water, through the roar in her head, she heard a scuffle. Fists. Grunts. Something thudded hard against the powerboat's console. She flinched.

Dylan moved around her, working the lines with tight-lipped grace, his lean body gleaming with sweat and sunlight. Margred barely noticed him. All her attention was on the other boat. The other boat and Caleb.

She strained to see him, to touch his spirit, to reassure herself he was alive.

And then she felt it, acrid as ashes blowing in the wind, ominous as a stain in the water. *Demon.*

Her heart plummeted from her throat to her stomach. Her hands twisted in her lap.

Dylan sensed it, too. He looked at her, his face white. "Swamp them."

Summon the seas and bury them?

Margred shook her head. "I cannot. Not without capsizing the boat and drowning your brother."

"Do it," Dylan said. "Or I will."

She snarled. She could hear the sounds of struggle, a gasp, a thump, a grunt of pain. *Honey, I can handle one middle-aged lawyer.*

But Whittaker would fight with the strength of the possessed. And Caleb could be hurt. Wounded. Bleeding.

Margred stretched shaking hands toward the dock. "I must bind him. The demon."

"How?" Dylan demanded.

She was not listening.

Desperation flooded her veins. Her mind swam with fear. She pushed her worry aside, diving below the frantic surface of her thoughts, reaching deep within for the clear wellspring of power that bubbled from her soul. The magic responded, flowing over and in her like music, like water, fluid, sparkling, irresistible. Her element. Hers. With a glad cry, she opened her mouth to drink it in, flung wide her arms to embrace it.

The boat bumped into the dock, jarring her concentration.

Dylan swore.

Margred opened her eyes.

Caleb was pinned against the side of the boat, one arm raised to deflect the demon's blows. Shot. He'd been shot. His shoulder bloomed black with blood. His lip was split and bleeding. Whittaker loomed over him with a fierce, fixed grin, his fists battering, bruising. Hard. Again.

Each dull impact struck her soul. The magic shattered and fled, leaving her empty, human, helpless. She wanted to throw up.

The demon's presence reached across the water like a furnace blast. Her courage dried up. Her resolution evaporated. Caleb warded the demon's fists with his injured arm, his good hand wrapped around the demon's throat. But blood dripped from his shoulder into the sea, and his arm trembled. He could not hold Hell at bay forever. He could die. He was dying.

"Help him," Margred screamed at Dylan.

Dylan vaulted from the boat.

She stared at Caleb's fingers gripping, pressing on the cords and vessels of the demon's neck. Fighting—still—as the demon battered him with its fists, as his life blood oozed away. She did not feel any braver. But she could not let him fight alone. With a sob, she summoned her pathetic store of human courage, gathered up the remnants of her selkie magic.

The demon's punches slowed. It scratched at Caleb's hands, trying to pry his fingers from around its throat. Whittaker's eyes widened and bulged. His body jerked. Shuddered.

Fire shot to the sky, rushing upward from the boat, a geyser of orange and red, a gush of smoke. The reflection flickered in Whittaker's eyes, as if the fire were in his head, as if he burned from the inside out.

Margred flung her arms wide, casting her spirit like a net toward the flame. Power shimmered at her fingertips. For a moment, magic hung suspended in the air, sparkling like water droplets.

Dylan raised the gun by its muzzle and wielded it like a club against the back of Whittaker's head.

As suddenly as that, it was over.

The blaze died. The demon's presence snuffed out, extinguished. A breeze wandered from the sea, sweet and salt, dispelling the mist of magic. Margred drew her breath on a sob and scrambled over the side, intent on one thing.

Caleb.

He staggered upright. Groaned. Whittaker's body slumped at his feet.

Relief and pain and tenderness flooded Margred's chest. Her eyes swam with unfamiliar moisture. She blinked it away, stepping over the body on the deck to reach Caleb's side. She had to touch him, to reassure herself he was safe.

With trembling fingers, she brushed the hair back from his forehead, stroked the swelling around his eyes and his poor, split lip.

They both winced.

"Are you all right?" she asked.

He captured her fingers and brought her hand to his lips. The gesture made moisture well again in her eyes. "I'm fine. You?"

"He shot you," she said, her voice rising in indignation.

"Yeah." Caleb eased his good arm around her waist. "Hurts like a son of a bitch, too. But I've had worse."

She buried her face against his shirt. His arm tightened. She rested against his heart, absorbing his strength, the sheer comfort of his presence. He pressed a kiss to her hair.

"What did you do?" Dylan demanded.

Caleb spoke over her head to his brother. "Crushed his windpipe."

"He's gone."

Caleb nudged the body on the deck with the toe of his boot. "He didn't get far."

"The demon," Dylan said impatiently. "I can't sense him. Where is he?"

Alerted by the tone of Dylan's voice, Margred raised her head from Caleb's chest, disturbed by the rhythm of his heart, alarmed by a vague awareness of something . . . wrong. She tested the air.

"I do not smell demon," she said.

Only a tickle at the back of her throat, a sly hint of sulfur on the wind . . .

"That's good." Caleb stood solid as a monument, the blood sliding down his arm to stain the deck. "Isn't it?"

Margred exchanged looks with Dylan, worry worming in her chest.

"Demons are immortal," Dylan said. "He wouldn't choose to die with his human host."

Caleb frowned. "I thought you bound him."

Margred flushed. "There wasn't time."

It sounded like an excuse, even to herself.

Caleb nodded, accepting her rationale.

Dylan was less forgiving. "He didn't just disappear."

The creases deepened on Caleb's forehead. "Why not? Demons don't have matter, you said."

"Not their own," Margred answered. A creeping sense of *wrongness* burrowed to her heart. "They borrow the form and substance of others."

She stepped from the comforting circle of his arm to cast

her senses wider, trying to track that disturbing trace of hell-fire clinging to the boat. But it was stifled, banked, hidden from her somehow.

Dylan cocked an eyebrow.

She shook her head, frustrated. *Nothing.*

"Then I know where he went," Caleb said steadily. "The demon. Tan."

Margred looked at him in surprise. He stood rigid above Whittaker's body, his face carved in stone. His right arm hung uselessly from his shoulder. His left hand clenched at his side.

"Where?"

"What are you talking about?" asked Dylan.

Caleb drew a short, sharp breath. "I feel something—I can feel him—pushing at my brain." He met Margred's gaze, his eyes as stark as death. "You can't find him because the demon found another host. He's in me."

22

"I CANNOT DO IT. THE DEMON'S SPIRIT IS TIED—tangled—with yours." Maggie's face was white as bone. Her voice shook. "I cannot separate out the threads to bind him."

Well, shit.

Caleb stood, absorbing the blow, accepting the truth of her words. He could feel Tan working within him, spinning along his sinews, knotting up his will, laying down lines of fire sticky as spider floss and strong as steel cable.

Maggie's gaze sought his. Fear swam in her eyes. "There are magic handlers among our people. Wardens. We could send for one to help you."

Caleb swayed on his feet, ignoring the burn in his blood. His brain felt thick as cotton. The demon inside him snickered and spun, sending red-hot filaments twining along his nerves, choking out thought and memory. Like that nasty dwarf thing in one of Lucy's fairy tales. What was its name?

Caleb frowned, struggling to remember, wresting bits and pieces of himself from the demon's control.

Rumpelstiltskin, that was it. The story his sister liked was Rumpelstiltskin.

"I don't think we can wait," he said.

Maggie took his hand. Caleb appreciated her attempt at comfort. Against the fever rioting inside him, her fingers felt cool and strong. But how could she bear to touch him, knowing who—what—inhabited his body?

"Perhaps the prince . . ." Maggie bit her lip. "Conn's skills are greater than mine."

"And he is not so . . . intimately connected with the demon's host," Dylan said.

Maggie growled low in her throat.

"But you could do it," Caleb said to Maggie. "If this—thing weren't inside me."

"I . . . If I could drive him out, yes. But I don't have the power."

"That's okay," Caleb said. "I do."

"You?" Dylan's voice dripped scorn. "You're human."

Exactly. He was human. And so he could do one thing Maggie and Dylan couldn't do.

He could die.

Caleb looked down at his hands, sticking from his wrists at odd angles like a department store mannequin's, awkward, alien, not his. Not wholly his any longer. Grasping the heavy slack of the anchor chain, he raised it from the deck of the boat. *Don't think about it. Do it. Do it before he can stop you.*

Caleb wrapped the chain around his waist.

Comprehension blossomed in Maggie's eyes. She caught her breath. "No. Oh, no."

"I saw you with the dolphins that day," he said to her. "You have power in the water."

"What are you going to do? Drown yourself?" Dylan asked.

"Yes." *While he still could.* Grimly, Caleb hauled on the chain. Blood smeared the links. His shoulder was on fire. "He won't stay to die with a human host, you said."

Dylan's eyes narrowed. "So Margred traps the demon as he escapes? It might work."

"I can't let you die!" The words burst from Maggie.

Her fierceness warmed Caleb. But it didn't change anything. He was a soldier, trained to weigh the cost of every action against its outcome. He had served under a desert sun where the shadows and the choices sprang in sharp black and white. If he hesitated now, if he failed, Maggie would die at his hands, and all hell would break loose—literally.

Caleb hitched another loop of chain around his waist, his good hand yielding reluctantly to his commands like an unfamiliar prosthesis. He could feel the demon's will eating through him like worms feasting on a corpse. What would happen when they were seated in his brain? When they reached his heart?

"There are worse things," he said evenly, "than death."

He tugged on the chain, testing it. He wouldn't escape that. Not underwater, with a wounded arm. He couldn't break it either, even with the demon's strength.

Caleb took another deep breath, looking around at the bright, flat water, at his brother, silent on the dock, at Maggie's pale face and dark, expressive eyes. Even frightened and exhausted, she was the most beautiful woman he had even seen. He would have liked to kiss her one last time.

He didn't want the demon inside him to touch her. To contaminate her. He could feel its contagion raging like an infection in his blood, taking him over, making him into something he hated and feared. He thought of what Whittaker had done to the selkie Gwyneth and shuddered.

There are worse things than death.

Yes. His head throbbed. But he would have liked to live. He would have wished to spend the rest of his life with her.

"Gwyneth's pelt is in the sea chest at the foot of Dylan's bed," he told her. "Take it, and be free."

"Don't worry," Dylan said. "I'll take care of her."

Bastard.

Maggie turned on him, eyes flashing. "Coward. Ass. Take care of your brother."

"I can't," Dylan protested. "He's right. This is the best way—the only way—to defeat the demon."

"You cannot simply let him die."

"I have no choice."

At least his brother understood.

Or maybe—the thought bit Caleb like a fly—Dylan was just glad to get rid of him.

Maggie stamped her foot. "When the demon leaves him, you must bring him up, out of the water."

"His body."

"Him," Maggie insisted. "Save him."

Caleb shook his head. His vision flickered red at the edges. His skull felt squeezed. "No. We can't risk Tan—"

"I will deal with the demon," Maggie said. "Let your brother do his part."

Caleb met his brother's black, unfathomable gaze. "I need to die."

"I know."

"Don't let him take me again."

"I swear."

Caleb nodded, satisfied. Gathering his strength, he shuffled the length of the boat, dragging his heavy limbs like the chain behind him. His skin felt close to bursting.

"Caleb!" Maggie's cry was anguished.

He turned back to look at her. So beautiful. So achingly alive. The sun beat warm on his head. The air on his lips was salty and cool. For precious seconds, every sunlit detail— the blue sky, the silvery dock, Maggie's hair lifting in the breeze—cut sharp and clear as glass.

He didn't shirk from what he was about to do any more than he would shrink from throwing himself on a live grenade to protect his squad. A man did what he had to do.

Out of instinct.

Out of duty.

Caleb held Maggie's gaze for one long, last moment. *For love.*

But he had to act now, while he still could. Before his body wasn't his to command, before the demon took him over, before the sweetness of Maggie's love tempted him past the limits of his strength.

"I love you," he said.

He stepped off the boat.

And the water closed over his head.

*   *   *

Margred knelt on the planks of the dock, staring down at the gray-green water, trying to distinguish the last release of Caleb's breath from the ocean foam. Her heart pounded in her chest, measuring time with each frantic beat.

Two minutes. Three. *Agony.*

How long could he hold his breath underwater?

How long could he survive with his body wracked by a demon and his heart pumping his oxygen-bearing blood into the sea?

She could not bear it. She jumped to her feet. "Now. Bring him up now."

"Steady," Dylan murmured.

Her lips pulled back from her teeth. "This is not working. Bring him up."

Dylan raised one eyebrow. "And waste his sacrifice? No."

She paced the rough boards, straining her senses, casting for a hint of Caleb's presence. She could feel the demon raging beneath the surface, incandescent with hate, blazing with frustration. Beside that outpouring of elemental energy, Caleb's life force was a pale flicker, a tarnished thread stretched almost to breaking point.

He was dying.

Alone.

While she hovered like a vulture above the surface, waiting for his body to shut down so she could bind the demon's escaping spirit.

She twisted her hands together. The reserves in Caleb's lungs must be almost exhausted. How long before they were gone completely and his brain began to die? Another minute? Four?

"If you love me, you've got to trust me. Trust us."

But she had never done anything like this before.

They had failed. *She* had failed, and Caleb and both their peoples would pay the price.

Margred stared at the sun-glazed surface of the ocean, feeling Caleb's courage rise to her in tiny bubbles like breath. *"You can do it. You have power in the water."*

She had power in the water . . .

Taking a deep breath, she jumped, fully clothed, into the sea.

The clothes, she realized almost instantly, were a mistake. Her full skirt wrapped around her legs, impeding her movements as she kicked her way to the bottom. Her human eyes were not designed to work in the filtered light. That was all right. She did not need to see.

Like a fish at the end of a line, she swam through cool, murky water teeming with life, drawn by the glinting thread she recognized as Caleb. Her nostrils were sealed underwater. She could not smell demon. But she felt the elemental's presence like an ache in her sinuses, like ash in her throat. His menace breathed like a beast in the darkness beneath her, baleful, hungry, huge.

Margred shivered, flailing her thin, weak human legs, her long, pale human fingers.

She followed Caleb's dwindling spirit and the demon's dark spoor down, down, to where Caleb's blood curled like a plume of smoke through the water.

Almost . . . *There.*

Her heart stopped.

Caleb drifted in his chains, his strength gone, his air gone, his skin like wax. His body swayed to the gentle urging of the surge like unheard music.

A terrible mix of hope and grief swelled her lungs. Her throat constricted. Her chest burned. Was she just in time? Or too late?

The current nudged Caleb's head, lolling on his neck. His lids lifted lazily.

And the demon looked out of his eyes.

She stumbled back.

Tan, Caleb had named him, or he had named himself. The old Welsh word for "fire." His spirit flamed.

The thin, bright thread connecting her to Caleb snapped. Her mouth opened in a silent cry of grief.

The demon was trapped, drowning, dying with Caleb, but he looked at her with hate and no thought of defeat in his eyes. He was older than she was. She could feel his age press on her, centuries of malice and resentment and power, immortal, elemental. He did not believe he could lose.

Margred's heart quailed. The pressure in her sinuses built.

She did not believe he could lose either.

Tan saw her—another body, another *host*—and hurtled himself at her, a fireball at her head, smoking through the water in a gout of fury and will that sent her tumbling and scraping along the ocean bottom. She fought for balance, for boundaries, for breath.

"You have power in the water."

But she could not *breathe*.

Dimly, she was aware of Dylan's great black seal form plunging through a cloud of bubbles. Too late. Tan's malice overwhelmed her. He was fire, seeking, consuming, hot. He assailed her, the tender tissues of her mouth and eyes, the secret places of her womb and soul, shriveling, probing, possessing. Margred recoiled. He was strong, stronger than she was, an elemental fixed on her destruction. She was only human, and Caleb was dead.

Just for a moment, temptation licked along her nerves and flickered in her brain, a spark, a flame. If Tan took her over, if he possessed her, her demon lover, would she be made immortal again?

"There are worse things," Caleb had said, *"than death."*

Ah.

She stopped thinking. She stopped breathing. She could feel her heart—her puny, human, broken heart—still beating. She was not defeated yet. If Caleb had died . . . Loss shuddered through her. Well, it was up to her to make sure he had not died in vain. She pulled the water to her, called her power to her, drank it in like blood, like wine. Lifegiving. Intoxicating.

She felt the demon's surprise, his pain and surprise, as her magic rose within her like water and flooded her, enveloped her, enveloped them both, forcing him back, forcing him out. She cast her spirit around him, arched like the curl of a wave, shining as pearl.

Tan, I bind you!

She poured her soul in a shining silver membrane that wrapped him, trapped him, like a globe of melted glass. The demon's rage pulsed like a heartbeat through the translucent walls. Colors battled and slid over the curved surface, red and blue, green and gold, as Tan battered and blazed against her. Layer upon layer, each one harder, stronger, more opaque, exhausting her spirit, extinguishing his.

Layer after layer encompassing him, encasing him, in a great, blue green, glowing ball, until the demon's fire snuffed out.

And everything went dark.

*   *   *

Maggie.

She floated like one of the seaborn, a thing of tide and foam, without body or conscious thought. Without pain. Without memory. Was this death? It was very peaceful. *"There are worse things than death."*

Oh, Caleb . . .

A shaft of pain pierced her, light in the darkness. She winced from it, struggling to stay, to drift in the cool, quiet dark.

"Maggie."

The voice disturbed her, hard and urgent, like a stone

flung into a pond. It rippled through her, drawing her toward the light. She floundered, gasping. She did not want to go there. She did not want to remember . . .

Caleb was dead.

"Maggie, honey, come on."

He did not sound dead. He sounded . . . hoarse. Upset.

She opened her eyes and saw his haggard face above her, haloed by the sky. She blinked. Coughed. "Where are we?"

Selkies did not go to Heaven . . .

Caleb made a sound between a laugh and a groan. "On the dock. Dylan pulled you out of the water. He rescued us both."

Dylan wavered into view, a shadow behind Caleb's shoulder. "A waste of effort. You're going to bleed to death anyway. Unless you do something about that gunshot wound. Ah, that brought her around," he said, satisfaction in his voice.

"Shut up," said Caleb.

He was going to bleed to death . . .

Margred struggled to sit. Her hands burned. Her legs bled, scraped raw by the rocks. She hurt everywhere, her joints, her lungs, her throat, her womb, as if the magic filling her had stretched things, moved them around, pushed all her internal organs out of the way.

Caleb looked even worse—drowned, battered, shot—his lips blue, his face stark, his eyes exhausted. Vulnerable.

Worry wrenched her heart.

"You need a doctor." She turned to Dylan. "You must take us in your boat."

"I am at your service, always," Dylan said dryly. "Anything else?"

Caleb shook his head. His face was drawn with pain. "We need to stay here. Radio the marine patrol."

Dylan raised his eyebrows. "Why? I could have you to World's End before their boat gets here."

"A man is dead," Caleb said. "There will be an investigation. I need to stay with the body until the scene is secured."

"Oh, please. Do you really want to involve your human police in what happened here? What are you going to tell them?"

"The truth," Caleb said evenly. "As much as I can. Whittaker followed us here, he shot me, and I killed him in self-defense."

"And how do you plan to explain your long-lost selkie brother?"

"I'm not. I'm not going to mention you at all. I want you and your boat out of here before the police arrive."

"I don't want them here. This is my island."

"Yours."

The brothers faced off like two bull seals on the beach.

"Yes." Dylan's smile flashed like a knife. "A bequest from our mother."

"I searched for you," Caleb said abruptly.

Margred, watching, understood him well enough now to recognize the gift he was offering. Caleb wanted his brother to know he had not forgotten him. The children of the sea flowed as the sea flowed, uncaring and unconnected. But Caleb's roots struck as deep as an oak tree. His shelter extended to everyone around him. In seven hundred years, she had never known anyone as committed, as concerned, as compassionate as Caleb.

"I searched for you both," he continued. "Driver's license, county property tax, graduation records. I never found you."

"I never intended you to," Dylan said coolly. "I don't like visitors."

Caleb nodded, accepting the rebuff. "Then get the hell out. Take your gold and the pelt with you."

Margred's reaction was instinctive, selfish and sharp as a child's who sees her toy taken away. *No. Mine.* Caleb gave the sealskin to *her.* Every intuition honed in seven hundred years of survival told her to snatch it and return to the sea.

"Take it, and be free," Caleb had said when he thought he was dying.

When they both thought he was dying.

But Caleb lived.

Margred's breath snagged. And she could not imagine her life without him.

Dylan scowled. "The pelt is not mine to dispose of. Or yours either."

Caleb rubbed his face with a blood-encrusted hand. "You leave it here while they search the island, somebody from CID could decide it's in violation of the Marine Mammal Protection Act and turn it over to the feds as evidence."

He wasn't trying to take the pelt away. He was trying to save it. Save her. His consideration stung her eyes.

"Fine," Dylan said. "I'll take it. For now." He looked at Margred with flat, black, challenging eyes. "You'll want it when Caleb is through with you."

23

~

THE LONG SUMMER EVENING STRETCHED INTO
night before Caleb pulled into his driveway. Beyond the
black spruce, the ocean sparkled, dark waves caught in a
silver net. The crescent moon, as white as a sail, rode
bright-edged billows of cloud. Beautiful. Peaceful.

Lonely.

He switched off the engine and sat staring at the reflected light in his windows, too sore to move, too weary to
think. Trying to summon the will and a reason to get out of
the Jeep.

He should have gone to his sister's. Maggie was there.

He didn't want to sit alone in the dark, nursing his
wounds and a drink like his father.

But he hurt, and he stank. He needed his pills, a shower,
and a clean shirt. He climbed heavily from the Jeep, setting
off a chorus of pain as all his injuries, new and old, made
themselves heard.

He had refused to be medevaced to the hospital in Rockport. He'd had enough of hospitals. According to Donna
Tomah, the bullet had plowed straight through the fleshy

part of his upper arm, missing the collar bone, the bundle of nerves above it, and a major artery below. He would recover.

Of course, he looked and felt like shit.

Regina's eyes had widened when she saw him. She had dropped by the station to deliver pizza to Sam Reynolds and Evelyn Hall, encamped more or less permanently in Caleb's office. Caleb didn't know if the state cops had been assigned to him as jailors or nurses, but as the evening and the case progressed, Reynolds at least began to treat him more and more as a colleague.

"Wow." Regina set the pizza on the counter above Edith's desk. "The weasel lawyer really kicked your ass, huh?"

"Pretty much," Caleb admitted.

"Mom said to tell you she thought you were tougher than that." Regina's teasing tone failed to disguise the concern in her eyes.

Caleb's smile cracked his split lip. "I am. He had to shoot me before he beat me up."

Regina laughed, as he intended, and fingered the little gold cross around her neck. "Seriously, Cal, everybody's glad you're . . . you know." She stopped, searching for a sentiment that wouldn't violate New England standards of reticence. "Here," she finished.

"Me, too," Caleb had said.

Here on the island.

Here, alive.

He wouldn't be if it weren't for Maggie and his brother.

Dylan had surprised him, Caleb acknowledged as he limped up the walk. He hadn't expected his brother to be there for him at the end. But Dylan had definitely saved his ass. Caleb even had a vague memory of his brother administering rescue breathing—something he was sure Dylan would prefer Caleb forget.

And Maggie . . . Caleb shook his head. He didn't know exactly what she'd done on the bottom of the ocean to defeat Tan, but whatever it was had drained her of color and almost of life. When Caleb came to, she'd been lying cold and stiff on the planks of the dock like an ancient warrior on his shield.

He'd thought . . . Oh, God, he'd been so afraid that he had lost her, that she was gone somewhere beyond his reach, even beyond death. A selkie without a soul. But she'd come back to him.

She'd come back.

Even with the scar fresh on her forehead from the demon's attack, even after seeing what Tan had done to her murdered friend Gwyneth, Maggie had turned to fight. For Caleb's sake. When the chips were down, she hadn't folded. She hadn't run.

Loyalty and grit, Caleb thought. A man couldn't ask for anything more.

Except for her to stay.

He stumbled over something in the shadows of the porch. Somebody had left a package by his front door, a bundle, a—

Sealskin.

Caleb froze, his hands clenching on the thick, coarse fur. Its musk rose in the darkness. Gwyneth's pelt. So his brother had already been by.

Something else to deal with, Caleb thought. Tomorrow. Tonight he just wanted to eat, to sleep, to breathe, to be. To be with Maggie.

After he showered, he would drive to his sister's to find her.

And take the pelt with you? a voice whispered in the back of his mind.

He ignored it. He'd deal with the pelt tomorrow, too.

He unlocked the door and stopped, struck by a smell. Coffee? Freshly brewed coffee in his empty house. A pair of sandals lay in the middle of the living room rug. A breeze blew from an open window in the kitchen.

His heart hammered.

"Maggie?" His voice was hoarse. Hopeful.

She uncurled like a cat from the cushions of the couch, her dark hair soft and loose on her shoulders, wearing a blue dress that flowed over her curves like water. Bare feet. Webbed toes.

The sight of her punched him in the gut.

"There you are," she greeted him. "Are you hungry?"

He was stunned. "You don't have to cook for me."

"I didn't." She tilted her head to smile into his eyes. "I brought dinner home from the restaurant."

Home.

His throat tightened. "That sounds good."

He ran one finger down her warm cheek, as if to assure himself that she was real. Then he did what he had wanted to do eight hours ago on the dock and every second since.

He kissed her.

Her mouth was soft and welcoming. She tasted of coffee and sugar and, impossibly, of the sea. Had she been crying? But he had never seen her cry.

She stood on tiptoe to deepen the kiss, her hand touching the bare skin at the back of his neck, and Caleb stopped thinking, stopped questioning, let himself be totally in the present, in this moment, with her here and eager in his arms. It was enough. It was everything.

When he raised his head, his split lip throbbed softly and Maggie was trembling along the length of his body.

"Dinner can wait," he said.

"It could. I cannot." Her slow smile teased him. "I want to hear about your day."

He cleared his throat. "Now?"

She tugged his hand. "While you eat."

He let her lead him to the kitchen. The scent of the salt wood flowed through the open window. The evidence of her presence was everywhere—a bright towel hung haphazardly on the back of a chair, an empty mug in the sink, a dusting of sugar on the kitchen table. She was here. She was back. A weight rolled from Caleb's shoulders.

She'd lit the emergency candles he kept in case of power failure and laid out a pair of wineglasses left from his first marriage. The trappings of romance? Or simply the way Regina had taught her to set a table?

But Antonia's didn't use candles.

"Sit." Maggie tugged at him again. "Tell me what happened. That woman, the square one—"

"Evelyn Hall."

"She would not let me in to see you."

He watched her open the wine with graceful, practiced movements. "In an investigation, you want to keep the witnesses apart." And the suspects, he thought but did not say. "So they can't make up or change their stories."

Maggie bristled. "You were shot. Do they think you made that up?"

Her fierce defense made him smile. "No, they could see that. One of the techs dug a bullet out of the dock they'll be able to match to Whittaker's gun. But Reynolds knows—suspects—I'm not telling him everything."

The white take-out bag rustled. "What did you tell him?"

Caleb leaned back in his chair. "That Whittaker was afraid you had remembered him. That he came after you to stop you from identifying him as your attacker. Based on that, I suggested they had probable cause to search his house in connection with the other woman."

Maggie tilted her head. "And did they?"

"Yep."

She set a plate in front of him. With a shock of pleasure, Caleb recognized the lobster rolls and tortellini salad he'd served her at their first picnic on the beach. Did she remember?

Of course she did.

She sat opposite him, leaning across the table. "What did they find?"

He set down his fork. "You sure you want to talk about this now?"

"Why not?"

"It's not very"—Caleb paused as the specter of his ex-wife rose to scold him—"pleasant for you to have to deal with."

Maggie's eyes flashed. "Gwyneth's murder was not *pleasant*. Seeing you possessed by a demon chained on the bottom of the ocean was not *pleasant*. This is what is. You have been fighting my battles all day. The least I can do is listen."

Caleb regarded her with wry appreciation. He would never compare her to Sherilee again.

Baldly, briefly, he described what the evidence team had found: tools they believed matched the marks of torture on Gwyneth's body; traces of blood in the floorboards and drains.

"So." Maggie drew a long breath. "It is done, then? This explanation satisfies them? You are not a . . . person of interest any longer?"

"It will take days—weeks—for the crime lab to process all the evidence. But Reynolds told me his lieutenant is already pulling detectives from the case."

Maggie reached across the table and touched the back of his wrist. He turned his hand over, linking his fingers with hers. They sat quietly, holding hands among the dishes. Caleb's chest expanded. His throat ached with a mingled sense of peace and loss. This was what he wanted, what he'd dreamed of. Someone to share the end of the day. Maggie, in his house and in his life.

Her grip tightened on his fingers. She smiled her siren's smile into his eyes. "You are tired. Come to bed."

He was exhausted. And sore.

But not, he discovered when she turned to him under the covers, too tired to love her.

They lay on their sides, facing each other, her leg over his thigh, her breasts brushing his chest. Her eyes were dark and heavy with desire.

Caleb threaded his fingers through her hair, stroking it back from the half-healed scar on her forehead. She cupped his battered jaw, her thumb grazing the puffiness under his eye, and kissed his shoulder above the bandages.

His body responded, thickening, swelling.

"Maggie, I don't know—I've lost a lot of blood," he said awkwardly.

She smiled, feathering a kiss on his broken lip. "It will be all right," she promised.

And it was.

They came together in small, incremental movements, with soft, open-mouthed kisses and quiet, indrawn breaths. He slipped inside her—soft, hot, wet—holding still as she pulsed around him. Tenderness welled. Spilled. *If this was the last time . . .* But he wouldn't let himself think that. To be in this moment, to be with Maggie . . . It was enough. He would make it be enough.

They rocked together, wrapped in each other, lapped in pleasure, until the gathering storm within them broke in ripples and murmurs, soft and welcome as rain. He felt her crest, the sweet contractions milking him, drawing out his own release.

She sighed against his throat.

He exhaled into her hair. "Maggie."

"Love." She rested her palm against his chest. "My love."

He twined his fingers with hers; raised their clasped hands to his lips and then to his heart.

Joined, at peace, they drifted into sleep.

*   *   *

Margred awoke to a great sense of well-being and the sun tickling her eyelids. Something warm and heavy lay on top of the bed covers. She smiled and stretched out her foot.

Not Caleb.

She opened her eyes.

He sat fully dressed on the edge of the mattress. And bundled in front of him was the brindled bulk of Gwyneth's pelt.

Margred felt a chill that had nothing to do with the open window. "What is this?"

"It's yours."

Margred sat up. "No, it's not."

"Gwyneth is dead," Caleb said quietly. "You said you could take her pelt if it came to you. As a gift."

"Yes, but—"

"So I'm giving it to you." Caleb's eyes remained steady on hers. Only his hands clenched in the fur to hide their trembling. "Take it."

Margred regarded him in disbelief. Lovely, noble, exasperating man. "I don't want it. Caleb, when I saw you under the water . . ." *Drifting in his chains, his strength gone, his air gone, his skin like wax . . .* "I thought you had died." Her voice broke, and tears pricked her eyes, hard, real, human tears. She blinked them back impatiently. "I knew then I did not want to live without you."

The grim line of his mouth relaxed. "You don't have to. I'll always be here. I'll love you as long as I live. As long as you'll let me."

She searched his gaze. "And that would be enough for you?"

He inhaled audibly. "It has to be. I'm not my father, Maggie. I don't want to change you. I love you for who and what you are."

Her hands reached over the fur to clasp his.

"Then we have a problem," she said. "I am not . . . what I was."

"Beautiful? Gutsy? Caring? Smart?"

She was pleased he saw her as all those things. But she was not casting for compliments. She needed to make him understand.

"I am not selkie. I do not have my powers any longer."

Caleb's eyes narrowed. "But you bound Tan."

She blinked. "I . . . Yes."

"And you called the dolphins."

She smiled, remembering. "I did, didn't I?"

"Being selkie—it isn't about your skin. It's something deeper. Something inside you. You're different, Maggie. Amazing. Magic." His gaze, his hands, were warm and steady on hers. "You're . . . you."

Margred stared at her hands, linked with his. Her human hands that had learned to wash dishes and set a table and soothe her lover's hurts. Her selkie hands that had summoned the rain and bound a demon.

Was Caleb right?

She was not what she once was.

Maybe she was more.

"Maybe I am not changed," she acknowledged. "But I have grown."

Like a child learning to stand on its own two sturdy legs, like a bride leaving her mother's house, she was ready to leave the cradle and bosom of the sea and walk on solid ground.

"I don't want to visit you to take my pleasure," she continued. "I want a real life with you, to sleep with you and talk with you. To grow old with you. To have children with you."

And she would never leave them, she vowed. She would never leave *him*. She could live on land and still be of the sea.

"How about dying with me?" Caleb challenged her.

She nodded. "I told you. I would not want to live without you."

"Maggie . . ." His eyes were gray and troubled as the northern sea. "I'm not a religious guy. But . . . only humans have souls, you said. Is one life with me enough for you? Is it worth giving up eternity?"

Only humans asked so many questions.

Only humans had such doubts.

And such faith.

Margred smiled. "I love you," she said. "I believe you love me. I do not believe the God of love would let such a thing happen if our love was meant to die with these bodies."

"God help us both, then," Caleb said. "Because I'd go to Hell to get you back."

*   *   *

They stood on a hilltop overlooking the sea, the sweep of horizon sharp and curved as a line drawn by pencil. Below, the boundary between land and sea blurred with every wave that rushed and retreated over the rocks.

Margred shook out her hair, the taste of brine on her lips, her bare feet planted on the sun-warmed soil among the buttercups and blowing grass. In the distance, strings of lobster pots crossed the water like lines of bright embroidery stitches, but no boats, no swimmers, no kayakers broke the far, wide, wrinkled surface of the ocean.

"Maggie." She loved the way he spoke her name. Caleb stood behind her, upright and strong as a lighthouse on the headland. "Are you sure?"

She had never been more certain of anything. "I lived in the ocean for seven hundred years. The sea is in my blood, always. But you are my heart."

She held the sealskin in her arms, the coarse, rippling fur, the warm, sleek weight of it. And when the surf rushed in again, she dropped it into the sea.

A harbor seal popped its bullet-shaped head from the water to watch as the waves plucked and dragged at the bundled pelt, carrying it, rolling and unfolding, out to sea.

Margred sighed. Smiled.

And turned to find Caleb waiting for her, a look in his eyes that made her heart turn over.

"Let Gwyneth have eternity." She gazed into his dear, battered face, more precious to her than the land beneath the wave. "I have you."

He kissed her among the rioting wildflowers while the ocean foamed on the rocks below.

Hand in hand, they descended the sunlit hill.

THE NIGHT THE ONLY ELIGIBLE MAN ON THE IS-
land got married, Regina Barone got drunk.

Getting laid would have been even better.

Regina looked from Bobby Kincaid, whose eyes had
taken on the wet glaze of his beer bottle, to fifty-three-year-
old Henry Tibbetts, who smelled like herring, and thought,
Fat chance. Anyway, on an island with a year-round population of eleven hundred, a drunken hookup at a wedding reception could have serious consequences.

Regina knew all about consequences. She had Nick,
didn't she?

The wedding tent's tiebacks fluttered in the breeze.
Through the open sides, Regina could see the beach where
the happy couple had exchanged their vows—a str
shale, a tumble of rocks, a crescent of sand bord
restless ocean.

Not your typical destination weddi
Maine in August, was hardly Saint Croi

Regina hefted a tray of dirty glassware and then spotted her son, standing beside her mother at the edge of the dance floor, jigging from foot to foot.

She felt her mouth and shoulders relax. The glasses could wait.

Setting down her tray, she crossed the big white tent. "Hey, good-looking."

Eight-year-old Nick turned, and she saw herself in miniature: dark, Italian eyes; thin, expressive face; big mouth.

Regina held out both her hands. "Want to show me what you've got?"

Nick's initial wariness dissolved in a grin.

Antonia Barone took his hand. Her mother was in full Mayor Mode—a hard red slash of lipstick and her two-piece navy dress. "We were just about to leave," Antonia said.

Their eyes clashed.

"Ma. One dance."

"I thought you had work to do," Antonia said.

Ever since Regina had offered to cater this wedding, her mother had been bitching about her priorities. "It's under control."

"Do you still want me to watch him tonight?"

Regina suppressed a sigh. "Yeah. Thanks. But I'd like to have a moment first."

"Please, Nonna," Nick added.

"It's not my decision," Antonia said, her voice suggesting it damn well should be. "Do what you want. You always do."

"Not recently," Regina muttered as they moved away.

But for the next ten minutes, she enjoyed the sight of Nick hopping and sliding, clapping and turning, laughing and carrying on like any other eight-year-old.

The music shifted and slowed.

Couples took their turn on the floor.

And Regina, her sandal straps biting into her toes, delivered Nick back to her mother.

"Midnight for us, kiddo. You go home in the pumpkin coach with Grandma."

He tipped his head up to look at her. "What about you?"

Regina brushed his dark hair back from his face, letting her hand rest a moment on his smooth cheek. "I've got to work."

He nodded. "Love you."

She felt a burst of maternal love under her breastbone like heartburn. "Love *you*."

She watched them leave the white rental tent and climb the hill toward the parking lot, her square mother and skinny son casting long shadows on the park grass. The setting sun lingered on the crest, firing the bushes to fuchsia and gold like the enchanted roses in a fairy tale.

It was one of those summer evenings, one of those days, that almost made Regina believe in happy endings.

Not for her, though. Never for her.

She sighed and turned back to the tent. Her feet hurt.

Mechanic Bobby Kincaid was tending bar for the free beer and as a favor to Cal. Bobby earned good money in his father's garage. These days every sixteen-year-old on the island with lobster money burning a hole in his pocket had to have a car. Or a pickup.

Regina sidestepped as Bobby attempted to grab her ass. Too bad he was such a jerk.

"Hi, Bobby." She snagged a bottle of sparkling wine from the ice-filled cooler and wrestled the wire cage around the cork. "Let's do a quick refill of all the glasses, and then I want those cake plates off the tables."

"Hey, now," rumbled a deep male voice behind her. "You're off duty."

Regina's heart beat faster. She turned. *Strong, tanned hands, steady green eyes, and a limp he'd picked up in Iraq.* Police Chief Caleb Hunter.

The groom.

Plucking the bottle of Prosecco from her grasp, Caleb filled a rented champagne flute and offered it to her. "You're a guest. We want you to enjoy yourself tonight."

"I am enjoying myself. Any chance to serve something besides red sauce and lobster rolls . . ."

"The menu's great," Cal said. "Everything's great. Those crab patties—"

"Mini blue crab cakes with chipotle aioli and roasted red pepper sauce," Regina said.

"—are really something. You did good." His eyes were warm.

Regina flushed all over at the compliment. She *had* done well. With less than a month to plan and prepare, with only a clueless bride and the groom's awkward sister for support, Regina had pulled off the wedding she'd never had. The rented tent was warm with lantern light, bright with delphinium, daisies, and sunflowers. Crisp white linens covered the picnic tables, and she'd dressed up the folding chairs from the community center with flowing bows.

The food—*her* food, mussels steamed in garlic and white wine, bruschetta topped with basil and tomatoes, smoked wild salmon with dilled crème fraîche—was a huge success.

"Thanks," she said. "I was thinking I might talk Ma into adding some of these appetizers to our regular menu. The mussels, maybe, or—"

"Great," Cal repeated, but he wasn't listening any longer.

His gaze slid beyond her to his bride, Maggie, dancing with his father.

Margred's dark hair had slipped free of its pins to wave on her neck. She'd kicked off her shoes so that the hem of her flowing white dress dragged. She was looking up at Caleb's father, laughing as he executed a clumsy turn on the floor.

The naked intensity in Cal's eyes as he watched his wife closed Regina's throat.

In her entire life, no man had ever looked at her like that, as if she were the sun and the moon and his entire world wrapped up in one. If anyone ever did, she would jump him.

If Cal ever had—

But he hadn't. Wouldn't. Ever.

"Go dance," Regina said. "It's your wedding."

"Right," Caleb said, already moving.

He turned back a moment to smile at her and order, "No more work tonight. We hired the youth group to give you a break."

"You know you have to watch those church kids like a hawk," Regina called after him.

But that was just an excuse.

The truth was she would rather schlep glasses and scrape plates than have the same conversations she'd had before with the same people she'd known all her life. *How's the weather? How's your mother? When are you getting married?*

Oh, God.

She watched Cal circling the dance floor with his new bride—slowly, because of his limp—and emptiness caught her under the ribs, sharp as a cramp.

Grabbing her glass and the open bottle of Prosecco, she walked away from it all, the music, the lights, and the dancing. Away from Bobby behind the bar and Caleb with his arms around Margred.

Regina's heels punched holes in the ragged strip of grass. Drawn by the rush and retreat of water on the rocks, she wobbled across the shale. A burst of foam ran toward her feet. She plopped onto an outcrop of granite to remove her sandals. Her bare toes flexed in the cool, coarse sand.

Ah. That was better.

Really.

She poured herself another glass of wine.

The level in the bottle fell as the moon rose, flat and bright. The sky deepened until it resembled the inside of a shell, purple and gray. Regina rolled her head to look at the stars, feeling the earth whirl around her.

"Careful." The deep male voice sounded amused.

She jerked upright. The contents of her glass sloshed. "Cal?"

"No. Disappointed?"

She'd spilled on her dress. Damn it.

Regina's gaze swung to the tent and then swept the shore, searching out the owner of that voice.

There, standing barefoot at the edge of the surf as if he'd just come out of the sea instead of simply wandering away from the wedding reception.

Her heart pounded. Her head buzzed from the wine.

Not Caleb. She squinted. He was too tall, too lean, too young, too . . .

His tie was loosened, his slacks rolled up. The gray light chased across his face, illuminating the long, narrow nose; the sculpted mouth; the eyes, dark and secret as sin.

Regina felt a pulse, a flutter, of pure feminine attraction and scowled. "I don't know what you're talking about."

He laughed softly, coming closer. "They look good together—Caleb and Margred."

She recognized him then. From the ceremony. "You're his brother. Dylan. The one who—"

Went away.

She'd heard stories. She was drunk, but she recalled the basics. How, twenty-five years ago, his mother had left the island, left her husband and Caleb and her infant daughter, Lucy, taking with her the other son. This one.

"I thought you were older," Regina said.

He went very still in the moonlight. "You remember?"

Regina snorted. "Hardly. Since I was, like, four at the time." She plucked the wet silk from her breasts. She'd have to make a trip to the mainland now. There was no dry cleaners on the island.

"Here." A flash, like a white flag in the dark, as he pulled out his handkerchief. A real gentleman.

And then his hand was on her chest, his fingers spanning the tiny gold cross that lay beneath her collarbone, the heel of his palm pressing the handkerchief right between her breasts. Warm. Intimate. Shocking.

Regina sucked in her breath. Not a gentleman at all. Asshole.

She knocked his wrist away. "I've got it."

Beneath the wet material, her nipples beaded. Could he see, in the dark? She mopped at her dress with his handkerchief. "What are you doing here?"

"I followed you."

If he hadn't just groped her breasts, she'd be flattered. "I meant, on the island."

"I wanted to see if they would really go through with it."

"The wedding?"

"Yes." He refilled her flute, emptying the bottle, and handed it to her.

The gesture reminded her sharply of his brother. Despite the breeze off the water, her face felt hot. She felt warm all over. She gulped her wine. "So, you just showed up? After twenty-five years?"

"Not quite that long."

He folded his long body onto the rock beside her. His hip nudged her thigh. His hard, rounded shoulder brushed her shoulder. The warmth spread low in the pit of her stomach.

She cleared her throat. "What about your mother?"

"Dead."

Oops. Ouch. "Sorry."

Let it go, she told herself. She wasn't getting anywhere swapping dysfunctional family stories. Not that she wanted this to go anywhere, but—

"It's pretty strange that you never came back before," she said.

"You only think so because you never left."

She was stung. "I did, too. Right out of high school. Got a job washing dishes at Perfetto's in Boston until Puccini promoted me to prep cook."

"Perfetto's."

"Alain Puccini's restaurant. You know. Food Network?"

"I take it I should be impressed."

"Damn straight." Pride and annoyance simmered together like a thick sauce. She drained her glass. "He was going to make me his sous chef."

"But you came back. Why?"

Because Alain—the son-of-a-bitch—had knocked her up. She couldn't work kitchen hours with an infant, or pay a babysitter on a line cook's salary. Even after she'd forced Alain to take a paternity test, his court-ordered child support barely covered day care. His assets were tied up—hidden—in the restaurant.

But she didn't say that. Her son and her life were none of Dylan's business.

His thigh pressed warm against her leg.

Anyway, men looked at you differently when you had a kid. It had been a long time since she'd sat with a man in the moonlight.

Longer still since she'd had sex with one.

She looked at Dylan, lean and dark and dangerous and close, and felt attraction run along her veins like the spark on a detonator fuse.

She shook her head to clear it.

"Why did you?" She turned the question back on him.

His shoulder moved against hers as he shrugged. "I came for the wedding. I'm not staying."

Regina quelled an unreasonable disappointment.

So it didn't matter how he looked at her, really. She leaned down to dig the bottom of her glass into the sand. It didn't matter what he thought. After tonight, she'd never see him again. She could say anything she wanted. She could do . . .

Her breath caught in her throat. *Anything she wanted.*

She straightened, flushed and dizzy. Okay, that was the wine talking. Loneliness, and the wine. She wouldn't ever really—she couldn't actually be considering—

She stumbled to her feet.

"Easy." He caught her hand, supporting her.

"Not usually," she muttered.

His grip tightened as he stood. "What?"

She shook her head again, heat crawling in her face. "Nothing. Let me go. I need to take a walk."

"I'll go with you."

She wet her lips. "Bad idea."

He lifted an eyebrow. He did it beautifully. She wondered if he practiced in the mirror. "Better than you turning an ankle on those rocks."

"I'll be fine."

To anyone watching from the tent, they must look like lovers, standing hand in hand at the surf's edge. Her heart thumped. She tried to tug away.

His gaze dropped to their clasped hands. His fingers tightened. "You are warded."

She scowled at him, aroused and confused. "What are you talking about?"

He ran his thumb along the inside of her wrist, over her tattoo. Could he feel her pulse go wild? "This."

Regina swallowed, watching his thumb stroke over the dark lines, the pale skin. "My tatt? It's the Celtic sign for the triple goddess. A female empowerment thing."

"It is a triskelion." He traced the three flowing, connected spirals with his finger. "Earth, air, and sea, bound together in a circle. A powerful ward." He looked up at her, his eyes dark and serious.

Too serious. She felt a jolt in her stomach that might have been nerves or desire.

"So, I'm safe," she said breathlessly.

His beautiful mouth curved in the moonlight. "As safe as you want to be."

Goose bumps tingled along her arms. She shivered, as exposed as if she stood naked by a window.

"Safe works for me," she said. Or it had until recently. "I have responsibilities."

"Not any longer. Caleb told you not to work tonight."

Regina blinked. He'd heard that? He was watching her with his brother?

Caution flickered. She hadn't been aware of an audience. She hadn't been aware of him at all except as Caleb's brother, a tall, dark presence at the back of the wedding, on the edges of the celebration.

Her toes curled into the sand.

She was aware of him now. He was barely touching her, only that light grip on her wrist, and yet she felt the heat of him all along her body. His eyes glittered black in the moonlight, absorbing the light, absorbing the air, growing bigger, darker, enormous as he leaned close, closer, tempting her with that well-cut mouth, teasing her with the promise of his kiss. His breath skated across her lips. She tasted wine and something else—dark, salt, elusive—heard a rushing in her ears like the sea. She opened her mouth to breathe, and he bent over her and covered her mouth firmly, warmly, with his.